Amondo Duckworth

4228 N.13th ST

Milwaukee, WI 53209

(262)-772-6740

keefestreetentertainment@gmail.com

BETRAYAL OF A STICK-UP KID PT.1

by

Amondo "Mister 2212" Duckworth

Prologue

Early Monday morning bobby stood in the living room of his two-bedroom apartment going over plans for a money-making move in his head. The living room was plush, especially for a getaway spot. The black leather furniture had been sent over from Italy because it matched the black and white marbled tiled floors. Bobby looked at his watch and decided to call KD, a young boy he considered to be his worker and send off. After a few rings the phone was answered. "What it do?" "I got some business fa' you and ya' boy if you want it." "Let me call an see what up." "a 'right, get back to me." KD hung up and looked at the custom-made tommy gun clock that hung on his cheaply painted wall. "He need to get up any way." KD said as he dialed the number. He let the phone ring knowing it would be answered. "Hello." The voice said sleepily. "Wake up we got money ta' make." Rock sat up in his bed rubbing his eyes. "I'm woke." He said as he yawned. "Hold on." KD replied then clicked over, when the phone rang, he clicked back over. "You still there?" "Yea, I'm-." "Bout time!" KD and Rock had been going through this for two years, and the routine never changed. "Everything ready to go?" KD asked. Bobbie didn't like talking on the phone, but KD didn't care. Bobby told them about his connection to Shaymo, and what he had in mind. "So, what's up?" he asked. KD was the first to speak. "I'm wit' it long as the money good." Rock sighed. "I'm in, but we gotta hit 'em hard the first time." Bobby had expected that from rock because he was always more cautious than KD. "You ain't gotta tell me nothin'." Bobby replied. "Is it worth it?" KD asked. Bobby realized that KD was second guessing him a lot lately. "Is you in or not?" KD was fed up with the way bobby talked to him, but he knew he had to play things cool. "Call us when you ready." KD replied then hung up and called his homeboy solo. After they hung up bobby quickly called Shaymo. "Yeah!" came an agitated voice

2

after three rings. "Sha, my man, what's up?" Shaymo was having trouble placing the voice. "Who this?" "nothin' like forgettin' a friend, this bobby." "Augh, what's goin' on?" "Remember that conversation we had a while back?" Shaymo thought for a few seconds. "Yeah, what about it?" "I'm ready when you ready." "I thought you was out tha' game." "Naw, after yall got hit I decided ta' lay low and focus on tha' shop for a while." "a 'right, where you plan on settin' up?" "At the proper arms." "ain't that the same place you showed me last time?" "Yea." Shaymo sighed. "Meet me at my spot in bout an hour or two." "Bet." Bobby replied already seeing the dollar signs. "Call when you on the way." Shaymo heard the click and thought about calling back, he didn't appreciate being hung up on. "Who was you talkin' to?" shaymo's girlfriend tiffany asked as she walked through the door. "don't worry bout that, just find me somethin' ta' wear." Tiffany rolled her eyes and walked to the walk-in closet. Shaymo smiled to himself as he watched her. He was on top of the world, he was only twenty-seven and rich in the ghetto sense. He had gotten plugged with the wild boyz and with their help had built an empire and bankroll from the ground up. Tiffany came from the closet holding a pair of black, white and red nikes that she had bought him, she also had a pair of black guess, and a white t-shirt. "This straight?" she asked holding out the outfit. Shaymo looked up to see what she had picked out. "Yeah, that's cool." He said as he walked in the bathroom. Tiffany sat on the bed and shook her head, she was getting fed up, but the money was too good to let go.

KD sat in the living room of his one-bedroom apartment talking on the phone with his homeboy solo in Atlanta. KD could hear the constant drip of water from the kitchen sink, and even though he could afford better, he was comfortable. "Money still bubblin' like water on tha' stove down there?" "fa' sho, I told you to come get in where you fit in." solo replied. "I know, but I told you when I come that way I wanna have my own crib an all that, I ain't tryin' ta live off nobody." Solo knew how KD felt, he had felt the same way when he decided to leave

Milwaukee. "a 'right, so when you gon' make ya' way down here?" "It shouldn't be much longer; I been stackin' my bread." While they were talking something occurred to solo. "speakin' of moves, how you bobby, an rock been getting' on?" "ain't shit changed, bobby still think its sweet." "Well, plan ya' move right, ain't no need to rush." "I already know, but I can't wait ta' shake these niggas." "Like I said, ain't no need to rush." "Yeah, I know I just hope this move be enough fa' me ta' move around." KD replied. "I feel you on that, but you'll know when tha' time right." The line clicked as they talked. "Hold on real quick." KD said before clicking over. "what's up?" "it's a go." Bobby replied. "a 'right, I'm a call rock, then call you back." "Just hurry up." KD clicked back over. "hey 'lo, I got some shit ta' take care of I'm a call you later." "a 'right, just remember what I said." "Fa sho." KD replied and hung up then called rock. The phone rang twice before it was answered. "Hello." "Hold on." KD said and clicked over. "Rock?" "Yeah, I'm here." "Bobby you there?" "Yeah." "what's good?" "Everything set." Bobby replied. KD hung up, grabbed his pistol then headed outside, once he was outside, he looked around, the neighborhood never changed, his friends were still on the same corner hustling and smoking weed, females and little kids were still walking through; they had just gotten a little older, and others were still just hanging out watching life pass them by. After peeping the scene for a few seconds, he made his way to his car, other than expensive clothes, and strip clubs, his car was the only thing he had spent money on. He had bought the plain Monte Carlo from a friend of his with money from his first lick, then he put gold flakes in the paint, and brand-new spokes on the tires. When he got in the car, he rolled rock back. "What it is?" "Get ready, I'm on my way." "a 'right." Rock replied. KD hung up and rock waited for a few seconds then called the airport. "Mitchell International Airport, Shauntel speaking." "What up?" he said. "Hey baby." She replied. "Is my tickets ready?" "You know I keep tickets on standby for you." "I just wanna be sho'." "I know, I know." She replied agitated. "Is the car ready?" "Yeah, you gave me the money, didn't

4

you?" she had been asked the same questions every time he went on a lick. "You sure you don't wanna go?" "I already told you I can't just take off and go with you." She replied. "Love you." "I love you to." He said as he hung up. They had met at a ponderosa a little over a year and a half ago, she had asked for his number, and he showed off by paying for her and her friends to eat, and they had been together ever since. Rock looked at his watch and knew KD would be pulling up in the next fifteen to twenty minutes, so he took a quick shower, got dressed then rolled a blunt. When he finished, he checked the clip of his nine. He knew when KD arrived because the bass from the music was making his window rattle. Rock knew his neighbors would complain about the music, so he quickly made his way outside. Once he got in the car, he looked around to see if anybody was looking out of their window. "Pull off, I don't want these mu'fuckas trippin'." Rock always did his best to stay low key and KD was just the opposite. When KD pulled off rock took the blunt he had rolled out of his pocket and lit it. They were four blocks from rocks house when KD's phone rang, he turned the music down and answered. "Yeah." "Where yall at?" "Headed yo' way." "I had to change the plan up." Bobby said. "What you mean you had to change the plan.?" Bobby was tired of KD's attitude. "Just listen." "I am listenin'" KD replied calmly. "I want yall to go get martin." "Fa what?" "Cuz, he Comin' wit yawl." "Hell naw!" KD replied. "Do what I said an go get him." KD took a deep breath to calm himself. "Any other changes?" "Naw, that's all." Bobby replied and hung up. It took them ten minutes to reach martins apartment, when they pulled up rock got out and rang the buzzer. "Yeah!" martin answered quickly. "let's go." "I'm headed down." Martin replied. Rock headed back to the car. "I don't know why we gotta bring this nigga." KD said when rock got in the car. Rock knew that KD had never liked martin, so he kept quiet. A few seconds later martin came out of the building dressed in all black like them. Rock got back out of the car and let him in. "you strapped?" KD asked when he got in. "of course I'm strapped." Martin replied as rock got back in. "my pops called me at the last minute and told me he wanted me to ride." KD sighed and put in his favorite Tupac CD. Rock knew that the cd KD put in helped him to zone, and he had a bad feeling about this move, but knew he couldn't back out, so he remained quiet and decided to let things take their course. "I wanna be first through the door." Martin said breaking the silence. "ain't no first, we gon' play it how its suppose to go." Rock didn't bother to get into the discussion because he knew that they were going to play it how it went. "Pops told me; it was on me if I wanted to go in first." "And I said, we gon' play it how it go, so leave it alone." Martin mumbled under his breath, but KD didn't notice.

Bobby was sitting at his black marble table thinking and waiting on Shaymo's call. It was still hard for him to believe that within the last two and half years he had turned dirty money into a mini mansion by the lake that only a seldom few knew about. His thoughts were interrupted when his phone rang. "Hello." "I'm headed to the spot in a few, you ready for me." "Yeah, I'm ready." Bobby replied smiling to himself. "I'm a make two more stops, so give me bout twenty or thirty minutes." "No problem, so when I get there, you want me to ring the bell or what?" "I'll call you when I get there." "a 'right." Bobby replied before he hung up and called KD. "I just got off the phone wit' Shaymo, he'll be at the spot in bout twenty, thirty minutes." "We ready." KD replied and hung up. "he'll be here in twenty, thirty minutes so, this should be a hit an run, no longer than a couple minutes, if that." Rock and Martin nodded. KD kept watch for Shaymo, he would know it was him because his hummer was known throughout Milwaukee. "Money in the bank." KD said once he saw the hummer. Rock nodded as they sat waiting to see what Shaymo would do. After a few seconds Shaymo got out of the hummer and took a piss, giving everyone a chance to see who was in the driver's seat. "it's a bitch in tha' truck!" "Fuck that bitch." KD replied. Martin didn't have to look over at KD, he knew by the tone of his voice to drop the subject. Shaymo finished and got back in the truck. "What tha' fuck he on?" KD asked. Rock

6

was wondering the same thing. "He probably just peepin' the scene, you remember how the fed's tried to snatch 'em last time?" martin replied. "Yeah, I remember." "It don't matter, we got all day." KD replied as he watched the constant ebb and flow of the neighborhood. When Shaymo got back in the truck he saw the look on tiffany's face. "what's wrong with you?" "I-I got a bad feelin' bout this." "don't tell me that fed shit still got you spooked." "It ain't that, I-its-I just got a bad feelin' bout this." She responded nervously. She couldn't explain it, but she knew she had to convince him. "baby think about it, bobby call you talkin' bout clickin' up then tha' feds hit, an now everything done calmed down an you back ta' getting' money he call outta nowhere." "You know we got hit cuz Shug was workin' fa tha' feds, it didn't have nothin' ta' do wit' bobby." She knew that shug had worn the wire in hopes of getting rid of Shaymo and Pokey, but something didn't feel right about the meeting. "Baby, we don't need this money, just pull off." Shaymo looked at the building that housed one of his spots and wondered if she was right. "Fuck it we n here now." He replied. "I'm tellin' you we don't need this money." Shaymo had tuned her out as he began dialing Bobby's number. "Well, can we get something ta' eat after this? I'm still hungry." "You been hungry a lot lately, is you pregnant?" Shaymo asked as the phone began to ring. "Naw, I'm just –." Shaymo held his hand up cutting her off. "I'm where you need ta' be." He said then hung up. "What was you saying?" "I ain't pregnant, I'm just hungry, wit' all this runnin' round I ain't ate nothin'." "You sure?" Shaymo asked looking down at her stomach. "Yeah, I'm sure, I think I'd know if I was pregnant." She replied with an attitude. "Just ta' make sure, we gone stop and get a pregnancy test when we done." "Whatever Shay." She replied rolling her eyes. "You gon' fuck 'round an lose some of yo' teeth, I'm sick of yo' attitude." "Sorry baby." She replied knowing he wanted to feel in control. After ten minutes passed Shaymo got impatient and checked his watch for the third time. "Where tha' fu-." Before he could finish, he saw bobby's blue beamer pulling in front of the building. "Bout time." KD and

Rock were relieved when bobby finally got out and headed to Shaymo's hummer. "Hand me a mask." Martin said eagerly as his father and Shaymo moved toward the stairs leading to the front door. "We ain't usin' em." "What you mean we ain't usin' 'em?" "Look where we at, if we get out tha' car wit' mask on we gon' be in jail before we get tha' money." Rock and Martin realized that KD was right. "Well, what we waitin' fa?" KD didn't respond as he reached under his seat and out three folded paper bags. "Here." He said as he tossed them each a bag." "What tha' fuck these fa'?" "You don't want nobody seein' ya wit' a gun, do you?" KD replied as he pulled a .45 off his waist and wrapped the bag around it, then watched as they did the same. "Crack yall doors a lil'." "Fa what?" martin asked confused. "Just do it." Martin slowly opened the door. As they were opening their doors bobby and Shaymo walked up the stairs leading to the apartment building. KD hopped out of the car and ran toward the building with rock and martin behind him. They made it to the building as Shaymo reached the door. "Lay it down, you know what it is." KD said motioning them to the ground. Bobby turned as if he was going to run. "don't move." Rock said pointing his gun at him. Tiffany put her hand on the .380 and waited calmly as things unfolded. During the excitement they had forgotten she was in the truck. "Lay yo' bitch ass down an don't move." KD said pushing Shaymo to the ground. When they began going through his pockets she had seen enough, and quickly swung the driver's door open, causing martin to turn her way, when he did, she squeezed the trigger three times hitting him twice in the chest and once in the leg. As martin fell to the ground his gun went off hitting Shaymo, KD pulled the trigger on his .45, the muffled shots came one after the other slamming her into the door of the hummer before she fell to the ground dead. As bobby ran to check on his son KD ran to his car leaving them to deal with martin. "What the fuck you doin'!?" bobby yelled. A few seconds later he pulled up to shaymo's hummer. "Help me get martin outta here." Bobby said as he and rock picked martin up off the ground. KD ran to the hummer, grabbed the

8

bags and tossed them in his car. "Fuck them bags! Help me get martin outta here!" bobby snapped as he and rock half carried, half dragged martin towards the car. KD hopped back in the car. "Rock! Let's go!" Rock couldn't believe what KD was doing. "don't do th-." They all heard the sirens as KD pulled off and left them with martin's body. "I ain't got nothin' ta'-." "I know, just go, hurry up!" Rock took the guns and ran down the block toward the college campus, once he reached the campus, he threw the guns in the sewer. Bobby stayed with the bodies knowing that he would have to come up with a good story, but at the same time he was plotting revenge, KD had not only robbed him, but might've cost him his only son. The police pulled up just as people began to come outside. "Get your hands up! Don't move!" The officers screamed. "Get help! My son need help!" bobby yelled as he put his hands up. As one of the officers called for an ambulance, a short blond, twenty something year old woman came out of the apartment building. "Officer! I got the license plate of the car the guy pulled off in." bobby knew that the plate number wouldn't lead to KD's car, he had taught him to use stolen plates. As more police cars pulled up a crowd began to form. "Somebody tapes this scene off before it gets trampled." One of the officers said as he kept people away from the bodies. Officers quickly got the scene under control and began interviewing everyone. Bobby told them that he and his son had come to visit a family friend and that there were people at the hummer talking and the next thing he knew gunshots rang out. As he talked three garbage bags floated by on the breeze. KD knew there was no turning back, he had finally seen his chance to get away from bobby and took it. KD knew that when the streets got the news of shaymo's death that bobby would put a price on his head just like pokey would do, but at that moment the excitement, and the adrenaline rush had him. As he continued to drive his greed kicked in and he wanted to see what he had taken from the lick, so he pulled into the gas station and reached into the back seat. When he unzipped the bag he couldn't believe it, the bag was all money, so now KD knew

9

he had caught Shaymo during his pick-up. He rezipped the bag and reached for the other one. When he unzipped it, he saw the six bagged up pounds of weed and three quarters of cocaine. It wasn't what he thought, but it was better than nothing. Before he rezipped the bag he took out a small amount of weed to roll a blunt and got out of the car, the weed had a pungent smell that followed him into the store. As he went to the counter a female came from the back with bread, a soda, and a meat that KD knew by the smell was pork, which he didn't eat. "Damn, you got some of that fa' sell?" The woman asked as the scent caught her by surprise. "Yeah, I got you." KD said as he went to grab a box of sandwich bags. "No drug dealin', I'll call the police." The man at the counter said. "What you say?" KD said as he put the baggies on the counter. "No drug dealin', I'll call the police." KD smiled before pulling the gun. "don't ever threaten me." He said before putting the money on the counter. Once KD was outside he went to his car and waited on the woman too come out, as he waited, he grabbed the bag that contained the weed and popped open the baggies and waited, when the woman came out, he blew the horn. The woman quickly made her way to the car. "Let me get a dub." The woman said. KD fixed the bag and as he was about to hand her the weed the police pulled in. "damn." KD said as he started the car. "what's goin' on?" "Here you go." KD said handing her the weed. The woman dropped the twenty-dollar bill on the seat. KD quickly pulled off when he saw the man in the store point at his car. The officers got on his walkie-talkie and gave the description of the car as they got into the squad car and proceeded to chase him. KD knew he would go to prison if they caught him, and they were catching up fast. KD didn't panic until he saw the other squad cars join in. "fuck!" he said as he turned the corner. KD knew he couldn't jump out at the rate of speed he was going, so he made a quick left and slowed down enough to jump out. When he jumped out one squad went to stop the car that had continued down the street, the other squads chased KD. KD was running for his life or so he felt, one of the officers gave a warning shot and KD kept

10

running, as he made it to another gain way, he saw two squad cars and as he turned back the sound of the shotgun froze him. "Lay down! Don't move! Hands spread out!" the officers said. And as he did what he was told he realized that he was going to prison and worse than that he was broke. "Never got ta' count the money." He said to himself.

CHAPTER 1

Kevin Imani Drake walked out of the twenty-foot steel gate that led to freedom, he was escorted by to guards as was Waupun correctional institution policy. He knew that no one would be waiting on the other side of the gate and that's the way he had set it up. KD had been planning his return to the streets since the beginning of his incarceration, he had kept his ears to the street and changed his plan accordingly. As the gate opened the guards handed him his ticket and check. "don't come back, this ain't the place for you." One of the guards said. "I ain't comin' back, so don't worry bout me." He said as he looked back and shook his head in disgust. KD knew what was waiting for him when he got to Milwaukee, and he couldn't wait. As he walked, he opened up the check and looked, the money he had gotten from family and friends had mostly been spent on canteen, lawyers and court cost, so he would have to build from the ground up; the check was enough to get him some clothes and that was about it, but he still wasn't worried. When he made it to the bus station, he cashed his check and called the first person on his list. "b, what up?" he said when the phone was answered. "What up my nigga? I been waitin' on yo call." Brian said excitedly. KD laughed. "I'll be in tha' mil in like an hour or so, is everything ready, cuz I wanna hit tha' ground runnin'." He replied seriously. "Yeah, it's good, yo car waitin' fa you, and I'll be there with the keys." Brian replied. "a 'right, my bus should be comin' in so let me get off this phone." KD said as he listened to the buses being called. "Yeap, we waitin' on you." Brian said before hanging up. KD got on the bus twenty minutes later and watched as the world flew pass the window, knowing that soon he and his people would run the streets of Milwaukee, and no one would be safe if they were hustling. KD watched as the different people got on the bus, but he didn't care he was focused on getting money and not going to prison again, he had told himself it would be court in the streets if it came down to it and he meant that, but he also knew that he didn't really want to die. He decided he needed to get some sleep before he got too Milwaukee, so that he could get started with a clear mind. When he got off the bus two hours later, he stretched and walked to the parking lot to see if his car was there, when he saw it, he smiled and headed into the station to call Brian. Twenty minutes later Brian was there with the keys. "I'm glad you out, everybody waitin' to hear from you," Brian said as he handed KD a cellphone. "that's you." He said. KD took the phone and called a few people. "Where my keys?" he asked holding out his hand. Brian dug in his pocket and handed him the keys. "let's go, I need a bath, haircut and all types of shit." He said with his first real smile in ten years. As they walked out KD looked around and shook his head. "I miss being able to see shit without a fence or wall around it b." KD said as he took a cigarette, he had gotten from one of the passengers on the bus out of his pocket and lit it. "I won't take it for granted this time." He said seriously. When they finally made it to the parking lot KD realized that he was truly free, no more bitch ass correctional officers telling him when to eat, shit, sleep and talk, no more listening to niggas lie about they life or the people they knew, he was free. "Is the tank full?" KD asked. "I took care of it myself, this mu'fucka good, all you gotta do is drive this bitch." Brian replied. KD got in and sighed. "Damn b! I'm home!" He yelled. "Nigga pull up out this mu'fucka, we got shit ta' do." Brian replied laughing and shaking his head with a smile. As they were driving through the city KD realized that he hadn't called the one person who truly

12

held him down. "Damn! I ain't called Trina yet." He said. "that's the first person you should've called, she bout ta' snap." KD dialed the number he had dialed more than any other in the years he'd been away. "Hello." She answered softly not recognizing the number. "Hey baby, what's up?" "Nigga where tha' fuck you at! You got released at nine 'o' clock this fuckin' mornin.'" She snapped. "It took me two hours to get too Milwaukee." KD replied with a laugh in his voice. "I don't find shit funny get here asap nigga." Trina replied seriously. KD knew she had every right to be angry but wasn't going to keep letting her go off like she was. "Chill that bullshit! I just got out, I'm takin' in tha' sites I'm headed that way as soon as I handle some other shit." He said. "Whatever, you had me worried, just get here." Trina said softly knowing he had just got out and not wanting to ruin his day. "Okay, baby and I'm sorry fa' not callin' asap." He replied. "Okay, I love you." Trina said happily. "I love you to baby." KD said before hanging up. "what's in the cd player?" he asked. "Master p." Brian replied knowing what was about to happen. KD quickly took out master p's cd and put in baby drew, a rapper from Milwaukee. "Play three." Brian said. KD changed the song and continued towards mano's house. When they arrived, they could hear the music coming from the speakers in the opened windows. Like almost everyone else KD knew, mano lived in the heart of the ghetto. The house looked like it was falling apart, the wooden stairs were uneven, and the paint was chipped there were patches of brown and uncut grass, empty chip bags, soda cans and blunt wrappers all over and where the protective railings were supposed to be there were only wooden beams nailed together. They took in the scene before getting out of the car and walking up the stairs to the front door. KD knocked hard, but no one answered, he turned the knob and opened the door. "Come on." He said motioning to Brian. As they stepped in keema stepped into the hallway. "Mano! KD and Brian here!" she yelled. "let 'em in!" he yelled back. "They already in the damn house! Turn the music down so we can fuckin' hear." KD and Brian laughed as the music was turned down and mano stepped into the hallway shaking his head. "don't act like yall ain't never been here before." Mano said as he walked toward the living room. "Star, what it do?" KD asked. "Shit, waitin' fa' you to get here." "Well, he here now, so let's get ta' business." Mano replied. "So, kd what's the deal? You said it was on when you touched." "Yeah, what's the deal?" Keema replied. "I already told yall what I was on, I just wanna make sure yall ready, cuz when bobby find out I'm back it's gon' be some shit." "Fuck bobby, he like fifty he betta mind his own or get dealt wit'." Mano replied knowing the history between them. "Well, get Doobie an them together, we goin' to my girl crib ta' talk about our first move." "I'm on it." Mano replied as he picked up his phone and said doobie's name. "They headed our way." Mano said after a few minutes. "So, we on?" keema asked. "Yeah, we on, so let's get this money." KD replied as he smiled and stood up. After getting off the phone with KD Trina decided to go upstairs and lay down, an hour later she was woken up by someone knocking on the door. "Damn! Two 'o' clock, it was just twelve-thirty." She said as she glanced at the clock and slipped her shoes on. "Who is it?" she yelled making her way down the stairs. "it's me baby" "hold on! Here I come." She said as she made it to the bottom stair slightly out of breath. "I'll get yo' key made tomorrow." She said after opening the door. As everyone walked in Trina glared at KD. "Stop being rude and introduce me to yo' friends." "a 'right, let's go in tha' livin' room." Trina locked the door and followed everyone to the living room. "Make yall self at home." She said. "Yall can chill, it's cool." KD said gesturing to the couch. Keema rolled her eyes when she saw Trina smiling. "Introduce everybody." KD looked at her and she knew he was telling her to chill, then he started the introductions. "Tara, Star, this my girl Trina, baby these my homegirls." "what's up yall?" KD saw the look on keema's face but continued the introductions. "These niggas right here is my boys Doobie, Mano, Brian and his lil' brother Zoe." "what's up?" Trina replied. Everyone gave their acknowledgments. "a 'right, let's get ta' business." KD knew that everybody there knew about what happened with him, bobby and rock,

14

so he skipped past that and told them about his plan to hit the candy store. "Okay, so what 'bout guns an shit?" Doobie asked. "I'm workin' on that, as a matter of fact I gotta make a call about that in a few minutes." "I don't know nothin' bout shootin' no gun." Keema said. "Me either." Star replied. "a 'right, we'll get that took care of." KD replied. "an how you gon' do that?" Keema asked with an attitude. "I'm a take yall to a shootin' range." KD replied. "Nigga! You on paper an we both felons, I ain't goin' to no shootin' range." "You ain't gotta go, but if you think I would get myself or yall into some shit you trippin' I gotta plug." KD said as he grabbed his phone and began to dial. "Hello." The raspy voice on the other end answered. "Grip, I need you ta' meet me at my girl crib." "a 'right, I'll be there in a few." "I'm here." KD replied and hung up. "Baby, who is Grip?" "One of my guys from middle school." "So, he gon' be gettin' money wit' us?" Keema asked. "Naw, that's the plug I was tellin' yall 'bout." Everyone was surprised that he was really moving so fast. "I'm a like bustin' moves wit' you." Zoe said. "Stick around lil' man we gon' teach you some shit." KD replied. "Oh! Word on the street is rock back in the mil, an him and bobby don' got a lot closer while I was gon' so we'll see what they on." At twenty-five after two KD's phone rang. "Yeah?" "I'm on tha' block come stand on the porch." Grip said as he slowly drove down third and Keefe. "I'm on my way outside now." KD replied as he hung up and walked out the front door. A few seconds later he walked in with grip. Grip was six foot one, two hundred forty pounds and as black as squid ink. "Everybody this grip, that's my girl Trina, my homegirls, Keema, Star and Tara, and them my niggas Doobie, Mano, Brian and his brother Zoe." "what's up everybody.?" Everyone replied politely, but to Trina, Grip looked shystie just like Brian. Trina wondered if KD could really trust them, but she kept her thoughts to herself. "Yall chill, we gon' talk some business then ride out." He said as he and grip headed to the kitchen. "She got any sisters?" "Naw." KD replied knowing it was a lie. "Damn shame she ain't got no sisters." Grip replied shaking his head. "Did we come in here ta' talk about my girl or business?" KD replied

15

half joking, half serious. "Both." Grip replied and smiled. KD shook his head. "let's talk business." "a 'right, what's up?" KD explained the situation. "it sound good, but I need my money, you my boy, but business is business." "I'll make sure you get paid, I'm tellin' you it's straight, look out fa' me." "a 'right, just remember what I said, business is business." "I got you." KD replied as he and grip stood and headed back to the living room. "Everything cool?" Trina said speaking for the group which keema didn't like. When they made it out of the house grip walked to his truck and got in. KD made his way to the passenger side of his car and tossed Trina the keys. "You drive." "Who ridin'?" "Just Brian an Zoe." "They just got in Doobie car." KD looked out of the window and saw Keema an Star heading their way. "Well, Keema and Star gotta ride with' us then." Trina pulled the seat forward. "Why you not drivin'?" "Cuz I'm tired, I been drivin' all day an I got a headache." "Aww, poor baby, you want me ta' do somethin' ta' make it better?" "yeah, a couple things, but we'll talk 'bout that later." Trina punched him playfully. "Yeah, ya ass ain't that tired." Keema and Star made it to the car as Trina popped the locks to let them in. "what's up yall?" she asked as they got in. "shit, can't wait ta' get where we goin.'" Keema replied snappishly causing Trina to glance at her through the rearview. KD rolled his window down. "Grip! We followin' you." Star tapped KD on the shoulder as Trina pulled off. "We get ta' keep tha' guns?" "Yeah, unless they get hot." "Hot? They gon' be hot anyway." Star shook her head. "He tellin' you, you'd rather throw it than get caught wit' it." Trina continued following grip, but as she drove, she decided that she needed to have a talk with KD. Star began looking out of the window and mumbling to herself. "Star, you a 'right?" Keema asked. "Damn, you all in mine ain't you?" "I just asked a question." Star figured she should get things off her chest. "KD, no disrespect or nothin' but its somethin' shystie bout ya' boy Brian, I don't trust him." Trina was glad that someone else felt like her. "I got that same feelin'." Trina said happy to have it off her chest. "we'll find out in due time." KD replied. It was three-fifteen when they pulled up to grips house; it was an ugly two-family house that needed repairing. Grip waved them forward, so Trina pulled up on the side of him. "We gon' park 'round tha' back, follow me." She followed him as he pulled into the alley. He hopped out and opened the gate. "Park behind me." Trina pulled close to his bumper and turned the car off as everyone got out. "Here come Mano an Them." "tell 'em to park in front of the gate an walk 'round to the front." KD waited for them to pull up and park, then lead them to the front. When they made it to the front Grip was unlocking the door. Trina was the first person to see inside the house. "Oh my God." She gasped. Everyone looked at her wondering what had gotten that reaction. "Did that come out loud?" she asked embarrassed. "Yeah, it did." Keema replied. When KD looked at her she knew he was angry and tried to avoid eye contact. Grips living room didn't look like it belonged in the house they were in. "come in, make yall self at home." When they stepped in they saw the cherry wood table with gold clown faces embedded in it, he also had a small piano made of the same wood. He nodded toward the table. "I had it made cuz it reminds me of all of my struggles." They all felt like he had read their minds. "I know yall here on business, so follow me, I'm a show yall tha' basement." They all followed him down to the basement, and it was ghetto fabulous. He had a pool table, mini bar and three full wall gun safes, he took a key out of his pocket and unlocked them but left them closed. "Before I open these, I want yall ta' know, yall didn't get 'em from me and whatever you pick is yours once you touch it gloves or not." "Get it right, yall only get one chance, so get what you think you can handle, don't be on that holly wood movie shit." KD said. KD, Mano, and Star walked over to one of the safes as Grip pulled open the doors. "Damn! You gotta 'nuff shit ta' fight a war in this mu'fucka." KD said shocked by what he was seeing in front of him. "If I stay ready I ain't got ta' get ready." Grip replied with a smile. "I feel you." "a 'right, you know what yall came here fa' so handle ya' business." Grip replied looking at KD. "Naw, I'm a let my people pick first." He replied. No one made a move oward the safes because they were wondering if KD was testing them. "You tha' one runnin' shit, you first." Star said. "that's what I'm talkin' bout re-mu'fuckin'- spect." It was their second test and they had passed. KD pointed out a Benelli assault shotgun, Grip unlocked the glass and passed it to him, KD took it and weighed it in his hands. "What about bullets?" "I'm a get 'em ta' yall before we roll out." Trina walked over and pointed. "what's that?" "that's a nine beretta, you sure you can handle that?" Trina looked back at KD. "It hold ten shots an gotta lil' kick to it, but if you want it, it's yours." "KD gon' teach me how ta' use it anyway, so I'm straight." Trina replied. "I see you gotta rida." "All tha' time my nigga." Doobie quickly glanced at KD, shook his head then walked over and pointed at the same shotgun. Mano watched Doobie play with the shotgun, then shook his head and looked at KD. KD caught the look and shrugged. "I want those." Mano said pointing at two Glock nineteens. "They hold sixteen a piece, thirty-two wit' tha' extendo's." Grip replied as he reached in the safe, took them out and passed them to Mano. "Oooh-wee, I like these pretty mu'fuckas." He said as he pointed them. "I got some rhino slugs fa' them bitches." Grip replied as he watched Mano play with the guns. Zoe walked over to the second safe. "I want tha' fo-five." He said. Grip looked at Brian who had a look of surprise on his face. "that's a dessert eagle, I got two clips fa' you." Grip replied as Brian shook his head in disbelief. Trina stood waiting on Keema, Star and Tara to choose, but KD pointed to Brian. "it's on you." "I already see what I want." Brian replied as he turned his attention away from Zoe. "let's get a move on then." Grip said. Brian pointed at a tec-nine. "Yall ain't playin' is yall?" "Hell naw, we gotta be right when shit go down." He replied. Keema walked over to the first safe, then over to the second one and back again. "I want that one." She said. "that's a twenty-two, but I tell you what, I'm a give you one free." Tara, Star, it's on yall." KD said. Star walked over to the first safe. "I want that three-eighty." Grip grabbed it. "Yeah, this was made just fa' you." KD walked over to Tara. "it's on you." "I want that thirty-eight." "So, you want Betsy? I got two boxes of bullets for you." Grip replied as he took her in from head to toe. Trina turned to KD. "Baby can I get a twenty-two for tha' house?" KD nodded as he walked over to the second safe. "Let me get that fifty cal, an that twenty-two." Grip handed him the guns and KD gave the twenty-two to Trina, then looked at his watch. When Grip saw him look at his watch he closed and locked the safes. "Let me grab them bullets and shit, so we can ride out." "I'm wit' dat" KD replied waiting on grip to go into one of the safes. "No offense, but I need yall ta' wait fa' me upstairs." He said as he put the key in his pocket. "No problem, let's go yall!" KD replied. KD and the crew walked back upstairs with their guns in their hands. "I hope yall ready." KD said. As everyone voiced their readiness KD's phone rang. "Hello." "So, you can't call the ol' man an let him know you on tha' street huh?" "Who this?" KD asked knowing who it was. "You don't remember my voice?" "Bobby? What's up?" KD replied wondering how he had gotten his number. "I need ta' holla at you." "When?" KD replied showing no fear. "Today if possible." "I'll try ta' get there round four, four-thirty." There was a moment of silence. "Its three-twenty now." Bobby replied as if four wasn't soon enough. "I know but like I said I'll try ta' get there at four-four thirty." He said before hanging up. When Grip came upstairs, he had two large army duffel bags. "Put yall shit in here, it's time ta' go." He said as he placed the bag on the floor. Once everyone placed their guns in the bags KD handed the bag back to Grip and they all headed out to their cars. They followed Grip for what seemed like forever. When they pulled up to Rodger's gun shop and shooting range Grip got out of his truck and sat the duffel bags on the hood of KD's car. "I made sure yall got everything yall need." He said when KD grabbed the bags. "I appreciate it." "a 'right, I'm a go an see if he ready fa' us." Grip said as he walked toward the shop. KD took the few minutes grip was gone to call bobby back. "Yeah?" an irritated voice responded. "somethin' came up at tha' last minute, so I'll be ta' you at five, maybe six." "a 'right, just don't forget." Bobby replied. KD knew bobby was pissed off by the tone of his voice, but he was his own boss now and there was no looking back. He put the phone back in his pocket and motioned for everyone to get out of their cars, then he sat the bags on the ground. "Yall, know what yall here fa' come get yall shit." Everyone began talking and walking towards the bags as soon as KD had finished talking. "We gotta be a team! What the fuck!" He yelled, throwing his hands up in frustration. Star knew what he expected, so she walked over, picked the bag up and stumbled under the weight. "Yall actin' like yall don't know what tha' fuck teamwork mean! If we can't work ta'gether what tha' fuck, we here fa'?" she said sitting the bags down and unzipping them. KD turned and looked at Trina who was smiling. "let's go! We need ta' be ready when my boy get back." Everyone formed a line and helped pass out the weapons. "We gotta pull 'round ta' tha' side, he 'poss ta' be closed." Grip when he walked back out of the building. "Yall heard 'em we gotta move, let's get it done." After everyone got their cars moved, they followed grip in the building. "what's up everybody?" A short, half bald, middle-aged man asked as he stood in the middle of the shop. Everyone stepped forward and shook his hand. "a 'right, listen! My name is Rodger, yall seen the sign out there, I only have three rules, respect my shit, don't kill ya' self in my shit, an never make my shit hot." Everyone laughed at Rodgers joke then agreed to his rules. "let's make our way downstairs to the shooting range." He said as he turned and walked. KD and Grip followed everyone down to the shooting range and watched as his crew spent the next two hours shooting and being taught to shoot. When the bullets began to run low KD walked over to Trina. "Can you handle that now?" "Yeah, I got it, Rodger had to keep me from shootin' wit' my eyes closed though." She replied with pride. "Times up! Let's pack up and roll out." KD yelled. Trina waited until he was done and pulled him to the side. "Baby we gon' need more bullets." "I'll get it took care of." He replied as he walked over to Grip and Rodger. A few seconds later KD walked back over to Trina. "Go upstairs wit' Grip." As they talked Star made sure everything was carefully packed in the duffel bags before setting them in front of KD.

20

Trina followed Star upstairs so she could talk to grip. A few minutes later KD came upstairs with the bags and headed outside to put them in the trunk. "Baby I need you ta' drop me an Brian off at Bobby shop." KD said as they got in the car. Trina looked over at him. "Everything okay?" she asked worriedly. "Yeah, everything straight, why you ask me that?" "It seem like somethin' botherin' you that's all." "Naw, I'm straight, I'm just wonderin' why he called me." Trina didn't bother to ask who or how they got his number. "Why yall goin' ta' tha' shop? You don't even fuck wit' him." KD seemed to be ignoring her, but she asked again anyway. When KD didn't answer she looked at Brian in the rearview mirror, then looked back at KD and tapped him on the shoulder. "Baby." She said snapping her fingers causing KD to come out of the deep thoughts he was having. "What." Trina and Brian looked at each other. "You a 'right? You spaced out on us an shit." "My fault, what you say?" Trina sighed. "I asked if you was gon' be a 'right." "Yeah, I'll be straight." He replied. Brian rolled down the window to let the breeze in. it was five-fifty when they made it to the shop. "Can you pop the lock?" Brian asked knowing they needed to be alone. Trina popped the locks and let him out. When he walked in the shop Trina relaxed and sunk into the seat. "Why you trust me so much?" KD sat up in his seat. "keepin' it real, I know you'd never fuck me over." "that's it? that's the only reason?" "Naw, I been knowin' you to long, so I know you really fa' a nigga." Trina forced a smile, so KD wouldn't see her pain. "Aw, okay." Trina replied, she had hoped to hear him say that he trusted her because he loved her. KD opened the passenger door, got out, then kneeled to look in the car. "Baby, be careful while you drivin' check ya' mirrors, an when you get home give 'em they shit an tell 'em ta' call me tomorrow." She wanted to cry but held back the tears. "I'll call when everybody leaves." She said. "a 'right, let me know what happen." He replied then kissed her softly. "I love you." He said knowing that's what she needed and deserved to hear. "I love you to." She said with a smile. It was five after six when KD walked in the shop. "Bobby!" he called loudly. "In tha' back.!" "Why

21

it's so quiet?" KD asked as he looked around for Brian. When he made it to the hallway, he put his hand on the fifty cal. KD kept one hand on his gun as he reached for the doorknob with the other, but before he could touch it Brian opened it. KD walked into the office and saw a female getting off her knees, she was caramel complected with short hair and big breast with dark nipples. KD moved his hand away from his gun as the woman quickly made her way to the couch and grabbed her dress. "Naw, naw, stay like that he done seen a woman naked before." Bobby said. The woman looked at them. "b-but I -I don't know him." "You ain't gotta know 'em so shut tha' fuck up an do what you gettin' paid fa'." The woman rolled her eyes as she dropped the dress back on the floor and walked back to bobby's desk. "I gotta wait on Shaniece ta' come out tha' bathroom." Bobby sighed as he knocked on the wooden door behind his desk. "Shaniece! What tha' fuck takin' so long?" "I'm on tha' way out now, damn!" When she came out of the bathroom a few seconds later KD was shocked by her beauty. She was light skinned like Lisa Raye and could've passed for her. "I see how you gettin' down now." 'I'm just watchin' I know my limit; I might catch a lil' head or somethin' but other than that I watch." Bobby replied with a smile. "Anybody ever told you, you look like Lisa Raye?" KD asked turning his attention to Shaniece. "Yeah, every day." She replied sarcastically. "Stop talkin' an get back ta' what yall here fa'" Shaniece rolled her eyes then laid on the floor and spread her legs, the other woman got between them and began to rub her pussy against hers. Brian looked at KD and booby as he threw money on the women. "don't you got somethin' you can do? He don't need you in tha' room we bout ta' talk business." KD and Brian exchanged looks and to KD his look said it all, Bobby had Brian in his pocket and now KD knew it. Brian shook his head as he walked out of the office. "Now, let's talk business." Bobby said with a slight smirk when the door closed. "I'm listenin'." Bobby walked to a small table and pulled out a chair, KD followed him cautiously. "I know you gettin' a crew ta'gether an you think you got somethin' ta' prove, an that's all good, but

22

don't step on my toes and I won't step on yours." "Is that all?" "Just one mo' thing, the streets say you got ya' eyes on tha' candy store, I'm cool wit' Danny, so fa' tha' sake of peace, don't fuck wit' 'em." "Tell tha' streets they don't know what tha' fuck they talkin' bout." KD replied knowing that Brian had broken rule one again and would have to go. "Maybe they don't, but I just wanted you to know they talkin'." "This what you called me fa'?" KD asked with open hostility. "Partly." Bobby replied calmly. "My ears still open." "a 'right, this what it is, I been fuckin' wit' these niggas fa' bout two, three years now, an I know they holdin' and movin' some heavy shit." "Heavy like what?" KD asked greedily. "I'm talkin' bout two spots movin' bout a ki or two every three days, I'm talkin' ridiculous money an plenty yah." KD stroked his goatee as Bobby continued running down the lick. "The only reason I'm talkin' to you bout it is cuz I know how you built, an I wanna show you ain't no beef, no hard feelin's, the past is tha' past." KD looked down at the women changing positions, Shaniece was now behind the other woman, who had gotten on her hands and knees in the doggy style position. Shaniece caught him looking at the two of them and slowly licked the other woman's pussy lips. "Should you be talkin' in front of them?" "don't worry bout them." "a 'right, so what's tha' deal?" "These mu'fukas workin' spots on twenty-third and Scott and tenth and Cleveland, we gon' do it like back in tha' day, buy an hit." "How many people? Cuz if they rollin' like you say, they gotta have security." "that's where yo' people come in at." "What you talkin' bout?" "I see you done got smart over tha' years." "Yeah, especially since you want me involved." KD replied emphasizing the word you. "a'right, this the break down, while we goin' through the front door yo' people can go through tha' back that way we got 'em covered both ways." "You still ain't told me how many people be in these spots." "They always switch up, sometimes it seven, sometimes ten, ain't no tellin.'" "I can tell you know we not rollin' on no maybes." Bobby leaned back in his chair knowing that it would be hard to get KD to let down his guard. "that's how they work, what can you want me ta' do?"

23

Bobby replied as he glanced at the two women who were moaning and working up a sweat. "Go in like tha' people they fear the most." "don't talk in riddles, what you talkin' bout?" "tha' police, go in like tha' police, get some badges, uniforms, fix up a couple of them caprices and do it like that." KD replied with a slight smirk. Bobby knew KD was right, and it pissed him off, but he nodded his approval. "I like that, and I can still put these bitches ta' work." He said nodding toward the women. Bobby knew that he couldn't let KD get into the streets like he wanted to because if he did there wouldn't be room for him. "Let me holla at you bout it once I talk to my people." KD replied as he sat back on the couch and watched the women put themselves in the sixty-nine position. "I need to know in two days." Bobby replied hoping to put pressure on him. "what's our cut if we decide to move?" "bout a hundred fifty-thousand, but you gotta split it wit' ya people." "they keep that much in a spot? "he asked suspiciously. "naw, that's between tha' two houses, why hit one an stop?" KD nodded, liking what he was hearing, but he was still on point and cautious. "Anything else I need ta, know?" "yeah, shoot ta' kill cuz they not gon' play." "tha' way you talkin' we gon 'need vest." KD said as he glanced at the women. "if you can get 'em, get 'em, I got some walkie-talkies." As they continued talking KDs phone rang. "what it do?" "just made it home." "put Mano on the phone." Trina handed Mano the phone and unlocked the front door to let everybody in. "what's up?" "shit, just walkin' in, what's the deal?" "I got wrapped up on some other shit, so just let my girl handle my end and yall call me tomorrow." "no prob, my nig." "a'right, put Trina back on the phone." "hold on." Mano replied as he handed the phone back to Trina. "what's that moanin' I hear in tha' background?" "some dyke bitches Bobby got freakin' on each other." "you need ta' get home, ain't no reason fa' you ta' be partyin'." Trina said angerly. "baby stop trippin' I'm here on business that's it that's all, as a matter of fact come get me." "I'll be there as soon as yo' people leave." "well, handle that an call me when you on tha' way." "yeah, okay." Trina replied still upset. "I love you." "I love you to."

24

She replied. KD hung up and turned to Bobby. "we done?" Bobby stood and turned to the women. "that's enough, get yall ass up an get dressed." KD shook his head as Shaniece, and the other female walked to the couch and began getting dressed. "yeah, we done but I need a favor from you." KD smirked. "yeah, what's that?" "I need you to pick up rock from the airport two days from now." "what time?" KD asked too quick for Bobby's liking. "six in tha' evenin'." "at Mitchell?" "yeah, call me when you headed out and I'll give you the gate number then." "an I don't care what he say, when you get him bring him to tha' shop, we'll talk a lil' more." After talking business for another twenty minutes KD opened the office door and saw Brian walking out of the garage. "somebody blowin'." He said. "probably Trina crazy ass." KD replied taking his phone out of his pocket. "call me an let me know if yall in." "I will." He said, not knowing if he meant it or not. "remember, two days, I need to know in two days." KD knew Bobby was trying to pressure him into accepting the lick without talking to his crew. He knew Bobby and Brian were up to something, but he couldn't put his finger on it. As Bobby unlocked and opened the outside door his phone rang, and the horn blew again. "yeah, that's her I'm outta here." He said as he stepped outside. "I'll catch up wit' you, I'm tryin' ta see if Bobby can put me in wit' them hoe's he had in there." "yeah, I figured that." KD replied as he walked to his car. "what's goin' on.?" Trina asked when he got in. "shit, we was talkin' business, what's yo' problem?" he replied knowing she was mad. "was you fuckin' one of them bitches he had in there?" Trina asked as she pulled away from the shop. "naw, they was there before we got there?" "can I trust you?" she asked seriously. "What kinda question is that? as long as we been together you gotta ask?" "it's the type I want an answer to an don't be tryna make me feel guilty." "yeah, you can trust me." When they reached the express way KD turned on the radio, young Joc's song I know played and KD rapped along. Trina reached over and turned the music off. "do you really love me?" she asked. "I wouldn't have said it if I didn't mean it." She knew that with all of the things

25

that were going on she shouldn't be on him the way she was, but she was giving him her all and she wanted to make sure he wasn't playing games. "good, that's yo' key." She said pointing to the key hanging from the rearview mirror. It wasn't seven-thirty when they pulled up to the house. Once they were in, he closed the door and locked it. "Bobby want me ta' pick rock up from tha' airport Thursday night." "fa' what? You don't even fuck wit' them, it gotta be somethin' to it." She said as she took off her shoes. "Bobby say he gotta move that'll put a hundred fifty gees in our pocket if we go, but we gotta split it." Trina wasn't surprised that Bobby offered them a part of his move to stay on KD's good side, but she knew that out of all of them he had to be careful, because she knew they hadn't forgotten what he'd done. "you told 'em bout everybody?" "naw, but he know about yall and tha' move already Brian runnin' his mouth." Trina was quiet for a few seconds. "baby, I don't think we should hit this move, I gotta bad feeling." "why? What you think he on." He asked as they walked to the living room. Once they were in the living room, he turned the TV on and sat on the couch. Trina lay her head on his lap. "I just feel like somethin' bad gon' happen if we go, we goin' ta'gether, so what can go wrong?" Trina sat up. "I don't know but I don't think we should go." KD tilted his head back and stared at the ceiling. "baby, a lil' over sixteen gees a piece ain't no petty change." "I know but what good is sixteen gees if we can't spend it?" KD stood up. "ain't nothin' gon' happen he can't set up much in a few days and we need that money." Trina hoped he was right because she still had the feeling that bobby was on some shystie shit, and knowing Rock was involved didn't make her feel better. "baby, stop trippin'." He said seeing that Trina was deep in thought. "I told you this bother me." "I know baby but trust me." "what I'm a do if somethin' happen to you?" she replied as tears ran down her face. KD wiped away the tears as he held her. "stop, ain't no need fa' all that I'm a be straight." KD said as he let go. Trina walked to one of the cabinets and grabbed a bag of popcorn and KD followed, he knew she ate when she was worried. "watch out fa' rock to." She said. "I already know who he roll wit' but I'm a feel 'em out." He replied as they walked back to the living room. Once they were back in the living room KD picked up his cellphone and began to dial. "who this?" a man with a squeaky voice answered. "this KD" "augh, why do I get tha' pleasure of this call?" the man asked. "I'm fresh out, my money short, but I gotta couple moves lined up an I need nine vests." "damn! You touch down on some wild shit." "man, you know shit ain't changed, I'm bout money an a nine ta' five ain't gon' cut it." "I feel you on that so when you gon' need this shit?" "ta'day if you can swing it." "I don't keep that type of shit on deck, give me bout a week." KOKO said as he handed a piece of paper and cellphone to his girlfriend. "bobby." She mouthed as she read the paper. "let me make a few calls an if don't nothin' come through, I'll call you back." "a'right, holla at ya' boy." KOKO said. "fa' sho." KD replied knowing that more than likely he wouldn't call back. KD hung up and called Mano, after a few rings he hung up and called Doobie. "hello." "what it do?" KD replied. "shit, what it do?" "Bobby gotta move he want us in on." "so, what's tha' problem?" "nothin' I wanna know if yall gon' roll wit' it even though I don't need all of yall." KD replied as he shook his head at the bowl of popcorn Trina was offering. "why not all of us?" Doobie asked curiously. "Bobby got rock an some of his people comin' we goin' in like tha' police." "aw, I see, he wanna make it half an half huh?" "yeah, basically." "how yall gon' do it like that wit' out uniforms?" Doobie asked. KD didn't like the tone of Doobies voice, he knew that Doobie was jealous of him, he had known it when they first met fifteen years ago at the juvenile probation office. "I'm workin' on that now." KD replied calmly. "so, you should be straight then." "yeah." KD replied wondering if he should watch Doobie more carefully. "let me call you back." Doobie said when his line clicked. "a'right." KD replied as he hung up and then tried mano again. This time the phone was

CHAPTER 2

answered. "hello." "mano, where you been?" "Makin' moves, why? What's up?" "bobby gotta move he want me in on an we need some police fits." "I can make a call, my pops friend work fa' tha' police." KD knew that mano was his best bet because his foster father had been a police officer for almost thirty years before he retired to live in California. "you think he'll plug us?" "fa' tha' right amount of change he will." "can you holla at him asap?" "what's tha' rush?" "we need it before next Saturday." Mano picked up on we. "what's wit' tha' we?" "he want me ta' bring at least five of yall cuz we goin' in like tha' police." "I'll get on it as soon as I hang up." "I'm a get off this phone so you can look into that." "I'll let you know as soon as I know somethin'." Mano replied before he hung up. KD put the phone down kissed Trina, then pointed towards the stairs as he picked up the phone and dialed Bobby's number. "yeah?" he answered. "I'm puttin' everything into play." Bobby was happy to hear KD say he was in. "so, I take it yo' people rollin' to." "it look that way." "good, good I'm a make a few calls so that we'll be on the same page." "a'right, don't forget about pickin' Rock up at Mitchell on Thursday." "I won't." KD replied and hung up. That night he and Trina made love until midnight. The next morning, he left the house and drove to the shop, when he arrived, they spent an hour talking about the move and how they first met. After they finished talking KD left and called Trina. "hello." "what you doing?" "nothin' chillin', why?" "cuz I'm headed yo' way." Trina smiled as she thought about their night. "you want me ta' fix somethin' ta' eat?" "naw, I'm straight." "baby, is everything okay?" "yeah, but do me a favor, call Keema, Doobie, Brian and Mano." Trina knew something was wrong. "what you want me to tell 'em?" "tell 'em ta' meet me at the house in an hour." He replied as he made a right on Holton and locust. "okay." "oh, after I hang up, I'm gettin' rid of this phone." "baby, what's goin' on?" "nothin' ta' worry 'bout, I'll talk to you when I get there." "a'right, hurry up an get here, you got me worried." "I'll be there." He replied and hung up. When Trina hung up her mind began working double time. She picked the phone back up and dialed Keema's number,

28

the phone rang five times before it was answered. "hello, hello." "keema?" "this me, what's up?" "this Trina." "oh, girl, what's up?" "I don't know KD told me ta' call you, he want yall at tha' house in an hour." "who's yall?" "You, Doobie, Brian, and Mano." "what about Star and them?" Keema asked. "I don't know, he said you, Doobie, Brian, and Mano." Trina said still trying to piece things together in her head. "a'right, I'm bout ta' click over an call Mano." "go head." Trina replied. Keema clicked over and when the phone rang, she clicked back over. "hello." "yeah? I'm still here." "it's ringin.'" After a few rings it was answered. "who this?" "this Keema, and that ain't how you answer no phone." "what's goin' on?" "nothin,' I got Trina on tha' phone." Keema said quickly. "what up Trina?" "nothin' much KD want yall at the house asap." "I'm gettin' my car fixed so I'm a call Doobie fa' a ride." "a'right, let me finish these calls." Keema replied and hung up. "call Brian." Trina said. "what's his number?" "hold on, I gotta look for it." "you got Brian number huh?" Trina knew what she was thinking. "naw, I got tha' number ta' his shop." Trina replied as she made her way up the stairs. Once she made it upstairs, she went to her room, opened the bedside dresser and grabbed a pink envelope with the shops number on it. "hello." "if you ain't heard a dial tone I ain't went nowhere." "whatever, I found tha' number, its three-four-two forty-two hundred." "a'right, hold on." Keema replied before clicking over. A few seconds later she clicked back over. "you still there?" "I'm here." "it's ringin'." "low key cuts." "is Brian there?" "hold on a minute." "tell him Keema need to talk to him." Trina chose to listen without saying anything, but the bad feelings were back. They waited five minutes before Brian made it to the phone. "yeah." "what's up?" "shit, waitin, on my next cut, what's up?" "KD want us at Trina's in a hour." "a'right, I was takin' off early anyway." "that's all I wanted." "a'right, let me get back to work." "bye." Keema said with attitude. When Brian hung up Keema clicked back over. "well, I'm on my way." "a'right, call me when you halfway." After Trina got off the phone with Keema she went to the living room and sat down to watch TV. Ten minutes later she heard

29

KD'S key in door. "baby!" "I'm in tha 'livin' room." KD walked into the living room, sat next to Trina, then kissed her. "you do like I asked?" "everybody said they on they way." "good, good, I got some shit ta' talk ta' yall about." "is it bad?" "you'll find out when everybody get here." "why you get rid of ya' phone?" "I'm just takin' precautions in case it's some funny shit goin' on." "okay, why you ain't got Tara an Star comin'?" "cuz, I got some other shit I'm a talk ta' them about." Trina didn't understand, but she nodded any way. At eight forty-five they showed up even though Keema never called. "what up yall?" Trina said when she opened the door. "nothin' much where KD at?" Doobie asked. "in tha' livin' room." When they made it to the living room Brian was the first to speak. "what's tha' business?" "I got some news, but we gotta wait on Mano." "I thought Mano was gettin' a ride wit' you." Trina said looking at Doobie. "naw, he got his car fixed he said he was straight." "augh, okay." Trina replied. "that nigga a slow down his own funeral." Keema said. "hell yeah." KD replied with a semi laugh. A while later there was a knock at the door, KD knew that it was Mano by the knock. "who is it!?" "ya' momma nigga, open tha' door." KD opened the door. "everybody in tha' livin room." He said as he locked the door and followed Mano to the living room. "my bad I'm late I got pulled over." "fa' what?" Keema asked. "speedin.'" "you straight?" "yeah, I'm straight, but what's crackin'?" "I told you I need ta' get those uniforms before next Saturday, tell ya' mans I got money if the price right." Mano took his cellphone from his pocket. "I'm a call 'em now." He said as he dialed the number. The phone rang once before it was answered. "Allen." "this Mano, what's up?" "business as usual, what's up?" "I need a favor." "what kind of favor?" "the type I'm willin' ta' pay for if the price is right." "my type of favorite type of favor, what you need." "I need nine vest and eleven uniforms." "get me four an a half grand." "damn, can I get a discount or somethin'?" "since you're my favorite black guy get me three thousand-two hundred." Mano repeated the price so KD would hear. "ask him how long before you can get 'em." KD whispered. Mano repeated his question. "bout two hours after I see the money." Mano repeated what Allen said and KD agreed. "so, what now? Cuz we ain't got thirty-two-hundred." Mano said after hanging up. "don' worry bout it." "a'right, so why we here?" Brian asked. KD told them about Bobby's move and how he wanted it done. "how much we in fa'?" Doobie asked. "a hundred fifty gees, but we gotta split it between us." There was a little bit of excitement in the room. "hey! Hey! Listen, we still gotta make this move tonight, so let's focus on that fa' now." "a'right, tell us what's up?" Keema replied. "I got word from an associate that this store on the north side got a nice piece of money in tha' safe we need that." "so, what we sittin' here fa'?" Mano asked. "I gotta make sure we do it right, so Keema I need you and Trina ta' put on somethin' sexy." Keema headed outside and Trina made her way upstairs without asking any questions. Keema made it back before Trina came downstairs. "I'm glad I went shoppin' earlier, where you want me ta' get dressed?" "use tha' closet." Keema was making her way to the closet when Trina came down the stairs, she was wearing a shredded denim skirt, with a mini tank top and strappy open toed sandals. "damn Trina." Doobie said as he looked at her freshly oiled legs. "Don't stare to hard nigga." KD replied seriously. "girl, you look good in that, is them choo's?" Keema asked. "and you know it." "what you wearin'?" Brian asked. "you'll see in a minute." Keema replied as she stepped into the closet and closed the door. A few minutes later she stepped out in a pair of suede capri Gucci pants, a half top that barely covered her breast and a pair of Manolo's. Mano stared at her for a few seconds. "what's up wit' all this." He asked. "like I said I got a move set up, we get in wit' em on his move, but we doin' this fa' us." KD replied. "baby, why we dressed like this?" "I'm getting ta' that, but before I do, I got somethin' ta' get off my chest, one of us either workin' fa' Bobby or just plain runnin' they mouth, either way Bobby know about this move, if yall wanna work fa' him go do that, but If yall wanna work wit' me, keep yall mouth closed." Everyone talked a few seconds. "a'right! A'right, listen this deal, this mu'fucka Danny Royals own the store I was talkin'

31

bout, he straight trick he think wit' his dick, that's why yall dressed like that." "okay, why we still here?" Doobie asked. "we on our way out, get strapped up." Thirty minutes later they were sitting in front of royal's candy store. "Trina, you an Keema gon' walk to tha' door knock, tell 'em yall just got robbed an need ta' use tha' phone we'll do tha' rest." "a'right." Trina replied as she and Keema opened their doors and climbed out. KD and the rest of the crew waited for Danny to open the door when he did, they were through the door like clockwork. Once they made it back to Trina's house, they opened the bags and counted five thousand dollars. "look, we got five gees', but a lil' over three of it gotta go ta' what we need, the rest we can split, so that's only like three hundred a piece." Everyone knew that it wasn't what they expected. "Mano, call ya' boy." Mano took the cellphone out of his pocket and began dialing. After two rings the phone was answered. "Allen." "this Mano, I'm ready fa' you." "let me call you back." "you want this money or not cuz if not I can find somebody else." Mano replied angerly. "a'right, I'm on my way." Mano hung up. "we gotta go to the deep east." He said as they headed outside. "where?" KD asked once they were in the car. "down to Farwell and Brady." Fifteen minutes later they hit Farwell and Brady. "pull up in the subway parkin' lot." KD pulled in the parking lot and left the car running. Five minutes later Allen pulled in besides them. "get out the car." He said as he looked around. Mano got out the car. "whose your friend?" "that's my guy KD, he cool." "you know tha' routine, let's get it over with." Mano turned and faced Allen's car and let him check for guns and a wire." "you're good." Mano walked to Allen's trunk and unzipped the duffel bags. "it's good." Mano replied. Allen walked behind him as KD counted the money. "How'd you know I already had tha' shit?" "cuz you my favorite white guy." Mano said as he grabbed the bags and put them in the back seat and got in. "pull off and go left." KD pulled out of the parking lot and turned left. When they arrived back at Trina's house he parked, got out then went and unlocked the door. Trina crept into the hallway. "baby, everything okay?" "yeah, everything straight."

32

"where Mano?" "he on his way in." A few minutes later he walked up the stairs with the two long duffel bags. "you movin' in?" Trina asked laughingly. "naw, but can I get some help?" KD grabbed one of the bags and walked into the living room. "I want yall ta' try on these uniforms and see if they fit. Keema and Trina grabbed shirts, pants, and boots, then walked toward the bathroom. Once they were in the bathroom they began to undress. "girl, dat bra and panty set cute, where you get it?" "Victoria secrets." Trina replied. "I figured that." Trina continued to dress and Keema continued to stare at her on the slide. "girl, where you work out at?" Keema asked. "I don't work out." Trina replied with a laugh. "fa' real? You shaped like that and don't work out; girl look at this." Keema said as she turned and grabbed what she considered fat on her legs. "girl ain't nothin' wrong wit' yo' body." Once they were done getting dressed, they walked out of the bathroom. Trina bent over to tie her boots and felt Keema's hand on her ass. "bitch! What tha' fuck wrong wit' you?" "TR-Trina, I'm sorry, I'm so sorry." "bitch, don't ever touch me again." Trina said staring at her angerly. "I said I'm sorry b-but I'm feelin' you, you don't need KD shystie ass." "I'm strictly dickly." "I'm sorry fa' comin' at you, but like I said KD shystie, so be careful." "what you mean he shystie?" "augh, so he ain't tell you bout our fuckin' baby?" don't worry though, the baby died right before he went to prison." Before the words had fully sunk in Trina punched Keema in the face. "you got me fucked up bitch!" Keema yelled as she swung back and missed. Trina kicked her in the stomach then grabbed her by the hair. Everybody heard the commotion, KD and Brian were the first to make it to the hallway. "what tha' fuck goin' on!" Brian asked as he grabbed Keema. KD held Trina as she tried to fight him off. "get tha' fuck off me! Don't touch me you bitch ass nigga, don't touch me!" KD was surprised by her anger. "what you snappin' on me fa'?" "you had a baby by her? You got her pregnant?" "what tha' fuck you talkin' bout!" he yelled. Keema fought to get away from Brian "I ain't never fucked that bitch! An we ain't never had no baby, I don't know why she lying." KD replied knowing it was a lie.

33

"fuck you bitch ass nigga! Just remember what you just said." Keema yelled as Brian lead her to the living room. Trina wiped her eyes and looked at KD. "I remember you fuckin' her." "that was in high school, we wasn't even together." "you got her pregnant KD?" "naw, I ain't get her pregnant." "dat bitch tried ta' dyke on me." "what tha' fuck you talkin' bout?" he asked as they walked to the living room "dat bitch grabbed my ass an told me she was feelin' me, she gotta go." "we need her fa' this lick." When they made it to the living room Trina mugged Keema. "whatever." "if yall wanna handle shit after this move that's on yall, but fa' now let's focus on this move." "yeah, we gone handle it." Keema replied quickly. "bitch you got it comin." Trina snapped lunging at Keema. KD quickly grabbed her. "let that bitch go!" Trina yanked away. "get off me Kevin!" "so, I'm Kevin now, so you believe her?" "honestly, I don't know what ta' believe." Trina replied angrily. "everybody chill a'right." Brian said. It took a minute for everybody to calm down. "so, you want me ta' sleep down here ta'night?" "no, I just wanna know tha' truth." Trina said sincerely. "I told you tha' truth." KD replied. "I don't know if I believe you, but I do know me an that bitch gotta see each other after this shit over." "that's on yall." KD said as he shook his head. "okay, now that yall done figured out tha' bullshit, let's get back to business, ain't we suppose ta' be meetin' Bobby?" Brian asked. "damn! You right, can yall at least make through this without tha' bullshit?" KD asked. Keema rolled her eyes. "I don't know bout her, but I'm good." She replied. KD looked at Trina. "I'm good, business first." She replied as she went upstairs to take off the uniform. When everyone was dressed, they left and headed to the shop. When they pulled up in front of the shop KD saw two cars, one was Bobby's, the other he had never seen before. KD pulled up on the side of Doobie. "Brian, who car is that?" he asked. "I don't know." When they parked Brian got out and walked to the door, everyone followed and waited. Brian pulled the door open. "Bobby!" "come ta' tha' back, I'm in the middle of somethin'." Bobby replied as he turned on the hallway light. They all looked at each other before walking

34

down the hall to his office. When they walked in there was a muscular man in the office, he was short, but built like Mike Tyson. "who all these people?" KD put his hand out. "what's ya' name pimp?" "MC." The man replied as he shook KD's hand. "MC, this my girl Trina, my home girl Keema, my niggas Mano, Brian, an Doobie." Bobby picked up the bag that was on the floor and sat it on the table while looking at Brian. "I'm bobby, an yall here because I asked KD if he knew some people, he could trust to help me pull this move, I figure he told yall already." Bobby walked from behind his desk and sat on the edge, forcing MC to move to the opposite corner of the desk. "KD said yall need fireworks for this, so I bought everybody Glock forties and shotguns like tha' police carry, so yall should have everything yall need." "show 'em the car's we hooked up." Brian said excitedly. "follow me out back." Once they stepped outside Bobby lead them down a path that was hidden behind recked cars that were used for parts. When they stopped, they saw six caprices in different colors, KD hadn't expected them to look exactly like detective or under cover cars, but they did. "Bobby hooked us up." Brian said. An hour later they left the shop with the guns, after having made plans to pick up the cars the next night. "why you get those guns?" Trina asked on the way back. "we gotta roll wit' his way of doin' shit right now, plus I don't want him to know I gotta plug." Trina knew they had been through the subject of Bobby and Rock but decided to ask anyway. "baby do you trust them?" "naw, that's why I'm doin' thing's this way." When they got up the next morning it was like the situation between Trina and Keema never happened. "baby I'm a buy us new phones today." Trina said as she kissed him. "a'right, let me get up, I'm a roll wit' you." KD replied. "what you want ta' eat?" She asked. "I ain't really hungry, I gotta bust moves." "well, go take a shower an by tha' time you get out an get dressed I'll be ready fa' mine." Trina said as she headed to wake everyone up, but when she made it downstairs everyone was already woke. "yall hungry?" "naw, I'm straight." Brian replied. "what about you Doobie?" "yall got cereal?" "yeah, it's in tha' cabinet, go head." Trina turned to

35

Keema. "you hungry?" "naw, I don't want shit from you tell KD to ask me." "chill out." Brian said. "fuck her." Keema said as she stood up. "Naw, bitch get fucked up fuckin' wit' me." "chill!" Brian said again. "where KD at?" Doobie asked. "he in tha' shower" Trina replied as she stood staring at Keema. Doobie went upstairs and walked into the bedroom then knocked on the bathroom door. "KD come get ya' girl an Keema before they get ta' fightin' again." "here I come!" Doobie walked out of the room and back downstairs. "Trina, KD want you." He lied. Trina mugged Keema as she went up the stairs. When she walked in the room KD was getting dressed. "what's goin' on downstairs?" "that bitch down there tryin' ta' start shit." "won't you get in tha' shower." Trina slipped off her long tee-shirt and got in the shower. Ten minutes later she came out of the bathroom and got dressed. "you ready?" he asked. "yeah, let's go." "yall finally ready ta' go I see." Brian said when they made it downstairs. "the question is, is yall ready?" "let's roll." Doobie said. "you got some killa' wit' you Mano?" "fa' sho." "let me owe you for a three-five." Mano went in his jacket pocket and threw him a half full sandwich bag. "you don't owe me shit; we can smoke off that all day." "good lookin'." KD replied. When they left the house Doobie and Brian headed to Doobies car, Mano went to his car and Trina and KD went to their car. Keema walked over to KD's car. "can I ride wit' you?" "it's up to Trina." He replied. "well?" Keema said. "hell naw." Trina replied. "you know what, we can finish this shit whenever." "you ain't said nothin' but a word." "what's up then?" Keema asked as she backed up to let Trina out of the car. "yall chill out! How tha' fuck we gon' be a team an yall can't get along for two minutes.?" "fuck it, I'll ride wit' Doobie." When she reached Doobie's car, he opened the door and let her in. "what happened?" "that bitch still trippin'." She replied angerly. "yall need ta' squash dat shit." "fuck that hoe, I'm a squash her bitch ass." When they pulled off, they headed to the mall. When they arrived, they decided to park by the entrance. "baby, I'm goin' ta' footlocker." "fa' what?" KD asked. "I wanna see what new shoes came out." She replied. "a'right, give me tha' money

36

so I can get tha' phones." Trina reached in her pocket and gave him three one-hundred-dollar bills, then walked to the escalator. When she made it to the second floor she walked into footlocker and saw KD's friend Grip behind the counter. "what can I get fa' you?" "somethin' pimpish fa' KD." "snatch him some crispy airforce ones." "let me see a pair." "they over here." He said as he walked to the shelf. "what you think?" he asked picking up a black and gold pair. "he'll love these, let me get 'em in a eight and a half." Grip turned and walked toward the storage room. "I'll be right back." A few seconds later he came out and walked back behind the counter. "you ready ta' get rung up?" "yeah, I'm ready." The shoes came to ninety-five dollars. Trina handed him a hundred-dollar bill and walked out. When she made it back downstairs, she decided to buy KD a watch and walked into Sterns Jewelry Store. The clerk was a middle-aged woman with long hair who looked like she could have been a model. "Welcome to Sterns, can I help you?" "yea, uhm, I'm looking for men's watches." "My names Melinda, come this way." Trina followed her to a glass counter. "I want that one." "ma'am, that watch cost two-thousand dollars." "that's all?" "yes, that's all." Melinda replied with a smile. Trina went through her purse and pulled out a roll of money and counted out two-thousand dollars and sat it on the counter. Melinda quickly grabbed the keys off the cash register and walked back to the counter, she took the watch out, placed it in a box and gave it to Trina with a receipt. When she walked out the store, she saw KD with their new cellphones. "baby, what you done went an bought?" "some shoes for you." She replied. "good lookin'." KD replied as he grabbed the bag. When he opened the footlocker bag, he saw the Sterns jeweler bag. "what you get at tha' jewelers?" "oh, that's for you to." She said. "what is it?" he asked. "a watch." "good cuz I need one." He replied. "where everybody at?" Trina asked. "buyin' watches an gloves." "you ready ta' go yet?" "yeah, let's get everybody an get the fuck outta here, I don't want you spendin' no mo' of ya' college money." Trina knew after the move she would get it all back. It took fifteen minutes to get

37

everybody together and out of the mall. When they left the mall, they headed back to Trina's house. "what time is it?" KD asked as he drove. "ten-thirty." Trina replied. KD set his watch. "what you wanna do baby?" "get on dat bitch Keema ass." Trina replied quickly. KD sighed and laid back in his seat knowing that all he could do was wait to see what the rest of the morning would bring. When they made it back to Trina's house everyone parked, got out and headed up the stairs. Trina unlocked the door, walked in and turned on the lights. "make yall self at home." He said as he closed the door. Everyone took a seat as he and Trina walked into the kitchen. "look, all this drama shit ain't cool, yall need to squash that shit asap, so how can we make this a dead issue?" KD asked as soon as the door swung closed. "I just want my one on one an I'm good." Trina replied. KD nodded. "a'right, I need you to be cool, cuz I'm bout to call her in here." KD went to the kitchen door and opened it. "Keema, come here real quick." Keema walked into the kitchen. "what's up?" she asked. "Trina want her one's so this beef yall got can be over." "it's whatever wit' me." Keema replied. "tha' way you talkin' you act like you wanna go now." Trina said with a smirk. "look, yall both talkin' like yall ready ta' go, so let's just get it over wit' so we can focus on this money." KD said seriously. They both agreed that it would be over after the fight. "a'right, let's go get this over wit'" KD said as he stood to leave the kitchen. "let's go." Trina said quickly but anxiously. "where we doin' this at?" Keema asked. "outside." KD replied. Keema was the first out of the kitchen. "what's goin' on?" Doobie asked. "I'm bout ta' beat Trina ass." Doobie, Brian and Mano watched as Keema walked outside followed by KD and Trina. When they made it outside Keema was standing on the sidewalk waiting. "what up hoe?" Keema said calmly. Trina came off the stairs with no reply, swung and hit Keema in the face causing her nose to bleed. "bitch you ain't on shit, you just talk." Trina said waiting on Keema to react. "get this shit over wit' Trina!" KD yelled. When Trina looked over to KD, Keema punched her causing her to fall. "get up bitch, talk that shit now." She said. Trina got up and rushed Keema, but

38

Keema stepped back to avoid being hit or grabbed and in the process, she grabbed Trina's hair and pulled her down. "yeah bitch, what's up now?" Keema said as she connected with two punches to her face. "talk shit now." Keema said as she continued punching Trina. "Mano, break it up." Brian said when they saw that Trina was protecting her face and not swinging back. Mano ran off the porch and grabbed Keema who was still punching Trina in the head and face. KD grabbed Trina and walked her toward the house. "yall cool.?" KD asked. "it's cool, it's over, I'm straight." "both of yall go clean ya' self-up." KD replied. Trina headed upstairs and Keema sat where she was. "ain't shit wrong wit' me, I'm straight, just get me a towel." KD shrugged, picked up his cellphone and called Bobby's shop. "hello." "what's goin' on?" "nothin' much, why?" "is it cool if we come through?" "of course." Trina came down the stairs wearing a different outfit with her hair freshly brushed. KD looked up to see if she was okay, then went back to his conversation. "we'll be there in thirty-minutes." "I'll be here." Bobby replied and hung up. "yall sure yall cool?" KD asked. Keema looked at Trina. "it's cool wit' me, I don't know bout her." "I said it's cool, I'm straight." KD nodded and walked toward the kitchen and Trina followed. When they were in the kitchen KD looked her up and down. "you a'right?" "baby, I'm straight." Trina replied as they walked out of the kitchen and back into the living room. "yall ready ta' go?" everybody agreed and ten minutes later they were headed to Bobby's shop. When they made it to the shop, they parked and walked in. "what's up Bobby?" "I see you got ya' click wit' you, yall ready ta' get down?" "fa' sho." Doobie said. Everyone noticed that Doobie was the first to speak, but they all agreed. "so, what's up yall?" Bobby asked. "we just came to get the walkie-talkies." "all business huh?" Bobby replied as he walked toward his private bathroom. A few seconds later he came back with two bookbags and sat them on the table. "take what you need." KD picked out seven of the walkie-talkies and zipped the bag up. "what frequency we gon' be on?" he asked. "five and one." KD gave everyone walkie-talkies. "who else goin' wit' us." KD asked.

39

"the hoes you seen, two of my people, Rock, me, you and yo' people." Bobby replied. "well, let me get to work, you go do what you gotta do, and tha' quicker tha' better." KD shook his head and walked towards the door. As they walked out the phone rang, Bobby looked at the phone and finally decided to answer it on the fourth ring. "Bobby's auto shop, Freddie, what's goin' on?" when they made it outside Doobie looked back at the shop. "it just me or did he act like he didn't wanna answer the phone while we was there." "I noticed that to." Mano replied. "yall followin' me ta' tha' crib or what?" KD asked showing his irritation. "we goin' back ta' Mano crib ta' make sure everything ready fa' Saturday." Keema replied. "yeah, we only got two days ta' set up." Doobie replied. "a'right, just have everything set up so we be on point." When Doobie and Mano made it to their car's they waited on Keema and Brian. When they pulled off, they Mano. KD waited for a few seconds, then pulled off and headed towards Trina's house, thinking about all the things he and crew could do with a hundred-fifty thousand. When he pulled up to the house, he saw Rock hanging up his cellphone and put it in his pocket. KD pulled into the driveway and rolled his window down. "nigga, I been callin' you, why you ain't answerin' yo' phone?" "I gotta new number." "well, you could've let somebody know." Rock said as he walked to the car. "didn't know it mattered." KD and Trina got out of the car and Trina went up the stairs and let herself In. KD stayed outside with Rock. "I thought you wasn't 'possed ta' be here till tomorrow." "I decided ta' surprise yall." "so, Bobby don't know you here?" "naw, I gotta call 'em." "what's been goin' down wit' you?" KD had somethings he wanted to say too rock, but now wasn't the time. "shit, what's been goin' on wit' you?" "chillin' tryin' ta' stay out, an get money." "same ol' shit." "basically, so how was it in Memphis?" "man, it was beautiful, hoes everywhere, I been fuckin' so much my dick hurt." "I been holdin' shit down wit' Trina since I got out." "come down to tha' dirty we'll hit tha' clubs, you can fuck all you want." "I'm cool I like breathin' too much." Rock knew KD was holding something in. "what's up?" "what you mean what's up?"

"I'm sayin', you actin' different, what's up?" KD got in the car and opened the passenger door. "get in." Rock got in and KD pulled off. When they were a block down KD looked at Rock. "I'm a keep it one-hundred wit' you, I'm disappointed in you." "disappointed in me fa' what?" "fa' one, when I got popped off you disappeared on a nigga, that was some shystie shit." Rock sighed. "look, shit was hot an I wasn't gon' bite tha' hand that feed me." "so, you bite me! The one who was tryin' ta' make you the hand that fed you." He replied angerly. "it wasn't like that, I felt like we owed Bobby enough respect to be loyal." "so basically, you turned ya' back on me fa' him?" "naw, but I'm rollin' where tha' money at." "so, you sayin' fuck friendship when paper involved then huh?" "if that's how you lookin' at it then yeah." Rock replied. "well, I know where we stand now." KD replied. "what that mean?" "nothin', I just know you ain't tha' same nigga I grew up wit'" "naw, I'm not." When they pulled up to the shop Bobby was standing outside smoking a cigar. When he saw that Rock was in the car with KD he walked over. "what tha'- welcome home baby boy!" Rock opened the door and got out. "bobby, what's goin' on?" "same shit different day, how you feel?" he replied. "I'm good, it feels good to be back." Rock replied. "ok, be careful out here, shit done changed." "don't I know it." KD got out of the car. "what's up ol' man?" he asked Bobby. "nothin' new youngin'" Bobby said stepping into the shop. "KD, you got Rock uniform an shit?" "yeah, we got him plugged." KD replied. "he know what frequency ta' put tha' walkie-talkie on?" "naw, we ain't talked really, when you get ya' radio put it on channel five or one." "all ya' people know how we goin'?" "yeah, they know tha' deal." "look, I need some sleep, so I can be ready ta' roll out." "well, go lay it down, cuz we need you on point." KD left the shop and dialed Trina's number. "hello." "baby, call everybody an tell 'em ta' start checkin' shit, I'm on my way." "you want me to tell 'em anything else?" "make sure everybody know they gotta have a vest on." "a'right." Trina clicked over and called Mano on three-way. "yeah?" "mano, what up?" "what up my nigga?" "I want you to be seen in that caprice before we hit this lick."

41

"why? What's up?" Mano asked concerned. "I want whoever these mu'fucka's is to see twelve ridin' through a couple days before we run in." "should I have somebody else ride through wit' me?" "you make that call, but I need you to ride through fa' sho." "a'right, hey, speakin' of ridin' who you ridin' wit' when it go down?" Mano asked. "I'm ridin' wit' Bobby, who you ridin' wit'?" "I'm ridin' wit' rock." Mano replied. "make sure everybody straight an tell 'em to be masked up when they get out the car." "one mo 'day an we gon' be rich!" Mano replied excitedly. "wait til' it's over before you start talkin' an spendin' money." KD replied. "fa' sho." "baby, hang up." Trina hung up and clicked back over. "yeah baby." "tomorrow, when we pull up to the house call Tara and Star." "a'right." Trina replied. "give me a kiss fa' luck." Trina gave the phone a kiss, hung up, then called everybody to relay KD's message. On the other side of town, the two females Bobby had in his office were trying on their uniforms. "Shaniece, help me put this fuckin' uniform on." "hold on baby, I'm still puttin' mine on." A few minutes later Tammy walked into the bedroom. "why tha' fuck we gotta do this?" "cuz, if we don't, we gone be stuck doin' shit like two days ago." Shaniece replied. "so, you really gone kill somebody for forty-thousand?" Tammy asked. "for that much money I'd kill my momma." Shaniece replied. "you a crazy bitch, but I definitely feel you." Tammy replied. "help me wit' this vest it's heavy." Shaniece said. "I wonder why Bobby bought us vest." "cuz when the shootin' start you wanna be protected." Tammy replied. Shaniece and Tammy looked in the mirror. "damn, it's almost two 'o' clock, call Bobby." Shaniece replied. "why?" "to let him know this shit fit an we goin'" "he takin' shit to far wit' these vests." Tammy replied. "get wit' it girl, for forty-gees I'd wear a fuckin' bomb vest." "I ain't wearin' that heavy ass vest." "that's yo' ass not mine, call Bobby." Tammy walked out of the bathroom and into the hallway, picked up the phone and dialed Bobby number. "hello." "bobby, this Tammy, Shaniece said to tell you we can fit the uniforms and we rollin'" "a'right, tell her I said yall lay back til' Saturday." "I'll let her know." Tammy hung up, walked back into the bathroom and sat on the edge of the tub. "Bobby said just lay back til' Saturday." "a'right, help me outta this shit." "you think we can trust him?" Tammy asked as she helped Shaniece out of the uniform. "I wouldn't be doin' this if I thought he was on bullshit." Shaniece replied as she slipped out of her shirt and vest. "I don't like him." Tammy said after she slipped out of her pants. "well, when this over we ain't gotta deal wit' him." Tammy put on her jeans. "I know we gon' be straight baby." "good, now let's go to bed." "not yet, I got shit on my mind." Tammy replied. Shaniece didn't have on anything except her T-shirt, and she walked behind Tammy and kissed her neck. "like what baby? You always closin' me out." Tammy turned around. "baby, since Bobby double crossin' his friends, what's stoppin' him from doin' it to us?" "baby, we never did nothin' ta' fuck 'em over, why would he cross us?" "I don't know, but I don't like the whole set up." "what you talkin' bout?" Shaniece asked. "it's just a feelin'" "and what that mean?" "I just don't like tha' way he came at us." Shaniece looked at the uniforms piled on the floor. "I don't either, but forty gees is enough fa' us ta' bounce." She replied. They both headed to the living room and when they got their Tammy turned on the TV. "I can't wait to get outta Milwaukee." She said. "that's all I'm sayin', so chill." "you wanna smoke a blunt wit' me?" Shaniece asked. "yeah, I need to mellow out a lil' bit." "let me go grab a couple blunts from upstairs." Shaniece said before heading upstairs, grabbing four blunts and heading back downstairs. They sat an talked as they smoked one blunt after the other. Halfway through the third blunt Tammy turned the TV off. "I still don't trust him." "baby, fa' get Bobby, here hit this." Shaniece said as she passed the blunt. Tammy took three deep hits and gave the blunt back. "I love you bae." "I love you to." Shaniece replied. Tammy stood up and reached her hand out. "let's go upstairs." Shaniece put the blunt out, turned off the lights and followed Tammy upstairs.

.... SATURDAY...

CHAPTER 3

Back at Trina's house KD and Trina were talking. "Baby, somethin' ain't right wit' this move." "what's wrong?" "Bobby got us split up?" Trina replied. "we all goin' to tha' same place anyway, so it don't matter." "I know we goin' ta' tha' same place, but still, why Bobby want us to partner up wit' his people?" "it's his move." "we should get everybody together." Keema replied. KD liked the idea, so he got everybody together and told them about how Trina and Keema felt, they all admitted to having the same feeling, but they still wanted to bust the move. "Doobie, I want you to take my place ridin' wit' Bobby, Keema I want you to ride wit' Brian, and Trina, I want you wit' Shaniece." KD said after they talked. "who you gon' be ridin' wit?" Keema asked. "I'm a be ridin' wit' Rock bitch ass, and I'm a have Mano ride wit' tammy." "what about his other people?" Doobie asked. "fuck 'em we'll watch 'em as much as possible." When they finished talking KD dialed Bobby's number. "hello." "what's goin' on Bobby?" "nothin' much, waitin' on yall to get my people's, so we can go over these plans one more time before tonight." "yeah, speakin' of that, there's a change of plans?" "what you mean change of plans?" "we wanna ride a lil' different than what was planned." "a'right, how yall wanna ride?" Bobby asked trying to hide his anger. "Doobie gon' ride wit' you, Keema gon' roll wit' Brian, Trina gon' ride wit' Shaniece an Mano gon' ride wit' Tammy." "what's all this about?" "just bein' careful." "what you mean?" "it means, I'm a step ahead of the game." "KD, don't fuck this up." "don't worry bout it." "a'right." KD finished the conversation and hung up. "that's took care of so now all we gotta do is chill til' ta'night." After a few more minutes of discussion, they headed to the shop too pick up cars. It took thirty-minutes to get to the shop and get the cars, and another thirty-minutes to get Bobby's people together. When they met back at the shop Bobby was waiting. "we better have our shit together." He said. "we ready." KD replied. "let's get this money." Doobie replied excitedly. "KD, let me talk to you real quick." Bobby said as he approached KD. "a'right, I need ta' holla at Bobby tha' yall go chill." Everyone walked over to the couch and available chairs and sat down as KD, and Bobby left the room. "what's this all about?" Bobby asked as soon as the door closed. "like I told you, I'm being careful." KD replied. "so, you don't trust me? Even after I let the past go." "I didn't say that, but I do have three questions though." "shoot." Bobby replied. "first, how Rock know where Trina stay? second, how you get my number, and third what's up wit' you an Brian?" "as far as how Rock know where Trina stay, I don't know ask him, as far as how I got your number, your third question answered that, and to answer your third question, me and Brian momma went way back, when she died, I checked in on 'em and made sure he was good, that's it that's all, you good now?" Bobby replied. KD nodded. "yeah, I'm good." KD replied only believing that Brian had given Bobby his number. "a'right, let's go." It took ten minutes for Bobby, KD, and their crews to leave the shop and get to their cars. "KD, you got ya' vest on?" Mano asked when everyone was getting ready to get in their cars. "fa' what?" "man, you trippin'." Mano replied shocked by KD's answer. "Everybody load up, let's go, it's time ta' get ta' tha' money!" Bobby yelled. "let's do it." KD replied. Everybody got in their assigned car and pulled off headed to the southside. "so, it's five in the front and six in tha' back?" KD asked as soon as he got in the car. "yeah, why?" Rock asked. "we can kill tha' bullshit, what's really goin' on?" "what tha' fuck you talkin' bout?" "I'm talkin' bout you an Bobby being on sneaky shit." "maybe he always knew he could trust me more than he could trust you." Rock replied without looking KD's way. "so, I'm right it's some sneaky shit goin' on." "naw, I'm sayin' would you trust him if he pulled tha' shit you pulled?" Rock asked. "You know what, I ain't gon' speak on that." KD replied "you should, cuz tha' shit was foul." Rock said still not looking at KD. "if he had a problem why he ain't say shit?" KD replied angerly. "it's bout tha' money, not loyalty, he could give a fuck less about you leavin' us out there a million fuckin' years ago." KD was done with the conversation, so he took his cellphone out of his pocket and called Trina. "hello." She answered on the second ring. "I just wanted to make sure you was straight." "I'm cool, what about you?" "yeah, I'm cool, just remember what I told you." KD replied. "baby, why yo-." "just do what I said! And be careful." KD hung up as they pulled up a block away from the first house they were going to hit. Trina pulled her mask down and turned toward Shaniece. "if yall cross us, I'm a kill you first." "bitch, don't threaten me." "it's not a threat, it's a promise." Trina replied. "I'm here ta' get money just like yall." Shaniece said. "good." Trina replied. While everybody checked their radios and watches Trina kept watch. "we got ten minutes! Everybody straight?" "this gon' be in an out, right?" Dobbie asked. "it shouldn't take more than a few minutes, in an out." "what about tha' other spot?" Keema asked. "we'll cross that bridge when we get there." MC replied. "yeah, we gon' take it a step at a time." KD said. "do we shoot through tha' door or what?" Mano asked seriously. "five minutes!" Trina said looking at her phone. KD nodded and checked his watch. "we gon' follow police procedure, knock announce then kick, but be careful." He said. "it's usually five or six people in the house, but it could be more." Bobby said so everyone was one the same page. "any shots fired should be to kill." Bobby's friend Troy replied. KD looked at his watch. "three minutes, let's load up!" They all took separate directions to the house on twenty-third and Scott. The first four cars sped down to the house as the others crept through the alleys. When they got into position Bobby started the contact. "team five, we ready in tha' back." "team one settin' up in front." KD replied. "don't fuck this up." "team one, ready and waiting." KD replied ignoring Bobby's comment. "team five, out of cars, team one do tha' same." "team one set for run in." KD replied. "mask down." "knockin' now." KD replied as he knocked. "police! Open up!" he yelled. When Trina

46

heard him, she began to dial, and Mano knew it was time, so he kicked in the door. They went in prepared for anything. "police! Police! Lay down! Get tha' fuck down! Don't move!" They all yelled. Trina watched the action while she waited on Star or Tara to answer the phone. "yeah." Star answered. "get ta' tha' spot it's goin' down!" Trina replied. "where!" Star replied excitedly. "the first house, get here asap." "we on our way!" When Star hung up Trina opened the driver's side door, hopped out and threw the phone back in the car. "come on." Trina said. "who you just call?" Shaniece asked. "don't worry bout that, let's go." Trina responded. "this ain't how Bobby said it was gon' go?" Shaniece said. Trina cocked her forty Glock. "I bet it ain't, get ya' ass out tha' car and grab tha' shotgun." Shaniece grabbed and cocked the shotgun, pulled her mask down, hopped out the car and ran up the stairs. Trina felt something wasn't right. *"it's like they knew we was comin', it's too easy."* She said to herself as she ran in the house. "police! Police!" She yelled as she headed toward the stairs. When she got to the second stair she heard a door bang against the wall, before she could react, she heard two shots. She closed her eyes and waited on impact, but all she felt was a thick wetness spread across her face and chest. She grabbed her walkie-talkie. "I'm hit! I'm hit!" she yelled in a panic. She heard footsteps, then felt her body being dragged backwards, then she heard KD voice. "open ya' eye's, you ain't hit." She blinked then opened her eyes, she felt the wetness on her face, and wiped it away. When she looked at her hand and saw the blood, she panicked. "oh God! Oh God!" KD used his shirt to wipe away the blood. "Baby! Baby! it ain't yo' blood, you a'right." Trina sat up straight and wiped tears from her eyes, then looked down the stairs where she had seen the man with the gun, but all she saw was a boy with half of his face missing, laying in a pool of blood. "oh shit! Oh shit!" KD shook her. "calm down, it's okay, baby it's a'right." "I'm a be sic-." KD held her hair as she began to vomit. "Somebody get towels, hurry up! Hurry up!" Trina saw Mano

47

coming up the stairs with his shotgun and towels. He looked at KD, then Trina. "you a'right?" "y-yeah, yeah, I'm straight." Trina replied. "where Bobby at?" KD asked. "him an Troy in the attic." Mano replied. "help clean this shit up, so I can get rid of these towels." While they were cleaning up Trina heard a commotion, then four shots. Trina turned and saw MC fall against the wall as a man walked over him and pointed his gun at his face. Trina closed her eyes and squeezed the trigger six times. Mano swung his shotgun in the direction Trina was shooting and saw the man shaking throwing up blood. Mano pulled the trigger on his shotgun twice. KD picked Trina up, grabbed the towels and went to the stairs. "you a'right?" Mano asked. "yeah, tha' lil' nigga crept out tha' closet on me." MC replied. Mano pulled MC to his feet. "Trina saved yo' ass." MC looked up at Trina. "I owe you one." Trina nodded and checked for her extra clips. "baby didn't nobody come when they heard the shots, what's goin' on?" KD began to reply but stopped when he heard a female voice speaking accented English. "please, I gave you everythin' don't kill me, go! go!" MC went down the stairs, turned the corner and crept towards the living room. "baby, radio Doobie, tell him to hit me." Trina did as he asked. A few minutes later his walkie-talkie beeped. "team one, what's goin' on?" "we searchin' tha' house like planned." Doobie replied. "I need you here asap." "a'right, I'm headed yo' way." "team one, where you at?" "we at tha' end of tha' hall." KD replied. Doobie walked toward the end of the hall and saw KD, Mano and Trina doing room searches. "KD, what's up?" "who all on channel five?" He asked. "me, Rock, MC, and Troy." "change over to one." KD replied. "anything else?" "why didn't nobody come when they heard tha' shots?" Trina asked before KD got a chance. Doobie seemed ready to give an answer when KD's radio beeped. "team one, this team five." "what's up team five?" KD replied. "we hit tha' jackpot." Troy replied. "what you talkin' bout?" "we found seven bricks under the floor in one of the closets." "I'm on my way down." "I'll

48

keep searchin' up here." Trina said as she made her way to another room. "stay on point, an if it don't look right shoot it." KD replied. When they made it downstairs Shaniece, and Rock were coming out of the bathroom. "we found money in tha' wall." KD and Mano walked through the living room and saw Tammy with a shotgun and MC with his Glock forty keeping the few living people in the house from moving. When they made it to the bathroom Shaniece and Rock had the mirror pulled from the wall, and two plastic wrapped bundles of money laying on the floor. "jackpot! We done did it." "knock holes in every wall in this bitch." KD replied. Rock took the butt of the shotgun and smashed it into the wall creating another hole. "damn! We gon' be rich, look at this shit, it gotta be more than half a mil' in this house." After talking to Rock and Shaniece, KD radioed Keema and Brian. "where tha' fuck is Keema and Brian?" He asked when he didn't receive a response. "last time I seen 'em they was headed to the basement." Rock replied. "him an Keema? Tha' fuck they on?" KD waved it off and headed towards the attic. Once he got close, he radioed Troy and Bobby. "team five, what's up?" "team one, this is team five." Came the reply after a few seconds of silence. "I'm lookin' fa' Troy." "I'm in the attic wit' Bobby." Troy replied quickly. "a'right, I'm comin' up." As he prepared to go up the stairs, he and Mano heard a fight, they ran towards the living room where the sounds coming from. When they made it to the entrance of the living room, Mano went in first and saw Tammy holding her right shoulder. "what happened?" Mano asked. "the bitch stabbed me!" KD came around the side of Mano and saw Tammy holding her shoulder. "what happened?" "the bitch stabbed me, I let her up to piss an the bitch stabbed me." Tammy replied. "shoot her." KD said calmly. "what?" Tammy said unsure. "the bitch stabbed you, shoot her." KD replied. "get up!" The lady didn't move, so MC walked over to her and pulled her to her feet by her hair. When she was on her feet she spit in his face. "oh, you like ta' spit, huh?" MC said as he punched her in the face and

49

pushed her towards Tammy. "look at me!" The lady looked up at Tammy. Tammy then pointed her gun at one of the girls on the floor who couldn't have been more than sixteen and shot her four times. The lady screamed and Tammy knew she would attack her, so she took two steps back, as the lady lunged at her she squeezed the trigger twice, what had been the lady's head exploded in a ball of blood and flesh. As the body dropped to the floor, Tammy wiped away the blood that had splattered on her through the mask. MC took a deep breath. "let's get you cleaned up baby girl." After the drama was over KD's radio beeped. "team one, this team five, we comin' out tha' attic." A few seconds later Troy and Bobby came out of the attic with two duffel bags. KD tried to radio Keema, and Brian again, but still got no reply. "where tha' fuck is Keema and Brian!" KD asked angerly. "in tha' basement." Bobby replied. "who told you that?" "Mano, -speakin' of Mano, let me call 'em." Bobby replied as he pressed the button on his walkie-talkie. "Mano, come in, Mano, where you at?" There were a few seconds of silence before the response came. "I- I'm in the basement with Keema, Rock an Brian." "what tha' fuck yall doin' down there?" Bobby replied. "w-we searchin'" KD quickly got on his radio. "hurry up, we been here to long, we gotta get to tha' other spot." Mano didn't respond. KD hit his transmission button so everybody would hear him. "Everybody meet in tha' front ro-." Before he could finish, his emergency alarm rang. "what's up?" "you gotta get down here, you won't believe this shit." Brian said. Trina heard the transmission and felt that something wasn't right. *"Where tha' fuck is Tara and Star."* She asked herself. KD made his way to the stairs and turned the corner to go to the basement, when he disappeared from their view, they heard his voice. "fuc-." Before the word was completely out of his mouth, they heard the blast from shotgun. His body was thrown into the wall from the impact. "nooo! Baby noo!" Trina screamed as she ran down the stairs to where he lay. Trina grabbed her radio and hit the emergency

50

button. "KD down! KD down! Help! KD's down" MC and Troy ran toward the hallway. "block off the doors and stairways." They yelled. "somebody help me get KD up!" Trina yelled. when no one came to help she started trying to lift him up. While she was trying to lift him up, she heard the door swing open, so she quickly picked her gun up and fired a shot. "what tha' fuck! It's us! It's us!" The house was still in chaos. "oh shit! I'm sorry, help me get KD." They both ran over, grabbed KD and helped her pull him to the couch. They checked to see if he was still breathing. "he breathin' let's get 'em out of here." Tara replied. They grabbed his arms and legs, and started to lift, then they heard a shotgun being cocked behind them. They all turned around. "let 'em go an throw yall guns over here." "you shystie mutha'fucka I'm a kill you!" Trina said angerly. Tara looked at Doobie. "what tha' fuck you doin'?" She asked shocked. "what tha' fuck you think I'm doin'? bitch I'm gettin' me." They couldn't believe what was going on. "Doobie this shit crazy!" Doobie grabbed his walkie-talkie and pressed the call button. "Keema get yo' ass up here?" Trina couldn't believe what she was hearing. "Keema! That bitch." Keema and Brian came from the basement with two bags, they both looked back down the stairs as if waiting on someone, then Rock came up the stairs with a shotgun aimed at Mano's head. "get over there bitch ass nigga." They couldn't believe they were in the double cross together. "I'm a make yall bitches pay fa' this." Trina yelled still holding KD. "what yall do wit' Bobby and Troy?" Star asked. they laughed as if she had told a joke. "what tha' fuck so funny?" Star asked. "you'll see in a minute, but fa' now lay tha' fuck down." Keema replied. Trina had the twenty-two she had gotten in an ankle holster but didn't know how to get too it without being seen. a few minutes later she heard Bobby and Troy talking. *"this shit couldn't have went no sweeta, what you think troy?" "I think we should kill all these mu'fuckas."* Troy replied seriously. *"naw, that's too much just stick to the plan."* KD began to move. "that nigga still alive."

51

"good, let 'em see how it feel ta' have ya' life fucked up." Trina saw Bobby and Brian walk out, but they were bringing up bags from the basement. "watch these mu'fuckas Shaniece, Keema check 'em fa' guns." Brian said. "Doobie already did that." Keema replied. "do it again." Brian said as he walked out of the room again. Shaniece and Keema started getting comfortable and put the shotguns on the couch between them. Trina saw her chance and grabbed the twenty-two out of her ankle holster and waited. "Keema, you better check 'em like Brian said. "a'right, damn." Keema replied as she got up and walked towards them. "Star and Tara closed their eyes in silent prayer. "turn over bitch!" "a-a'right, just don't shoot." Trina replied. Keema looked at KD's slow moving body on the floor. "Shaniece, watch him while I check these hoes." "I got him just do you." As Shaniece turned and pointed the shotgun at KD, Rock walked into the kitchen. Trina knew she had to go for it. "turn over, slow." As Trina turned slowly Keema bent down and grabbed her arm, as she turned her on her back Trina pulled the trigger five times. Star sprung from the floor and lunged at Shaniece in hopes of tackling her. Shaniece pulled her trigger twice out of fear and for a few seconds everything seemed to freeze as Trina watched KD's body flopped twice from the impact. Trina ran screaming towards KD's body and everything went black. "wake up! Wake up!" Trina felt the heavy hand come across her face again. She prayed that it was a nightmare, but when she opened her eyes, she saw KD's body on the floor bleeding from the mouth, she also saw blood slowly dripping from the side of vest. "baby nooo!" "you got more than him to worry bout bitch." When her vision cleared, she saw Keema faceless body, then felt hands forcing her head up. She saw Stars naked body tied to a chair. "fuck you bitches!" "I'm glad you feel like that." Tammy replied as she walked behind her and put the shirt she had once worn around her neck and pulled. "Brian hold the sleeves." Tammy said as she reached in her waistband and pulled out Trina's Glock put it

52

to the back of Stars head and pulled the trigger three times. Trina screamed. Tammy walked around the chair and stood in front of Star and pulled the trigger four more times. Tara vomited. "Tammy let's go, radio Bobby an tell 'em come on." Brian said unaffected by what was going on. "what about him?" Shaniece asked pointing to Mano with the shotgun. "kill him." He replied. Shaniece pulled the trigger and the close-range shot ripped through Mano's vest as they came one after the other six shots in all. Mano died trying to push his intestines back in. For Trina and Tara everything went black. The only thing Trina would remember for a while was Tara waking her up. "come on we gotta go, get up." Trina felt Tara helping her up. then she felt air on her face. "KD, we gotta get KD." "Baby, K-KD, gone, he dead." Tara replied through her tears. "nooo! No-o-oo-oo!" Trina screamed. Trina didn't remember anything after being helped from the house. "no! where? What!?" she screamed as she woke up and looked around before realizing she was in Tara's bed. "where KD an 'em at?" "Trina, you don't-oh baby, they-they." Tara broke down crying. "they killed KD, they set us up." "nooo! not my baby, not KD, no-oo-oo." Trina broke down. Tara felt helpless, but she knew that there was nothing she could do for her, nothing except let her get it out of her system. Tara was still shocked that things had gone the way they had, not only had Star been killed, so had Mano, Keema, and KD, but out of all of them only Keema deserved it. Tara knew that they were blessed to be alive, but she knew it would be wrong to try to convince Trina of that right now. Trina continued to cry until she couldn't produce the tears, and even then, she continued to scream out for KD, she didn't know which way was up or down, it seemed like her whole world had come crashing down and there was nothing she could do to stop it. After thirty minutes she fell into a restless sleep, tossing and turning until she finally woke up. Tara watched in silence as Trina dealt with her pain, it hurt her to see Trina that way, but she was dealing with loss to. Tara dosed off in the chair, but quickly woke up when she began to see Mano dying as he tried to push his intestines back in. she had been through a lot in her life, she had been raped at a party in her hometown of Indiana two years before she moved to Milwaukee met KD and Mano, she knew that she would never live down what happened, so she went home, stole a thousand dollars, bought a gun for two hundred, then went back to the house where she had been raped, knocked on the door and patiently waited for it to be opened, when it was she began firing at the people in the house, she hadn't waited to see if anyone died. She got on a greyhound bus the same day and ended up in Milwaukee, she was homeless and almost broke, so she spent the money she had left on a hotel. She worked for the hotel when her money ran out, the agreement was she worked for them and lived free, but she needed money, so she got a job as a stripper and ended up meeting KD and Mano. The only people who cared for her were dead and she was too shocked to deal with it. Everything Trina was going through physically; she was going through mentally. Retaliation was a must.

CHAPTER 4

"your partners breathin'!" The paramedic yelled. "he's not my fuckin' partner, he's not an officer either." Detective Randall replied angerly. KD had waken up in the house on Twenty-Third surrounded by the police. They ignored the blood and slow breathing as they patted him down. While the officers went through the house, he began to cough up blood, and stopped breathing. "he's not breathin'! he's not breathin'! code twenty-two-one." One of the officers radioed in. the paramedics arrived within minutes, they loaded him into the back of the ambulance and sped off. "I found a phone it only has one number listed, want me to call it?" "yeah, call it." Chavez replied. Trina's cellphone rang twice, out of habit she looked at the caller ID. "it's KD number!" she yelled. "answer it! Answer it!" Tara replied excitedly. Trina hesitated, then answered. "h-hello." "this is detective Randall's; may I ask whose speaking?" "t-this is Trina Gibbs." "I'd like to speak to you in person." He replied. "w-what are you doin' wit' my boyfriends' phone?" "we'll talk about that when we're face to face." Trina remained quiet. "what's your address? I'll send a squad over." "I-I have a car, but what's wrong? What's goin' on?" "I called because he's been, because mister Drake has been rushed to the hospital." Trina couldn't believe her ears. "hospital? Where is he? Tell me somethin'!" "well, uh, this is real confusin' but he's in bad shape an might not make it, if he does, he's in a lot of trouble, that's all I can say over the phone." "a'right, I'll be there in twenty minutes." Trina hung up and turned to Tara. "what they say?" "he alive, he-he at mount Sinai." "you can't go in that shit, they'll take yo' ass ta' jail." Trina looked down at herself and saw that she still had on the police uniform. "oh shit! I gotta get rid of this shit, you got somethin' I can wear?" "yeah, I got somethin' fa' you, take that shit off, we'll get rid of it on the way to the hospital." Trina rushed to take off the boots and threw up. "I'm sorry, I didn't, oh my-." "don't trip, but you are gettin' checked while we at tha' hospital, you ain't finsta die on me." Trina went in the bathroom, grabbed some towels and cleaned up the mess. After cleaning up she got undressed and got in the shower. "you gon' be a'right!" Tara yelled. "yeah! I'm straight." As the water ran down her body, she began remembering things that had happened at the house. "baby you gotta make it through this." She as tears mixed with the water and ran down her face. Trina got out of the shower and dried off, then grabbed the clothes that Tara had slipped into the bathroom. "Tara! Where you at?" "gettin' my clothes out, is you out the shower?" "yeah, I'm out." "good, cuz I need to hop in there." "a'right but hurry up." Trina replied. Ten minutes later they were in the car. "you gotta big ass bruise from the side of yo' nose down to ya' cheek." Tara said as they drove toward the hospital. "you got some make up?" she asked surprised that she hadn't noticed the bruise herself. "yeah, but I don't know if it's gon' help." "well, I gotta do somethin', I don't want the police askin' questions." Trina replied. "girl what tha' fuck you think they called you fa'? he tha' police he don't give a fuck bout KD." Tara said as she passed Trina the makeup. Trina tried her best to cover up the bruise, but it didn't work." "fuck it! Fuck this shit." "girl, calm down, don't get all worked up." Tara replied. "I can't help it, this shit drivin' me crazy." Trina replied. "I know but, you can't go in their wit' ya' head all fucked up." Trina sighed and leaned back in her seat. Neither of them spoke during the rest of the ride to the hospital, they were both to busy trying to figure out what to expect when they got their; whatever it was they both knew in their hearts that it was going to be life changing. The only thing they didn't know was how. Tara looked at the clock that was mounted on the dashboard, Trina figured that Tara was trying to figure out how much longer it would take for them to get to the hospital, but in all actuality, she was trying to figure out how to keep her thoughts from causing her to lose her cool, and any distraction from her thoughts was a good one.

"Detective Randall, I'm doctor Peterson." Randall shook the doctor's hand and thought how easy it would be to break it. "Well, what's up doc? Is he gonna make it?" "we did our best, the rest is up to him and his body, those close-range shots fractured his ribs and punctured a lung, he bled a long time, has anyone been contacted on his behalf?" "his girlfriend's on the way here as we speak." "Good." "if he survives how long will he have to stay?" "about two or three weeks at least." Tara and Trina pulled up to the hospital and parked. Trina hopped out of the car and ran straight to the nurse's desk. "is Kevin Drake here?" the nurse was used to this type of thing. "let me check ma'am." To Trina it took forever. "he's in room 1-3k, IC unit." "which way?" "straight down the hall to the left, then go to the fourth door on the right." Trina took off running. "slow yo' ass down be'fa you hurt somebody!" Tara yelled. When she made it to the IC unit, she saw an officer standing in front of what had to be KD's door. "ma'am what's the problem?" The officer said as she arrived at a full stop in front of him. "I-I'm Trina Gibbs, I talked to detective Randalls." Tara saw two more officers going down the hallway. "what's going on here?" one of the officers asked. "this lady, uh, miss Gibbs says she spoke to you." "yeah, yeah, I did, she's cool." "could you both follow me?" "can we see him please? Just once." Trina asked as they started to walk away from the door. "uh, well, okay, but I have to be in the room." Randalls replied hesitantly. "a'right I just wanna see 'em, that's all." Randalls nodded and the officer in front of the door stepped aside. "he doesn't look good, so don't expect any serious miracles." "o-okay." Trina replied as she opened the door. "o-oh my God! Trina screamed, shocked by KD's appearance. "what's wrong?" Tara asked as she pushed her way into the room. "oh shit! She said softly when she saw KD lying on the bed with tubes in his nose, mouth, and side. The IV in his arm was dripping clear fluid into his body, but he was still ashen, and the bandages were stained with blood. Randalls pulled them out of the room quickly. "sorry, but ladies I gotta get you outta here." He said as he closed the door and began leading them away from the room and back down the hall to a room where there were two other detectives and a few chairs. "ladies, sorry we had to meet like this, so we'll try to get you outta here as soon as possible." A lady in a blue business suit said. "who is yall?" Trina asked. "I'm detective Williams." The man standing next to the woman replied. Detective Williams was six foot four, dark skinned, mean looking and had on a suit that looked like he'd slept in it. "I'm

Detective Coldburn." The lady replied. Tara and Trina could tell she was a bitch, she was wearing a pair of 'fuck me' pumps that matched her suit and looked to be about forty or so. "how are you ladies?" Coldburn asked. "well, I'm not doin' so good." Trina replied sarcastically. "and why is that?" Coldburn replied with the same sarcasm. "look! My man in that fuckin' room wit' tubes runnin' through his fuckin' body! So cut tha' bullshit." "a'right, let's do that." She said. "okay, umm-uh-." "miss Gibbs." Trina said helping the man out. "miss Gibbs, would you know of any reason your boyfriend would be dressed like a police officer?" "no, I don't." "what about you ma'am?" Williams asked pointing at Tara. "no, sir I don't." she replied. Coldburn shook her head and smacked her lips. "do you know anyone on the southside miss Gibbs?" she asked. "not that I can think of." "what about you?" Coldburn asked as she pointed at Tara. "my name is Tara harper, and no, I don't know anyone on the southside detective." "miss Gibbs, miss Harper, here's the situation, we found mister Drake seriously injured in a well-known drug house on twenty-third and Scott, upon searching the house we found five dead bodies, one of which we can pen on your boyfriend." Detective Randall replied. "N-naw, I-I don't believe that." Trina replied hoping she sounded convincing. "well ma'am we got bullets from one of the victims, a Star James and shells that match the weapon mister Drake was found with." Williams said cutting into the conversation. Trina shook her head and blinked away tears. "you said he was seriously injured." "yeah, it seems that he was shot three times close range with a shotgun, which was also found at the scene." "ain't it possible he was set up?" Trina asked. Detective Randalls decided to answer her question. "well ma'am we're looking into that due to witnesses saying they saw multiple people in police uniforms going in and out of the house, but as I said it's a well-known drug house, and no one could see faces, apparently they were all wearing mask." "well mister Randall, I don't know what to say." Coldburn smiled.

58

"miss Gibbs." "yes." "when was the last time you talked to or saw your boyfriend?" "I don't remember, but maybe early yesterday mornin.'" "what about you miss Harper?" Randall asked. "I'd say around the same, but I'm not sure." Randalls and Williams exchanged looks of disbelief. "miss Gibbs, where'd you get that bruise?" Coldburn asked after seeing the looks Randalls and Williams exchanged. "I got hit in the face with a baseball." "must've been a bad pitch huh?" "yeah, why?" "looks like it hurts, that's all, miss Harper do u play any sports?" "yeah, I play tennis and softball." "oh, I play softball for the police league." "oh, ok I play in tha' hood wit' friends." The smile on Coldburns face disappeared. "oh, um, well before you go, do either of you know this man?" Coldburn asked as Williams laid down a picture of Mano on the floor of the house with his intestines hanging out. Before Tara could stop herself, she gasped and quickly turned away. "miss Harper, I know this might be hard, but how do you know him?" "t-that's my homeboy, oh my god." The detectives looked at each other, then Williams gave Tara some tissue. "we're sorry ladies, we don't want to cause you any more trouble, if you can think of anything, I mean anything that could help, here's my card." He said as he passed Trina his card. Williams walked them to the door. "I hope everything turns out good for the two of you." He said solemnly. "thank you." Trina replied. Williams watched as they walked away then walked back in the room and closed the door. "those bitches are lyin' through their fuckin' teeth." "I know, but why?" Coldburn replied. "I don't know but I'm a find out." "yeah, I say we dig into this, real deep." Randall said as he stood up. "where do you think that bruise really came from?" Williams asked. "I don't know, but I'll bet my fuckin' job it wasn't a baseball." Coldburn replied. "I think it was the first thing that came to her mind, did you see how she ran her fingers across it? It was like she forgot it was there." Randall replied. "yeah, I was thinkin' the same thing, she was caught off guard by the question and that bruise looked new to me, and it wasn't swollen

59

much for a baseball to the face." Williams said as he thought about Tara. "what do you think about miss Harper?" Coldburn asked as if she had read his thoughts. "I don't know, she was kind of hard to read, I didn't see any real emotion until I put that picture of her friend on the table. "yeah, I think she might've been holdin' back, especially when you asked her when she last saw or talked to mister Drake." Coldburn replied. "well, we got some good observations, so let's work on what we got."

A WEEK LATER

"you watched the news lately?" Rock asked. "naw, why?" "ta see if everything went as planned." Bobby laughed ignoring Rocks comments. "Brian! Doobie! Come in here for a minute." Bobby yelled. A few seconds later they walked out of the back room. "yall still back there fuckin' on them hoes.?" Rock asked with a smile. "why not? They gon' be dead in tha' mornin' anyway." Doobie replied. "we good on them hoes, what up though?" Brian asked. "Rock think shit might not have went as planned." "rock, you worry too much, just lay low an be cool." Doobie replied. Bobby got up, walked to the back room and opened the door. "damn! Yall been back here working these hoe's ain't yall?" he said as the smell of sweat, sex and weed came to him heavily. "get you some Bobby, they broke in." Brian replied with a laugh. "I might as well, who got tha' best pussy?" "tammy!" both men yelled. Bobby

60

walked in the room and stood next to Tammy, then walked back to the door. "Brian, Doobie, come here." "what up?" Brian asked. "untie the bitch an turn her on her stomach." As they untied her, she began to fight. "get away from me! Let me go!" she yelled. Doobie quickly hit her in the head with his gun and she slumped to the mattress unconscious. After they flipped her over, they each gave Bobby a condom. "have fun." Brian said as they walked out of the room. "beer in the mini-fridge." Doobie said from behind the closed door. A few minutes later they heard the screams. They went to the door, opened it and saw Bobby sticking the top of one of the beer bottles in her anus. "yall wanna watch or somethin' mu'fucka! Close tha' door." Brian closed the door and the screaming started again. "he in there killin' tha' bitch." Brian said. "oh well, I got my nuts off." Doobie replied. As they walked away, they heard four gunshots from the backroom. "oh shit!" rock said as they ran toward the backroom and swung the door open. "what tha' fuck!?" Brian yelled. Bobby was zipping up his pants and holding his gun in a blood covered hand. "what happened?" Rock asked. "the bitch wouldn't cooperate." Doobie and Brian walked closer to the bed and saw the exploded and bloody flesh of her anus. "you put her gun in her ass?" Doobie asked. "fuck that bitch, finish this hoe off to." He said pointing at Shanice's unconscious body. They walked over to shaniece and squeezed their triggers. "take 'em outta here an burn em." As Rock and Doobie grabbed the car covers and gasoline, Bobby turned on the TV and watched the news. "let's go." Doobie said. "yall go head, I'm here." Rock replied and walked away. "Dave, I'm standing in front of the house that has been the center of a massive police investigation, it all started a week ago when six dead bodies and one seriously injured person were discovered by officers responding to a nine-one-one call reporting that officers were under fire, upon arriving at the scene police found this man Kevin Imani Drake seriously injured and dressed as a police officer, another male Robert Green was

61

pronounced dead at the scene, he was also dressed as a police officer, that's all that we have at this time, but we'll be following all of the late breaking news and reports on this case, this is Janet Breadmerson channel twelve news, back to you Dave." Bobby turned the TV off and threw the remote. "did you hear that shit?" Bobby asked from the doorway. "six fuckin' bodies! Six! That mean them hoes made it out, Fuck!" Bobby snapped. "I told you we should've killed all of 'em." Rock replied. "shut tha' fuck up, you sound like Troy, get them bodies the fuck outta here!" "did you see that shit B?" "yeah, I saw it, so now what?" "first, we get rid of these hoes, the uniforms and the cars, then we chill and wait." Brian and Doobie rolled the bodies up in the car covers. "help me get these bitches to the car." "where you parked at?" "by the back door, the trunk already open." When they placed the bodies in the trunk Brian grabbed the gasoline cans. "where we goin'?" he asked. "cherry street to the abandoned warehouses." "under tha' viaducts by the train tracks?" "yeah, make sure we burn everything." Doobie replied. "don't worry bout that, cuz I ain't goin' to tha' joint." Brian said. "me either, speakin' of that, you think we can trust Rock?" "he got his hands dirty like the rest of us, so if we go down, he do to." "yeah, you right, let's get this shit done an get back." Doobie said. It took fifteen them fifteen minutes to reach the viaduct and take the bodies inside the building, drop them on the floor, and pour the gasoline over them. "go get the other can." Doobie said. "we don't wanna draw no attention." "no shit, just do what I said." Brian went and got the other can of gasoline and poured it all over the bodies then threw a match on them. There was a loud gust as the fire caught. "Let's go! Let's go!" Doobie yelled. They both ran to the car and hopped in, never seeing the young boy. "that shit was easy." Brian said once he calmed down. "hell yeah, just the way it's 'posse to be." "hey, did you see the look on Tara an 'em face when dat shit went down?" "that was a kodak moment." Doobie replied. Twenty minutes later they were getting close to the shop when they saw a police car park on the side of the building. "what the fuck the police doin'

at the shop?" "I don't know, keep goin.'" Brian replied. "what you thought I was gon' do,

stop?" "call the shop." Brian replied worriedly. Doobie grabbed his cell phone off the

charger and dialed the number to the shop. "bobby's auto shop, bobby speakin.'" "what tha'

police doin' there?" "it's cool, it's just a friend of mine, we handlin' some business." "a'right,

we'll be there in a minute." Doobie replied before hanging up. "what's goin' on?" Brian

asked. "it's a friend of his, they just handlin' a lil' business." Doobie replied as he turned the

car around and headed back toward the shop. Even though neither of them spoke they

both wondered what business Bobby could have with the police, especially with all that was

going down, but then again it wouldn't hurt to have the police on their side, maybe after

seeing the news he was deciding to cover all of his bases and throwing them to the dogs to

save his own ass. They both knew it was a dirty game, because they both played it, the

only thing they could do now was wait to see what would happen, everything, well almost

everything was going as planned, so all they had to do was relax and prepare to spend the

money they had gotten for their parts in the lick. As they continued toward the shop Doobie

thought of ways to invest his money, he was far from stupid, he was a college graduate, the

only one in his family. He knew what the good life was supposed to be, he had lived it until

his father was indicted for money laundering and tax evasion, after his dad was found

guilty, he and his mother went from living in a plush suburb to living in the heart of Keefe

Street, the ghetto his father had fought to escape, now he was on his way up in the world.

Brian's mind was on the same thing, he and Zoe had lived in Detroit for most of their lives,

Brian was the oldest at thirty-two, and Zoe had just turned twenty; they had been poor for

as long as he could remember, his mother had taught him to strive and work for what he

wanted, and he had done just that, but he was always fascinated by the street life he had tried it in Detroit, he sold drugs for a while, but wasn't good at it, he tried stealing cars, but didn't make enough money, so he finally left Detroit and ended up in Milwaukee where he went to school to be an auto mechanic. Bobby had given him his first job and now that he had money it would be his last job.

CHAPTER 5

"officer, officer!" the nurse yelled. "yeah, what's goin' on?" Randalls asked. "T-that guy you brought in is woke." "bout fuckin' time, I'm goin' in to talk to him." "don't upset him, he's in a lot of pain." The nurse replied not really wanting to let him in KD's room. "I won't, I just want to ask him a couple questions." "alright, but he'll have to write down his answers, we don't want the tube in his throat to move." "no problem, you gotta couple sheets of paper and a pen?" The nurse went to her desk and brought back paper and a pen. He walked into KD's room and smiled. "mister Drake, how you feelin'? I'm detective Randalls, the nurse said you couldn't talk, so I brought a pen and some paper." Randall passed him the paper and pen. KD slowly grabbed them and began to write, when he was done, he sat the pen down. Randalls picked the paper up and smiled until he read KD's response. "Suck your! Mister Drake let me tell you somethin', I hold your life in my hands, and when I'm done with you,

you'll be in Marion federal prison suckin' dick for envelopes." KD winced in pain as he held back his anger. "good, we got an understanding, now I want to know everything from the beginning you sonafa' bitch." KD picked up the pen and paper then began to write again, a few minutes later he passed the paper back to Randalls. "now, that's a good boy, let's see what you've got to share with daddy." Randalls began reading. "I got you, you mutha fucka." KD grunted as if he was trying to speak. "you want me to keep readin'?" Randall asked. KD nodded slightly and winced in pain. "a'right, let's see I left off about here." Randall said as he began to read out loud, after a few sentences the statement stopped. "who!? Who did you rape? I need to know which one." Randalls said eagerly. KD held his hands out and winced from the throbbing in his head. Randalls handed him the paper quickly, hoping he wouldn't pass out. "write! Write everything." KD began writing and a few seconds later he passed Randalls the paper and pen. "a'right, I left off at, you realized you had actually fucked- so let's see who you fucked that's worth you spendin' life in prison." Randall read the paper. "you sonafa' bitch! You think this shits funny!?, you wanna play games! Let's play." KD rang the emergency button as Randall reached for the tube in his throat. "detective! What are you doing?" The nurse yelled. "I'm glad you're here, I pressed the button, it looks like this tube is wiggling or somethin'" "detective, the button is on the other side of the bed, I think you should leave." "yeah, I'll be goin' now." Randalls replied as if he hadn't been caught in a lie. "I'll walk you out." "oh, mister Drake, here's my card, let's continue where we left off." As Randalls and the nurse walked out of the door KD tried to smile and reached for the paper and pen that Randalls left behind. "I'll get that when I come back mister Drake." The nurse came back twenty minutes later, but he was sleep, so she picked up the paper and began to read, once she finished, she began to laugh, after straightening up the room she read the letter to herself again. That night as KD slept

65

nightmares crept in. The shotgun blast that knocked him into the wall, the voices he heard as he slowly gained consciousness, then more shotgun blast as someone stood over him or almost over him and pulled the trigger, then screams, the laughs, everything in his dream was played over and over in slow motion, he could feel the pain as the slugs impacted his body, he was dying, he had to get air, he couldn't breathe, then the police were everywhere, they were pointing guns and yelling, there was nothing he could do, his body wouldn't cooperate with his brain, which was good because there was no way he would've survived the gun battle. As the nightmare continued, he heard Tara saying he was dead, did everyone think he was dead? Why hadn't Trina been to see him or had she? Could she? He didn't remember her coming. KD was a high school dropout, he had grown up in Milwaukee on the east side, his mother had given up hope of him doing anything with his life and his stepfather didn't care about him either way if he didn't have to deal with him. He had always been hard to control, and he had been running the streets doing petty robberies, selling drugs and gang banging since he was eleven or twelve, he had always liked to take risk and it had finally caught up with him. He shifted himself in hopes of waking himself up, he was losing air again, he needed to breathe, He felt like he was being suffocated, he shifted a few more times before quickly opening his eyes. When he remembered where he was and how he got there he began to form his plans for revenge. The game is cold, but it's fair, KD thought to himself as he lay back staring at the ceiling plotting his next moves. "damn, where you at Trina?" He asked the empty room as the medication finally took over. He had hit the morphine button to take away the pain.

"girl, the police on some bullshit." "I already know, but we one step ahead of the game." "what you think we should do?" Tara asked. "I think we sh-." The phone rang, cutting off the

66

rest of Trina's response. "answer it." Tara picked up the phone then looked at her. "what!?" Trina asked excitedly but worriedly. "KD woke, it's the nurse she wants to talk to you." Trina ran and snatched the phone so fast that Tara tripped backwards over the cord. "h-hello." "miss Gibbs, I'm only doing this because-because I believe mister Drake is in big trouble." "put him on." "he can't talk, he actually wrote everything down, he told me to relay this message, get him the best lawyer you can find, bring him as much money as you can get together, and get everyone together and tell Grip he needs to see him asap." "is that all miss uh-." "yeah, that's all." "thank you." "no sweat miss Gibbs." The line went silent, and Trina looked at Tara. "what!? What!?" She asked. "call grip fa' me, I gotta make some calls." "what's the number?" "uh-i-its four-six-two, fifty-six eleven, tell him KD need to see him." "a'right." Tara replied as she dialed the number. Trina called her brothers and sisters and told them to come over. It was thirty minutes later when they arrived. Trina introduced everybody. "Wanda, Angela this Tara." Wanda and Angela both nodded. "these my brothers Drama and Drew." "what's up?" Tara replied. "tryin' to figure out what's goin' on." "yeah girl, what's goin' on.?" Wanda asked. "get ta' talkin' sis." Angela said as she sat down. Trina didn't know how to begin because she hadn't told them anything. As she thought of how to start, it came to her that nobody mentioned the bruise on her face. "well, spit it out." Wanda said. "yeah, we got stuff to do, and what happened to yo' face?" "you and KD got into it didn't yall?" Drew asked. Trina didn't know what question to answer first, so she stood their quietly. "is you okay?" Angela asked. "yeah, I need you to take me to the bank an the hospital, then I'll tell yall everything." Two hours later they were back at her house listening to everything that she wanted them to know happened in the last couple of weeks.

TWO WEEKS LATER

"I'm here to see Kevin Drake." "just a minute sir." The nurse replied as she walked over to the computer and began to type. A few seconds later she walked back to the small desk. "can you sign the visitor registration please?" The nurse handed the clip board and papers to him and watched as he signed. When he handed them back, she briefly glanced at the papers. "alright, mister Prince he's in on one-three k, IC unit, that's down the hall and to the left, fourth door on the right." "thanks." When he arrived at KD's door he walked in and saw him watching TV. "what's up nigga?" KD pointed to a piece of paper and pen. "you want that?" Grip asked as he looked in the direction KD was pointing. When Grip passed him the paper and pen, he handed one of the pieces back. "you want me to handle this for you?" KD pointed to the other pieces of paper then handed them to Grip. "damn, you got addresses, relatives names, hangouts, what else you got for me?" KD pointed to the closet where a bag Trina had brought was hanging. Grip handed him the pen and paper. "the bag? What's in the bag?" KD pointed to the closet again as blood came through the tube in his throat. "k! what's wrong?" KD pointed to the closet. Grip went to the closet, reached into the bag and pulled out a roll of hundred-dollar bills. "this me?" KD nodded before pressing the emergency button. Grip saw the light flash. "what wr-?" The nurses and doctors rushed through the door. "sir-sir, you have to leave now!" one of the nurses said as she picked up the phone and pressed a number. "we have a code blue in room one-three k, IC unit, repeat a code blue in room one-three k, IC unit." "w-whats goin' on? That's my family." "sir, just go out to the waiting area please." Grip walked out of the room, turned on his cellphone, and called Trina. "hello." "this Grip." "what's up?" "listen, I'm at the hospital an I just finished talkin' wit' KD, but he hit his emergency button, the nurses called a code blue." "what that

68

mean?" "I-I don't know, but its plenty of nurses and doctors in there." "let me talk to a nurse." Trina replied. "let me see if I can get one." "what's wrong?" Tara asked. "I don't know, I'm tryin' to find out." "what's goin' on?" Wanda asked. "I don't know we might have to go to the hospital." Trina replied. "why? What's wrong wit' KD?" Angela asked. "damn Angela, you ask to many questions, I just said I'm tryin' ta' find out." Trina replied in frustration. "what you want us to do?" Drew asked. "go get my phone off the table." Drew went to get the phone. When he gave it to her, she called the hospital. "Grip, you still there?" "I'm here." "I need you to come over here an holla at my little brother real quick." "I'm leavin' the hospital now." He replied. When they hung up Trina grabbed Tara's car keys. "yall ready ta' go?" "yeah, we ready." They replied. "Drama, Drew, KD guy comin' over here ta' get yall, just ride wit' em, he cool." "what we ridin' wit' him fa'?" Drama asked. "just do what tha' fuck I said!" Trina snapped. "a'right sis, damn." On the way out Trina turned an ran back to her room. "girl, what is you doin'?" "I forgot my ID an shit." Trina hated lying to her sister and friend, but she knew she had to do things a certain way. "anybody answered at the hospital?" Trina knew that she should've been at the hospital, but something held her back. "it's still ringin'" After a few minutes the phone was answered. "Mount Sinai, IC unit." "yes, can I speak with a nurse please." "one minute please." When the receptionist clicked off, elevator music came on. Trina looked at her watch. "this punk ass elevator music gettin' on my last fu-." "nurse Carrie speakin'" "yes, this is Trina Gibbs I'm callin' mister Drake." "miss Gibbs, he's fine, but he had us scared for a while, he's been out of surgery for fifteen minutes, we have him heavily sedated." "okay, umm, I was gon' come up there, but I'll wait til' he wakes up." "give me your number, and I'll call you when he does." "tell me when you ready." "go head miss Gibbs." "it's three-nine-three, five-zero-zero-nine." "I got it, I'll call you as soon as he wakes up, if I'm on duty." "that's cool." Trina hung up and sat the phone down. "I thought yall was goin' to the hospital." "I just called, he sedated, the nurse gon' call if he wake up." "so, what now?" Wanda asked. "let's just chill." "yall hungry?" Tara asked. "hell yeah." Angela replied. "I second that." Wanda said. "let's go get somethin' from subway." Trina replied. They grabbed their jackets and headed out the door.

"Drama, we'll bring yall somethin' back." Trina said as she opened the door. "a'right, but don't get no onions, lettuce, or tomatoes." He said. "a'right." She replied and walked out. Trina and her sisters had been gone for twenty minutes before Grip pulled up to pick up Drama and Drew. When Trina and her sisters got back no one was there. "they must've left wit' KD guy." Angela said. "so, they probably out gettin' into somethin', all they do is rap, smoke an get into shit." Drew was the oldest between him for a father figure, he had finished the tenth grade, but then dropped out and started trying to find his way into the music industry, he had all types of hustles and used his money to buy shoe's, clothes and studio equipment, and out of all his sisters Trina was his favorite. "Drama ain't no better, he wanna be just like Drew." Drama was the baby of the family and grew up idolizing Drew, he wanted to be in the music industry, he had dropped out of school in the ninth grade and moved in with some friends who turned him on to selling drugs and carrying guns, he was forced to move back in with his mother and two sisters after being arrested. "I know when they come back, I'm a cuss they ass out, look how they left my table." Trina replied looking at the cigar tobacco, and blunt ends. Trina knew exactly where they were, but she couldn't tell Wanda or Angela, because she knew that they wouldn't be able to handle that. "what you got ta' drink?" Angela asked. "soda, Kool-Aid, and water." "I knew I should 'a bought some pa'tron from tha' liquor store." "what I tell you bout drinkin'?" "I know, I know but it ain't like I be off my fuckin' square or nothin'" "yeah, okay let me find out you on some other shit Angela." Trina said half seriously. "whatever! Don't be all up in mine, let me do me." Angela replied smiling. "oh! So, I guess I ain't ta' be worried bout huh?" Wanda asked. "you could say that." Trina replied. "fuck you." Wanda said. "naw, fuck ya' man." "can he come over?" Wanda replied laughingly. Bobby, Doobie, Rock, Troy, and MC were at the shop having a meeting about how Trina and Tara made it out of the house alive, and how they would handle the problem. "look Bobby, we already got two witnesses that can link us to this shit an we don't know if that crazy mu'fucka KD gon' pull through." Rock said. "so, what yall think we should do?" Bobby asked. "I think we should start tying up loose ends asap." Rock replied. "I think yall just nervous." Bobby said knowingly. "I ain't nervous an I feel like Rock, and Troy, the sooner tha' better." MC said. "you to? Damn, why yall so scared of them hoes?" Bobby asked. "first off, I ain't scared, I just don't want 'em goin' to tha' police." "if they do that, they'll be fuckin' they self." Dobbie replied. "true, but bitches do some crazy shit, look at that one broad, locked her kids in tha' closet so she could go out and party, then when she got arrested, she waited five days ta' tell tha' police the kids was in the closet." MC replied shaking his head. "yeah, I mean look what happened when we left them hoes fa' dead, shit, we thought KD was dead when we left, I think we took enough chances." Troy said. "I don't think it's nothin' ta worry bout, they don't wanna go ta' prison, an as far as KD, if he pull through, he got caught red handed they gone slam 'em, I say we straight, so we should move on to somethin' else." Doobie replied. Bobby sighed. "well, I say we just chill, go about shit like we usually do and play it by ear, if anything come up we'll deal with it, but fa' now fuck all that shit, let's chill an fa'get this shit ever happened."

"I'm wit' that." Brian said as he opened a soda. Even though everybody had their doubts, they agreed that forgetting about it and relaxing was best. As they talked about how to deal with their everyday situations, Grip, Drama, and Drew rolled past the shop looking at the cars that were parked outside. "that one right there, that's Doobie shit, an that white one, that's Bobby's." Grip said as he pointed. "let's handle these niggas an keep it movin'." Drama replied. "that's why we here, when I pull ova' I want yall to grab those gloves, that black bag, the gas container, an tha' straps, they already loaded, just make sure yall put the bag back." "got you." Drama replied. "yall sure yall can handle that?" Grip asked. "yeah, we got it." Drew replied. Grip pulled over at the next corner and they did just what grip had told them. "yall ready fa' this shit?" Grip asked. "hell yeah." Drama replied. "you gon' park in front of the shop or right here? Drew asked. "right here, we gon' walk to tha' shop." "man, it's four o' clock in tha' afternoon." Drama replied looking at grip as if he had gone crazy. "that's what these fa'." Grip said as he reached under his seat and pulled out mask. "let's go." "who gon' pour tha' gas?" Drew asked. "drew, you do tha' gas, pour it on tha' cars, tha' shop, everything, as much as you can before it's empty, then throw the match an be ready." Grip replied. "a'right, I'm ready." Drew said before taking a deep breath. "let's do it." Drama replied. When they got to the shop he poured the gasoline, threw the match and watched as the fire spread. "get in place, hurry up." Grip ordered. Drew quickly threw the gas can in the fire and found a hiding place. Drama looked around to make sure that no one had crept out of the shop. On the ride over grip had explained what the consequences would be if they got caught, if either of them would have shown they were scared he would've dropped them back off and did the move by himself. Drew peeked his head out of his hiding spot, wondering what was taking so long for bobby and the rest of them to realize that their cars and part of the shop was on fire. "you think somebody picked 'em up?" Drama asked. Grip

72

put his finger to his lips and shook his head. Inside the shop they were finally back on business and splitting the money from the robbery. "let's see it's thirty-six ounces in a brick, so two hundred-fifty-two oun-." "hey yall smell that?" Brian asked interrupting the count out. "smell what? Rock replied. "you always talkin' bou-" Rock cut himself off as he began to smell it. "that's smoke." He said. "what tha' fuck is- open a window." Brian walked to the front of the shop and saw the flames. "this mu'fucka on fire!" he yelled as he ran toward the back. They all made their way out of the shop. When they made it outside MC saw his car was on fire. "my mutha'fuckin' Benz!" he yelled as he watched it burn. Drew lifted his mask before he was spotted and stepped out of his hiding spot. "I-I saw who did it." He said playing innocent. "I got a bill fa' you if you point 'em out to me." MC replied, falling for the set up. "h-he did it." Drew whispered as he pointed. MC turned in the direction Drew was pointing and was met with three close range shots to the face. "that's from KD mutha' fucka." Grip said with an evil smile. Rock heard the shots and reached for his gun, but Drama stepped out of the gangway. "if you like breathin' pimpin' you might wanna drop that an walk toward my guy in front of you." When Bobby, Brian, and Doobie heard the gunshots they hit the ground. "w-who tha' fuck is yall?" Rock asked. "shut tha' fuck up nigga." Drew replied. "g, pop that fat mu'fucka, but don't kill 'em." Drama said. "not a problem." Grip replied as he pulled the trigger twice. Bobby screamed. "shut tha' fuck up, fa' I decide to kill yo' punk ass." Grip said menacingly. "y-yall w-want m-money, it's in tha' shop." Rock volunteered nervously. "where in tha' shop?" Drama asked. "i-in tha' b-back sittin' on tha' table." "d, you heard tha' man, run in an grab it, hurry up, if ain't shit in there I'm a knock his brain through his teeth." Grip said not taking his eyes off Rock the whole time. Drew ran into the shop and headed towards the back, he grabbed a bag from under the table and threw as much as he could in it and ran out. "it's good, Let's go!" he said. "what's your name?"

73

Drama asked. "R-rock." "a'right Rock, you comin' wit' us." "f-fa what? Yall got what yall want." "cuz, I said so, now walk." As they began to walk Grip looked at Troy. "hey! You, the tall one." "y-yeah?" "g, what you doin'?" Drama asked as he pulled Rock to a stop. "don't trip, just get him to the trunk." "you sure?" "yeah, put him in tha' trunk and wait fa' me." "a'right." "now, back to you, nigga you know what this about right?" Troy wasn't sure if he should answer or not. "n-naw." "to bad my nig." Grip replied and pulled the trigger four times. "that's from KD to mu'fucka." When Grip ran, he heard the sirens getting closer. "fuck!" he yelled. When he turned the corner, the car was already running, so he jumped in. "drive normal, we can't afford ta' get stopped." Grip said breathing heavily. "where we goin'?" "to the shootin' range." "shootin' range? Is you crazy? We got a body in tha' trunk." Drew replied. "don't worry bout it, I got this." They drove for twenty minutes. "turn left right here, and go 'round back." "when they made it to the back, the doors were already open. Drama backed the car up to the door and popped the trunk. When he popped the trunk Grip and Drew pulled Rock out. Once he was out of the trunk Drew kicked him down the stairs, hoping he had broken his ribs. When they made it, downstairs Rodger was standing next to Rock. "what's up everybody?" he said. "nothin' much, just brought a distant friend down to see how we handle business." Grip replied with a smile that looked out of place. "well, everything you asked for is already set up, so have fun." "fa' sho, yall strap that mu'fucka up there." Grip said pointing to the mechanical rack that was supposed to hold the paper targets. "wit 'what?" Drew asked. "drama, go to the third booth and get the handcuffs, tape and baseball bats." When drama came back, they hung rock from the rack. When they finished taping up rock all three of them lifted him up on the track line, and roger pressed the green button. "how far out you want him?" Rodger asked. "bout five feet." Grip replied. Rodger pressed the button to bring the rack forward. "that's five feet my friend, just like you

74

asked." "drama, grab them bats." Drama grabbed the bats, he kept one and passed the other to Grip. "drama, you ever play baseball?" "hell naw, I ain't never played no fuckin' baseball." "well, you gone learn how ta' swing a bat today." Grip said as he reached up and ripped rocks shirt halfway off his body. Rock tried to talk through the tape as he struggled to get free. "calm down mu'fuka." Grip said as he stepped back and got into position to swing the bat. When he swung the bat, he aimed for rock's stomach. "that shit feel good! Take a swing drama, drew get you one to, Rodger you want one?" "nah, I'm just here ta' watch and learn." "you sure?" "yeah, I'm cool." Drama swung the bat and hit rock across the abdomen, then passed it to drew who hit him across the legs. "let 'em rest for a minute, we got all night." Grip said as he watched rock swing limply. "yeah, let me call sis real quick." Drew replied. Grip passed him his cell phone. "hello." "hey sis, come down ta' Rodgers, we gotta surprise for you." "I'll call when I get close." Trina hung up and shook her head. "Trina, what's wrong?" Angela asked. "nothin'." She replied before taking a deep breath and continuing. "yall wanna go somewhere wit' me?" "somewhere like where?" Angela replied. "the gun range." "gun range, naw I'm cool." Wanda said as she shook her head. "what about you?" Trina asked turning to Angela. "I'm cool." "Tara?" "let's go." Tara replied knowing that Trina really didn't want anyone but her to go. "I'll drop yall off." Trina said as they headed back toward her house. "we'll be back." Trina said when they pulled up. "if we ain't here, hit one of us." Angela replied. "a'right." Trina replied as she pulled off with Tara still in the passenger seat. "what's goin' on?" "you'll see when we get there." Twenty minutes later Trina called Grip. "yeah?" "we two blocks up." "a'right, just pull up in back." Five minutes later they pulled up to the back and parked. Trina knocked. "drew, drama, one of yall open the door!" a few seconds later Rodger opened the door. "come in ladies, I hope you like the surprise." "I hope so to." Trina replied. "girl, what the hell we here fa'?" "I don't know, just shut up and follow me." When they made it downstairs, they saw drew, drama and grip sitting on the couch in the outer office. "hey sis, Tara." "what up?" Tara replied. Drew, Drama, and Grip made their way into the shooting area. "look what we got fa' yall." Drew said as Rodger grabbed the box off the floor and pressed the green button. As the track moved forward Trina and Tara looked at each other. "how yall pull this off?" Tara asked. "a dog always go back to where it feel safe." "take the tape off his mouth, I wanna hear 'em scream." Tara replied angerly. Drama walked over to him and snatched the tape from his mouth. "w-what yall w-want?" "you don't know my voice?" Trina asked. "naw, w-who is yall?" "take the tape off his eyes." "what you mean take the tape off?" Drama asked nervously. "exactly what I said, now do it or I'll do it myself." Drama sighed as he ripped the tape off. "shit!" Rock yelled from the pain. "look at me! Look close you punk mu'fucka, I want you ta' see who I am." Trina said as she fought to control her emotions. Rock slowly lifted his head. "w-what y-yall gon' kill me?" he asked when he saw Trina and Tara. "naw, we got plans for you." Trina replied as she took a cigarette out of her pocket, lit it, then walked over to him. "I always wanted to know how burnt skin smelled rock, what about you?" Trina asked hoping she could go through with what she was planning, "drama, drew, hold his legs open." Tara said. "y-yall gon' wish yall was dead when bobby get ta' yall bitch!" rock said as he began to struggle. As they held his legs Tara unzipped his pants and pulled them down. "aww, look at that, he gotta winky between him legs." She said in a squeaky, childish like voice. "not fa' long he don't." Trina replied. "hold his legs tight." "we got 'em, just do what you gon' do." Drama replied. "light a cigarette." Trina said handing Tara one. "I need a light." "pick a part Tara." Trina said as Tara lit the cigarette. "mmm-mmm, the nuts." "go fa' it." They took their cigarettes and put them on his testicals. "already screamin', we just got started." Trina said angerly. "girl, I like the way you think." "yo turn, I hold, you

76

burn." "yeah, I can do that, this fa' star, kd, an mano." Trina grabbed his dick as Tara took a puff of the cigarette, then placed the tip on his dick. Rock screamed and began to struggle. "shut 'em tha' fuck up somebody." Drew and Grip walked over with the bats and signaled for drama to let go of his legs. "yall straight?" Grip asked. "we ain't even got started." Trina replied angerly. "do yall." Grip said as he sat on the couch. "Tara looked at everyone but remained quiet and waited to see what would happen. Drama and Drew were surprised to see their sister getting down the way she was, but they remained quiet. Rodger was wondering how much money he would get out of them, blackmail would be easy with the situation he had them in, everything was on tape.

CHAPTER 6

The fire department arrived at the auto shop accompanied by the police and ambulance after receiving an anonymous tip that the shop was on fire, and people were seriously injured. "mister Tills, can you tell me exactly what happened?" one of the officers asked. "all I know is we were countin' the shops take for the month an m-my friend Troy said he smelled smoke, so we came out to see what was goin' on an some dudes in mask was waitin' fa' us." "is that all sir?" The officer asked. "t-they took my friend Rock." The officers' eyes lit up and he seemed more interested. "can you give me Rocks real name?" he asked. "Terell Codlee." "spell that last name for me." "c-o-d-l-e-e." "a'right sir, do you need to go too th-." "ricks! I need to ta-." "don't you see I'm chec-." "sir! It's important, they found two bodies under the viaduct, a kid seen it all." The officer said hoping not to be disciplined for the interruption. "a'right, tell dispatch I'll be there in twenty, maybe thirty minutes." "will do

77

sir." Davis replied. Brian had heard the conversation and knew that it could be trouble if the little boy had gotten the license plate of the car. "you wanna go to the hospital?" "naw, I'm straight, but what about my boss? Is he a 'right?" "mister Skyy will be fine, the gun man didn't hit anything vital." Ricks replied. "t-thank you." Brian said glad for any good news. "no problem, hey! One more question mister Tills." "what's that?" "do you know why your friend was armed?" "no sir." "well, if you can think of anything else, here's my card." Ricks said as he handed him his card. "Davis! Let's go." Ricks yelled to the man who was holding back the on lookers. As Davis and Moby got in their cars and headed to the viaducts the fire department began rolling up their equipment and one of the firefighters walked over to Brian. "sorry about the shop man, wished we could've saved it." "thanks." Brian said. When the fire department and ambulance pulled off Brian got up and walked to his car.

Officer Allen Cantz also known as Al sat behind his desk looking at pictures of Robbie Green also known as Mano lying dead in a well-known drug house dressed in a police uniform. He laid the pictures down and continued reading the report that had been written by other officers that were on the scene, he sat the report down, picked up the phone and dialed an extension. "Fredricks." "This is Allen, what's up?" "I need to see you in my office, now." "a'right, I'll be there." Fredricks replied before hanging up. A few seconds later he walked into Allen's office. "what's up Al?" "you sure that nothin' they do is able to lead back to us?" "yeah, everything straight Al I-." A knock on the door stopped their conversation. "come in!" Allen yelled. "I-I'm officer Lyle, I was told to give you this sir." Lyle handed him a note written on the station's memo paper. "a'right Lyle, you can go." "thank you, sir." When Lyle left, he began to read the note. "son of a bitch!" he snapped. "what's the problem?" Fredricks asked. "they just found two burned bodied on cherry under the viaduct." "so, what,

78

it ain't got nothin' to do wit' you." "I hope not." "even if it does, they can't prove it." Fredricks replied. "like they'll keep their mouths shut." Allen said. "any proof?" Fredricks asked. "a lil' boy seen it all." "who's on the scene?" "Davis, Moby, and Ricks." "should I go?" Fredricks asked. "yeah, see what they got." "a'right, any word on if mister Drake made it?" "I'll check on that, you make sure shit gets handled." "I got it Al." Fredricks replied. When he was outside of Al's office, he stopped the tape recorder that he had in his pocket. After stopping at the front desk, he went to his office, grabbed his off-duty revolver, then headed to his car, once there he pulled off headed to the scene. A lot of things were running through his mind, none which he cared to focus on now, but if things went the way he planned he would have nothing to worry about. Fredricks had been born in Florida in 1970, his mother was a lawyer and his father was an alcoholic who couldn't hold a job, Fredricks was the oldest of two children and only got along with his mother, as a child he couldn't stand his sister or father so one day he decided the only way that he and his mother could be happy was to get rid of the father and sister, so one night while his mother was at a party and his sister and father slept he set the house on fire then walked to the neighbor's house as his father and sister died screaming for help.

Officer Davis and Moby had been on the scene for nearly an hour and had both spoken to the little boy named Willie, and his parents. Willie told them that he played on the side of the building throwing rocks through the windows, and that today he had saw a white car with two men in it, they had pulled up, gone in the trunk and pulled out two big blue bags and two red cans, they poured the stuff from the cans on the bags then set the bags on fire, got back in the car and left. After that he had ran home and told his mother. "that lil' boys smart." Davis said. "yeah, you think he might be in danger?" Moby asked. "nah, the guys didn't see him, and if they did, they didn't do nothin' then." "true, hey, I talked to Moore, she said they found tire tracks, so they're doin' a mold on 'em to see what they can come up with." "what they got so far?" "only what the boy saw, tire tracks, an maybe some footprints, which could belong to a hundred million homeless people." "fuck it, let's head back." Davis replied. "fine by me it stinks down here." Moby said as he crinkled his nose. As they made it back to their car, they saw Fredricks getting out of his squad. "what up fellas?" he said with a smile. "nothin' much, just finished lookin' around the scene, nothin' ta be found." Moby replied. "well, update me I'm late." Moby handed Fredricks his notepad. "just give it back when you're done." Moby said as he walked away. "no problem." Fredricks replied. As Davis made it to the car, he looked back in Fredricks direction. "I hate that fucker." "who doesn't hate tha' fucker? He never does any work an more than likely gets all the credit." Moby replied. "yeah, same shits been goin' on fa' years." Davis said with a smirk. A few minutes later Fredricks walked over and knocked on the window. Moby rolled the window down. "thanks." Fredricks said as he handed him the notepad back. "no problem." Moby replied. Fredricks nodded and walked back to his car. "fucker didn't even go talk to the family." Davis said as he watched Fredricks pull off. "you thought he would? That's work, you should've known better." Moby replied.

They had all been taking turns working on Rock. "Grip, that nigga dead yet?" Drama asked. "naw, he one of those die-hard type niggas." Grip replied. "should I put 'em outta his misery?" Trina asked seriously. "hell naw, he getting' what he got comin'." "damn girl, look at 'em." Rock's eyes were swollen shut from the constant pepper spraying, his body was one big bruise from the bats, and he had burns from the soles of his feet up to his chest. "make sure one of you cleans the blood up, I'm not goin' to prison for you guys." Rodger

80

said as he looked around. "we got it." Drama replied. "well Tara, finish him or not?" Trina asked recalling how she had run to the bathroom to throw up four times during the beatings and torture. "not just yet, Rodger you got a water hose?" "yea, why?" "go get it please." "a-a'right, but I'm not doing anything else though." He said nervously. "nobody said you had to." Tara replied as he walked up the stairs and unlocked the small glass door containing the water hose. A few seconds later he threw down the hose. "start pullin'." He said. "ok." Tara replied as she and Trina started pulling the hose. "that enough?" Rodger asked. "yeah, that's cool." Rodger made his way back downstairs then sat down. "grip turn it on." Grip walked up the stairs and turned the water on. "wake up, I want you to feel every minute of this." Tara said as she sprayed rock from head to toe. "turn the water off." Trina said. Grip quickly turned the water off and came downstairs. "you remember how Mano died don't you?" "I-auh-I." "well you gon' get off a lil' easier." She said as she swung the water hose. It hit him across the abdomen, chest and face. "send that bitch bout ten feet out." Tara said. "what you bout ta' do?" Trina asked. "don't trip." Tara replied as she went and grabbed a box cutter out of her jacket pocket. "yall might hear a lot of screamin'." She said as she walked toward the booth. "send 'em a lil' further out." Everybody looked at each other then walked around the booth. "I want him to feel all of this." "what you finsta do?" Trina asked curiously. "a lil' drawin' that's all, you wanna help?" "naw, I'm a watch." Trina replied. Tara walked over to Rock pulled his pants down and cut through his underwear. "I don't think you gon' survive this." Tara said as she placed the tip of the razor on his dick. "If you survive, I hope you can get use ta' sittin' down ta piss." She said as she gripped his dick and plunged the razor through his tip causing him to struggle and kick as he screamed. "don't die yet mu'fucka I want you ta' suffer like Mano." Tara said as she sliced through his dick. Rock continued to scream as the blood gushed from between his legs. "now you know how he felt." "let him down." "what!?" Drew replied surprised. "let 'em down!" Tara snapped. Drew got the keys and used a step ladder to uncuff him, when the cuffs were unlocked, he dropped to the floor with a thud. "j-just kill me." Rock said through swollen lips. "no problem mu'fucka." Tara replied as she sliced into his throat and chest. "Drew, hurry up an turn the water on." "turn it on as far as it'll go." Trina said. Drew ran up the stairs and turned the water on. "help me get this bitch outta here." "you can use my truck; I'll give you an hour an report it stolen if that'll help." Rodger volunteered. "thanks Rodger." Trina replied as he went in his pocket, took out the keys and tossed them to Grip. "good lookin'" Tara said as she walked behind him. "no pr-." His reply was cut short as Tara stuck her blade in his neck and sliced his throat. "what tha' fuck!" Grip yelled. "no loose ends, he'd snitched on us in a minute to save his own ass, is it a problem?" Tara asked. "naw, but that was my plug." Grip replied. "don't worry about it." Tara said as she wiped her blade clean. "Grip, Drama, get tha' bodies in tha' trunk, drew come wit' me." "let me grab my mask first." "bring me one to, Tara go start the car." Trina said as she tossed her the keys. "bring the gas down here." A few seconds later Drew walked out with a duffel bag and threw it in the trunk, Trina walked out behind him smoking a cigarette. "let's go!" she yelled. "what about the fire?" Drew asked. "light a cigarette, but don't put ya' mouth on it." Drew lit a cigarette and passed it to her. "I hate to do this, but oh well." She said as she threw the cigarette. The fumes jumped quickly because of the gasoline, and they all knew the shop would explode soon because of all the ammo. "pull off! Pull off!" Trina yelled. "what about the bodies?" Drew asked. "run the truck into the shop." Drama quickly started the truck. "y-you sure bout this?" he asked. "just do it an come on?" Drama put his foot on the gas and jumped out. "fuck!" he yelled. "is you bleedin'?" "I'm straight." "Trina we gotta get the hell outta here, lets go!" Trina ran to the car. "meet back at my house." Drama, Drew, and Grip ran to Grips car and got in. "let's go the police gon' be here any minute." Drew said. Drama got the car started and hit the gas. "slow down! We don't need ta' get pulled over." "a'right! A'right! I got this chill." Drew thought about all the things that had went down and couldn't believe that he was involved. He had been in fights and saw people get shot and stabbed, but he had never seen anybody get tortured and beaten the way they had done Rock.

"Doctor Peterson, do you think we should prepare for surgery on mister Drake?" "no, I think he's going to recover very wel-." "what about the code blue two days ago?" one of the nurses interrupted. "well, everybody has setbacks of some kind, in my opinion he's recovering faster than most people in his predicament." "what about you Nedson?" the nurse asked. "I feel that if he has another week at his current rate then we'll be able to turn him over to the pol-." "Turn the volume up, that's five maybe ten blocks from here." Doctor Peterson said as he pointed at the TV. Doctor Nedson picked up the remote and turned the volume up. "wha-." "shhh-quiet." Doctor Peterson said as he listened. "hello everyone, this is Nancy White bringing you late breaking news." The news reporter paused. "at five 'o' clock this evening police were called to the buildings right behind me when a child who was playing here says he saw two men driving down here and in the child's, words burn something, that something turned out to be two bodies, as of now the police do not know if they have found male or female bodies, but will be releasing a statement as soon as possible, this is Nancy White, Fox News." "oh my God, that's horrible." Doctor Peterson said shocked. "I feel sorry for that lil' boy." The nurse said as she shook her head. Nedson sighed. "I feel sorry for the world." He replied. "well now that everyone has something to feel sorry for, Nedson, Sharon, can we talk about getting this murderer out of here and into prison where he belongs?" Peterson said. "with all due respect, when he's ready to leave then he'll be released to the authorities, but until and that times comes, whenever that may be he will be in our care and treated as necessary to his condition and injuries like every other patient, is that clear?" Nedson replied. "yes, perfectly clear, but I will be taking this to the supervisor." "that's your right, but I'll stand by my recommendation." "is this meeting over?" "clearly." "good, have a nice day Sharon, Nedson." "what was that all about?" Sharon asked. "he feels that he's too good to be around mister Drake." Sharon shook her head. "well, I gotta get back to work, if you need me, just page me." "a'right, thank you." "no problem." She replied then walked out of the room.

Across town at Saint Joseph's hospital Bobby was preparing to check out when his phone rang. "h-hello." "did you see the news?" "yeah, I saw it, come get me." Thirty minutes later Doobie pulled up in front of the hospital and went inside. "excuse me, I'm looking for bo-." "hey! what up? I been waitin' on you." Bobby said once he finally saw Doobie at the desk. "my fault, it took so long for me to get here." "let's go." Bobby said ignoring the apology. They walked out of Saint Joseph's hospital and got into Doobie's silver ford explorer. "so, what's up? What we gon' do?" he said when they were finally in the truck. "it's business as usual until I say different." "what about tha' shop?" "I gotta get some money on the street, so I can find out who did this shit." "what about Rock?" Doobie asked. "did they call askin' fa' money?" Bobby asked. "naw, ain't nobody called." Doobie replied. "you think KD behind this shit?" Bobby asked as he watched the city fly by through his passenger side window. "I don't know, I mean KD a killa, but he was damn near dead when we left him." Doobie replied. "what that mean?" Bobby asked. "I'm sayin' he ain't got outta tha' hospital that quick, and even if he did, he on his way to tha' joint." Doobie replied. They pulled up in front of Brian's house fifteen minutes later. Doobie knocked. "who is it!?" "it's bobby, is Brian

84

here?" a few seconds later Brian opened the door. "what up?" Bobby asked after he saw Brian's nervousness. Brian clicked the safety back on the tech nine he was carrying. "shit, waitin' fa' tha' other shoe ta' drop." He replied. "what you talkin' bout?" "yall think this shit a coincidence? KD plannin' this shit, we should've finished tha' job." Brian replied as he looked at the door like he expected KD to rush in. "you gon' be a'right?" "ain't none of us gon' be a'right til' that nigga KD dead or locked up." "look, we just came over to let you know it's business as usual." Brian looked at Bobby like he had just realized he was there. "yall see tha' news?" "yeah, we seen it, but don't worry bout that right now." Doobie replied. "so, what we gon' do?" "I'm a put some money on tha' streets and see what I can find out." "let me know if you need me." Brian replied. Bobby and Doobie stood to leave, and Brian flicked the safety off the tech, then walked them to the door. "what you think?" Doobie asked once they were outside. "that nigga scared ta' death, I think it's time we send somebody to check on our friend KD." Bobby replied. "who you wanna send?" Doobie asked. "pass me yo' phone." Bobby replied. Doobie handed Bobby his phone and watched as he dialed. "who you callin'?" "my man pharaoh." Bobby replied as the phone rang. "word ta' life, this tha' God, what up?" Pharaoh answered, his New York accent coming through heavily. "this Bobby, what's goin' on?" "shit, chillin' wit' tha' Goddess Duke, why? What's up?" he replied. "I got a problem I need took care of; you think you can get to tha' mil' ta'night?" Bobby asked. "I can get there if tha' money right, how much you talkin'?" "twenty gees a clip." Bobby replied. "that's what I like ta' hear, I'm on tha' next flight." Bobby hung up then dialed another number. "hello." "Bruce I-." "dis ain't Bruce, hold on." Bobby could hear voices in the background before Bruce got on the phone. "who this?" "this Bobby, remember that nigga Pharaoh you was tellin' me about?" "yeah, what about 'em?" "I got it through the street he on his way ta' tha' mil'." "real talk." "of course." "can you get 'em somewhere?" Bruce asked. "I can try, I know a chic he fuck wit'." Bobby replied. "cool, cool." Bruce said through a smile. "you know this gon' cost you." "how much?" "thirty gees cash." Bobby replied. "how he comin' in?" "I'll let you know." Bobby replied. "call me as soon as you find out." Bruce said feeling himself squeezing the trigger on pharaoh. "no problem, just have that money ready." Bobby said before hanging up. "problem solved." He said as he handed Doobie the phone back. Doobie looked at bobby then shook his head as he put the phone in his pocket. "that's a slick move." Doobie said with a smile. "I can't afford ta' leave no loose ends when this shit over." "so, what's the deal wit' this nigga Pharaoh?" Doobie asked. "I met him in New York a while back, he cool." "okay so what's the deal wit' tha' nigga Bruce?" "Pharaoh got a short fuse, Bruce pushed one of his buttons at a party, so Pharaoh repaid the favor by robbin' him an his girl, strippin' em both ass naked an leavin' em outside they house fa' everybody ta' see." Doobie laughed. "that's some cold shit." He said. "that's why I called him." Bobby replied. "you sure yo' plan gon' work?" doobie asked. "yeah, that's why I told Bruce I was gon' call em' when Pharaoh come ta' get his money, Bruce a be their waitin' ta' collect his head." "so you really know a female he fuckin' wit'?" Doobie asked. "yeah, he fuckin' wit' Bruce ol' bitch." "that's some fucked up shit." "yeah, but that's how it go." Bobby replied.

Everyone was back at Trina's house, Drew and Drama were rolling blunts while Grip talked to Trina and Tara. "KD gave me a list of shit he want done asap, he told me to ask if you got his lawyer yet?" "not yet." "why not?" "he ain't told nobody who to get." Grip reached in his pocket and pulled out the paper KD gave him. "Peter Hopper, five-six-two, thirty-three o' three." Trina grabbed a pen and wrote down the number. "yall gon' be straight here?" Grip asked as he stood. "yeah, we straight." Trina replied walking to her room, then returning with her twenty-two. "Grip be careful." She said. "I will, hey Drew come outside wit' me real quick, I got somethin' fa' yall." They walked out to his car, Grip popped the trunk and unzipped one of the bags. "give these ta' Trina and Tara." Drew whistled softly and put the guns in his hoodie. "let me get one." "that's strictly business but take these for you and Drama." He said handing him a box of bullets. "I'll be back later." Grip said as he closed the trunk. "a'right." Drew replied as he walked back toward the house. "sis put that lil' mu'fucka up." He said as he closed and locked the door. "we need all the straps we can get, lil' or not." Trina replied seriously. Drew pulled the two forty-fours out of his hoodie and sat them on the table. "Grip said yall might need these." Drama looked at the guns. "ain't that a bitch, they get heat an we stuck wit' half empty clips." Drew reached back into his hoodie and tossed the box of bullets on the couch. "stop bitchin' all tha' time." "fuck you." Drama replied. "naw, fuck ya' girl." "I have, yours to." "yall still be ribbin' each other?" Trina said shaking her head. "why you say it like that?" Drew replied. "I thought yall was to old fa' all that." She replied. "we know when ta' get serious, believe me." "Trina, leave 'em alone, let 'em have fun." Tara said. Trina sighed and walked back to her room. "what's her problem?" Drama asked. "I don't know, shit been hectic so let her ger her time."

Grip drove back to the hospital and went to KD's room. When he walked in, he noticed that KD didn't have tubes in his throat or nose anymore. "what's up nigga?" KD lifted his head and looked at Grip. "w-what's up? Everything took care of?" he asked speaking softly and with trouble. "not everything, but some of it." Grip replied. "Trina get in contact wit' tha' lawyer?" KD asked. "she said she gon' call tomorrow morning." "is t-tha-?" "yeah, the shop gone, we got Rock, Troy an MC." Grip said cutting him off. "d-did they go after anybody?" "naw, they don't know who hittin' em' yet." KD cleared his throat and spit into a small cup.

"the police came an cuffed me earlier, so I'm a be gettin' sent ta' tha' county when tha' doctor approve 'em ta' come move me." "ain't no police out there." Grip replied thinking KD was hallucinating. KD slid his left arm from under the blanket and showed him the cuff. "they here somewhere, probably watchin' who comin' an goin' outta here, so just do what's on tha' list an tell Trina ta' take tha' block off tha' phone." Grip nodded and headed to the door. "I'm a call ya' mom's an 'em so they know not ta' come." KD nodded then turned to the news to see what had been going on in Milwaukee, even now he wanted to have his ears to the street. He hadn't survived as long as he had in the game by not knowing what was going on. "I thought you was leavin'." KD said when he noticed Grip hadn't left. "I wanna catch this first." "we come to you live with late breaking news, at seven 'o' clock last night police and fire departments from two counties responded to an out-of-control blaze at Rodgers guns and more, it was called in by a local bar owner who does not want to be identified, fire fighters and police made a grisly discovery when they arrived and got the blaze under control." "Jane, can you tell us what that discovery was?" "well Bill, they discovered a burnt truck with what appeared to them to be two bodies, this has been the second fire where bodies have been discovered, the police have not stated whether they think the two are related, more on this gruesome story tonight at ten, Jane Alexander fox-." KD turned the channel and looked at Grip. "not the first ones." Grip said as he shook his head. "come see me at the county." KD replied. "I'll be there my nig." Grip replied as he walked out of the room looking to see if he could spot anyone watching, once he was outside of the room he tried, but didn't spot anyone watching, so he focused on handling the third thing on KD's list.

CHAPTER 7

88

Detectives Fredricks sat in Allen's office. "what tha' fuck's goin' on out there? This shits gettin' outta hand and I want it stopped!" Allen snapped. "Al, we're out there, but we got nothin' the shit can't be connected." Fredricks said. "what does the lil' boy know?" Allen asked. "Shit, he couldn't describe nothin' all he said was a white car, two people." Fredricks replied. "Good, good, so that's one less problem we gotta deal with." Allen said with a slight smile. "yeah, one less with a million more waiting." Fredricks replied with a smile of his own. "what you smilin' bout?" Allen asked. "we need to talk." Fredricks replied seeing his chance. "about what?" Fredricks turned to make sure the door was locked, and the blinds were down. "you gonna need ya' bottom drawer stash for this one." "what stash?" Allen asked as if he didn't know. "look, I know you keep a lil' powder in there, so break it out, the door locked." Fredricks replied. "what the fuck is this about?" Allen asked again. "I need more money Al." "so does everybody else." Allen replied. "well, I'm in a position to do somethin' about it." Fredricks replied. "Fredrick you not gettin' more money." Allen replied. "well, I guess I gotta play this for the captain." Fredricks replied as he reached in his pocket and pulled out the tape recorder and pressed play. "I-I'm officer Lyle, I was told to give this to you sir." There was the sound of rustling paper. "a'right, Lyle you can go." "thank you, sir." Then the sound of the door closing and more rustling of paper. "son of a bitch!" "what's the problem?" "they just found two burned bodies on cherry, under the viaduct." "so, what it ain't got nothin' to do with you." "I hope not." "even if it does, they can't prove it." "like they'll keep their mouth shut." "no proof." "a lil boy seen it all." "should I go?" "yeah, see what I got." "a'right, stop it." Allen finally said. Fredricks stopped the tape. "you'll go down with me, so do what you have to." Allen replied. "I've done this with every conversation we've ever had, should I bring the box?" Fredricks said with a smile. "I don't believe you." Allen replied.

89

Fredricks smiled then reached in his pocket and pulled out another tape. "listen ta' this, it's the Coppanelli case." Fredricks pushed play. "I don't give a fuck if he's innocent make him guilty, I want this Italian fuck locked up forever, he gets nothin' no more guns, vest, no-." Fredricks stopped the tape and smiled. "how much you mutha'fucka?" "I'm not a greedy guy, I'm takin' in thirty-five a week now, so let's make it fifty-five an tha' tapes disappear." "you'll get it startin' tomorrow, but I want all of the tapes an no copies." "you got it, but you might wanna put that up." Fredricks said as he pointed at the plate and unlocked the door. As Allen placed the plate back in the drawer and checked his nose for residue there was a knock. "hold on for a sec!" he yelled. "we done here?" "fa' now." Fredricks replied with a smile. "come in!" he said finally. Fredricks opened the door and bumped into Pam Cotton, a five-foot four blond known for her thirty-eight double D breast and twenty-four-inch waist. "sir I figured you'd want to hear this before it hits the news." "I'm listenin'." "those bodies from the viaduct." "yeah, what about 'em?" "they're female an tha' test shows that the fabrics taken off of their remains is the same as our uniforms." "okay and?" "they think they found melted badges, so either they're police or they were part of the shit that guy Drake was involved in." Fredricks and Allen looked at each other. "I appreciate the heads-up cotton, good job." "no problem, Al." she replied as she walked out of his office. "Goddammit!" he snapped before taking a deep breath. "what else can go wrong?" he asked and immediately regretted it. A lot could go wrong, and a lot was going wrong, this was the first time that he felt everything was crushing down around him and he didn't like the feeling. "damn it!" he said as he rubbed his head and looked at Fredricks. Both men knew the consequences if things fell apart and neither of them wanted to deal with them. They knew at this point there wasn't much they could do. Fredricks sighed and walked out of the office, Allen got up, locked the door and put the plate back on his desk. Bobby sat at

Doobies house staring at the TV. "what the fuck they talkin' bout?!" He yelled hoping the fear he felt didn't show in his voice. "don't worry bout it, that's bullshit they couldn't have found no badges they just usin' scare tactics." Doobie replied. "scare tactics my ass, call Brian." Doobie walked to the table, picked up the phone and Dialed Brian's number. "ain't no answer, tha' scary mu'fucka probably saw the news and packed his shit." Doobie said as he hung up. As he headed toward the kitchen the phone rang. He quickly went back and answered. "yeah?" "what up Doobie?" "who this?" "tha' Grim Reaper nigga." "who on the phone?" Bobby asked. "some nigga talkin' shit." "hand me the phone." Doobie handed him the phone. "Pharaoh, this Bobby wh-." "shut up! Somebody wanna talk to you." Grip said. "B-Bobby, w-what's goin 'on?" "now you know, and I know tha-." "who tha' fuck is this!?" Bobby snapped. "don't worry bout that let's just make sure they don't end up like Martin." "W-wait pl-please! Don't hurt 'em tell me what you want." "I want you to listen." "o-okay you got my attention." Bobby said. "good, calm down an listen." "a'right, a'right." "now that you listenin', I need you to pick who you love more, I'll call back in a minute." "get to my house now!" Bobby yelled. Doobie quickly headed out. "be careful, this mu'fucka got my wife and daughter!" the phone rang as Doobie pulled off. "h-hello." Bobby answered nervously. "ya' minute up, so who funeral you goin' to?" "if you want money I-I can get you money you ain't gotta do this." "I tell you what, I'm a let you tell 'em who you love more." "w-wait I haven't picked." "well hurry up or I'm a pick." Bobby finally broke under the pressure. "you dead mu'fucka! Whoever you are I swear I'm a kill you! I'm a kill you!" he yelled hysterically. "anger won't get you nowhere Bobby" Grip replied calmly. "say bye ta' ya' wife an daughter." There was rustling in the background. "daddy!" "baby help on tha-." The gunshot sounded like a firecracker to Bobby, then he heard his wife's screams before they were silenced with a gunshot. Bobby stood shocked, but after a few seconds he realized

91

that he was losing everything and everyone he loved or was close to, the game was calling in its debts and there was nothing he could do to stop it. Bobby knew KD had to be behind this, he had underestimated him, but now he knew what he had to do.

It had been thirty days since his last set back and the doctors agreed that KD could be placed into police custody. Doctor Peterson was the first to volunteer for the call to captain Shortlin, he felt good knowing Kevin Drake was finally going to be transported too prison. "I feel a hundred percent sure that mister Drake can be moved without any medical issues." "good I'll send three of my guys to get him in an hour, if that's okay." "perfectly fine, we'll be waitin'." "doc, before you go, I got an undercover named Momar there, can you page him for me?" "sure, sure no problem, hold on a second." Doctor Peterson clicked over and paged Momar over the call system, then clicked back over. "I just called; he should be here any minute now." After a few minutes, a short, stocky man with a military cut approached the desk. "my name was called a few minutes ago." The man said. "you have a call." Doctor Peterson replied as he handed him the phone. "yeah?" Momar said as he put his ear to the phone. "Momar, this is captain Shortlin, I need you to stay for another hour, I'm sending three officers to get Drake." "no problem." Momar replied. "and make sure you keep the notes on everyone who came to visit, and inform the staff, that mister Drake gets no more visits or phone calls." Shortlin said before hanging up. "no more visits or calls for Drake." Momar practically yelled. "a'right." The nurse replied as she grabbed a pen from the desk and wrote the restrictions on her chart. Twenty minutes later nurse Carrie walked to KD's room. "it's time for his medication." She said as Momar eyed her name tag. "go ahead, I'm just here to keep the visitors out." Nurse Carrie walked in and turned on the lights. "mister Drake it's time for your medication." KD sat up and rubbed the sleep from his eyes. "what?" "it's time for your medication." She repeated realizing KD had been sleep. "I'm not

92

supposed to be tellin' you this, but I overheard one of the doctors on the phone, the police will be here to get you any minute now." "I kinda figured that, can you hand me the phone?" Carrie handed him the phone, KD was confused when the front desk picked up. "I'm tryin' ta' make a call." "mister Drake, I'm sorry, but I was told no visitors or phone calls were allowed. KD slammed the phone down. "ain't that a bitch!" "what's wrong?" The nurse asked. "I can't have visitors or use the phone and I need to make a call." Carrie looked towards the door. "this is the second time I've risked my job for you, this better be important." She said not knowing why she wanted to help him. "believe me, it is, and I'm a make sure you straight, that's my word." Carrie took the cell phone out of her pocket. "hurry up." She said as she handed him the phone. KD dialed the number quickly and waited for an answer. "yeah! Who this?" "this KD nigga, they movin' me ta'night, move on to the next one." He said hanging up and handing her the phone. "you jus-." "hello." A voice interrupted from the doorway. "can I help you?" Carrie asked as she eased her phone into her pocket. "yeah, I'm officer Delaney this is officer Kimbrough and his partner Lennon." He replied as he stepped aside to let the other officers in. "I guess you're here for mister Drake." Delaney looked Carrie over from head to toe then smiled. "well, those two came for him, I came to take you too dinner." Carrie wondered if he had seen her slip the phone in her pocket. "as much as I might like that, my boyfriend wouldn't." she replied with a smile. "well, if he's ever dumb enough to lose you, I'm at district five." "if he's ever dumb enough, I'll call you." She replied as she headed out of the room. "excuse me gentlemen." She said as she squeezed past them. Lennon watched her walk away. "hey, Delaney, you see tha' ass on her? Like two fuckin' midgets." Delaney didn't bother to look. "let's just get this fucker outta here." He replied pointing toward KD. "go get a wheelchair, I'll shackle his legs." Twenty minutes later KD was checked out of the hospital and taken to the Milwaukee

County Jail. He wasn't worried because so far everything was going the way he figured it would, the robberies were one thing, but murder and betrayal was a cause for revenge and revenge meant death for all of those who decided to go against him. KD knew that Bobby had waited ten years to get revenge, but KD was prepared to battle to the death to make sure Bobby wouldn't walk away from the war he had started.

Trina decided it was best to lay low after the discovery of the bodies at the gun store, she was flicking through the channels when the news caught her attention. "about two weeks ago we reported on two horrible crimes that occurred under the viaduct behind me, first a ten year old boy witnessed two unidentified men start a fire in the very building he was playing in, after escaping the fire he told his parents and they called nine-one-one, upon the arrival of the Milwaukee police and fire department the blaze was put out and two bodies were discovered, both burnt beyond recognition, today the coroner and police released the names of the two victims, they are twenty-eight year old Tammy sholes and twenty-six year old Shaniece Dunbar, both are residents of Milwaukee, but their families could not be reached for comment, we'll be bringing you more developments as the they happen, this is Lucinda watts channel twelve news." Trina dropped the remote and reached for the phone right before it began to ring. "h-hello." She answered nervously. "did you see the news?" Tara asked excitedly. "yeah, I was just about to call you." Trina replied. "you think we got somethin' ta' be worried about?" "naw, we didn't do shit." "what if tha' police wanna talk?" "we never heard of 'em." Trina replied. "a'right I gotta go." Trina turned off the tv, picked up the gun Grip had given her, then went to her room to lay down. Fifteen minutes later she was asleep, the nightmares came quickly, there were gun shots and screams, she tossed and turned, but didn't wake up, the scenes played themselves over and over, but instead of seeing KD, she was running, she was being shot and she was dying. She could hear the

94

laughter of those who had betrayed their trust, then she saw Star walking towards her with no face, she finally woke up just short of screaming out and being covered in sweat.

Doobie and Bobby were at the airport waiting for Pharaoh's flight to arrive, they had chosen Mitchell International Airport because of its closeness and seclusion. flight one 'o' seven Pan Am from New York, unloading at gate four, flight one 'o' seven unloading at gate four. The announcement came over the pa system. "that's his flight." Bobby said as they headed toward gate four. "can we trust him ta' handle this shit?" Doobie asked. "he can handle it, he real wit' his shit." Bobby replied as he took out his phone and dialed Pharaohs number. "damn son, my feet just touched ground, give me a minute." Pharaoh said with a tone of hostility. "meet us at the restaurant wit' tha' neon blue light." Bobby replied. "yo, hold up God, what's this us shit? You know I get down by my lonely." Pharaoh said through gritted teeth. "just get ya' bags an meet us at the restaurant." Bobby replied coolly. "word life yo, we gotta talk dun." "just get hurry up." "I'll be there in a minute." Pharaoh said, hanging up as he reached baggage claims. After getting his bags he walked to the restaurant and saw Bobby. "pharaoh what's up?" Bobby asked standing to shake his hand. "same ol' dun, smokin' haze, gettin' money and keepin' tha' Goddess happy." "good, good, now let me introduce you to my right-hand man, Doobie come over here and meet my mans." Bobby said motioning him to come over. Doobie walked over and eyed Pharaoh. "if you need somethin' let me know an I'll see what I can do." "a'right, a'right, word ta' mutha yo' word ta' mutha." Pharaoh replied with a slight smirk. "let's go, we got business ta' handle." Bobby said as he looked around. "let's do that cuz I need ta' start checkin' niggas profiles." Pharaoh replied. "what you mean profiles? You plugged wit' tha' people or somethin'?" Doobie asked. "hold tha' fuck up son, you just said some ill shit yo, fuck you mean am I plugged wit'

95

tha' people dun? I don't fuck wit' no police son." Pharaoh snapped. The three of them headed outside as people turned to see what was going on. "chill! I ain't got time fa' yall bullshit." "fuck you mean chill? Ya' man's just disrespected me to the highest degree son." "it's over! I ain't got time fa' this shit, so it's over!" Bobby snapped. "cool, no hard feelin's, it's over, now when I'm a get my tools an shit?" Pharaoh asked. "Doobie, you took care of that right?" Bobby asked rhetorically. "yeah, he good." Pharaoh smirked. "okay, I dig it yo', but I gotta get some nuke, this ground walkin' shit ain't fa' me b." "what tha' fuck is nuke?" Bobby asked. "weed dun, weed." Thirty minutes later they pulled up to one of Bobby's duck off spots. "yo, I'm a need a car ta' get around." "let's go in an talk." Bobby replied as he got out of the car. "pop tha' trunk, I'm a need my bags." Pharaoh said. "we got you a room at tha' village inn." Doobie said as he walked toward the trunk. "don't go through my shit yo'." Pharaoh said jokingly. "I ain't gon' fuck wit' yo shit, an watch ya' mouth, we ain't in New York." Doobie replied. "was I suppose ta' take that as a threat dun? Cuz if so, you got some work ta' do God" "yo b, where you find that clown?" Pharaoh replied as he walked up the stairs to go in the house. "he far from a clown, be cool a'right." Pharaoh looked back and saw Doobie walking their way. "I'm cool dun." Bobby opened the door to let them in. "let's talk business." Bobby said as he sat down. "that's what tha' God came fa'." Pharaoh said as he dropped down heavily on the couch. "it ain't no secret that I been havin' problems wit' a few people, they killed my two best hitters, kidnapped another, shot me twice, robbed us, burned down the shop an killed my wife an daughter." The last words caused his voice to crack and tears to roll down his eyes. "damn dun, who you into it wit? Tha' mob, what tha' fuck you do?" Doobie waited to see if Bobby would tell the truth. "I'm not into it wit' tha' mob, it's just a lot of hatin' goin' on cuz we gettin' money an niggas ain't eatin' like

96

they want to." Bobby replied. "sound like yall should stop starvin' niggas." Pharaoh replied with a smile. Doobie pushed himself to his feet from the chair he was sitting in. "this shit ain't funny nigga, what tha' fuck you smilin' bout.?" He snapped. "that's yo' last time illin' out on me, next time you step wrong I'm a make you swallow my fuckin' tim's feel me." Pharaoh replied cracking his knuckles. "miss me wit' that sh-." Pharaoh cut Doobie's words with a right to his jaw that caused Doobie to flip over with the chair he was in. "I told you to leave me tha' fuck alone." Pharaoh said as he kicked Doobie repeatedly. "Pharaoh that's enough!" Bobby yelled. "naw dun, we past that I'm a show this clown he need ta' respect me." Pharaoh said as he grabbed the cordless phone and began hitting Doobie in the head with it. "I was being cool yo' but you wanted ta' play tough son." The gunshot caused Pharaoh to freeze and turn around. "I said, that's enough, you proved ya' fuckin' point." Bobby snapped. Doobie was slowly getting up from the floor. "y-you got it comin' nigga real-." "shut up! Get ya 'self together." Bobby said with a deep sigh. Doobie stumbled to the bathroom as blood dripped from his nose, lip, and a cut on his head. "pharaoh, watch ya 'self ya' hear me." "I hope I ain't gotta murk ya' mans, but if he come at me, I'm a put it to 'em that my word dun." Pharaoh replied. "I'll call you at tha' hotel." Bobby replied. "a'right but what about gettin' me some blaze yo'?" pharaoh asked. "we'll take care of that on tha' way." Bobby replied. "well, let's go." Pharaoh replied. "Doobie, I'll be back in a few minutes, I gotta drop pharaoh off." "can you snatch some Hennessy, ice and squares?' Doobie called from the bathroom. "yeah but stay on point an don't answer tha' phone unless my number come up on tha' caller ID." Bobby said. "a'right." "yo Doobie, my bad fa' snappin' off yo'." Pharaoh said with a smile. "yeah, we'll see." Doobie replied. Bobby pushed pharaoh towards the door. "I told you ta' chill." Bobby said. "I was apologizin' ta' ya' mans." Pharaoh

97

replied. "I know what you was doin', just remember that's my right hand." Bobby said seriously.

"a'right b, I'm done wit' it, but what's up wit' my wheels?" "they at tha' hotel, on the second

floor of the east wing parkin' garage, it's a black-on-black Dodge Viper, but don't use it when

you handlin' business, it can be traced back ta' me." Bobby said as they got in the car. "no

problem b, now all I need ta' know is how many niggas I gotta deal wit'?" "we gon' go step by

step, first I need you ta' take care of a bitch that's helpin' these niggas." Bobby replied. "just

point me at her an I'll handle tha' rest." Bobby smiled as he reached into the arm rest. "here's all

you need ta' know." He said handing him a piece of paper and a picture. "consider it done b."

pharaoh replied putting the paper and picture in his pocket as bobby pulled off.

CHAPTER 8

Officers Delaney, Kimbrough and his partner Lennon transported KD in an unmarked van.

Delaney sat in the back with KD. "mister Drake, you alright?" "yeah, I'm straight, why?

What's up?" "well, I gotta bet with the fellas up front, a hundred dollar bet actually, and I

wanna know if you plan on goin' into protective custody cuz of the wheelchair and all." KD

shook his head. "what tha' fuck I need protective custody fa'? that's fa' bitch niggas an

snitches." KD replied. "I'm glad ta' hear that because when they fuck you, I'll get a hundred

dollars out of it." KD laughed. "you watch too much tv." "mister Drake, I know people

who'd kill you then fuck your corpse if they thought it would get them out." Delaney said

seriously. "you ain't scarin' me wit' that sh-." "we're here, you a'right back there Delaney?"

"I'm fine, just havin' a chat with our friend mister Drake." He replied. When the van stopped, Kimbrough and Lennon climbed out and walked to the back of the van to open the doors. "let's get this fucker in there so we can go." "a'right, lift him up." Kimbrough and Lennon lifted the front of the chair and Delaney lifted the back, but as he did, he tipped the chair. "catch him! Catch him!" he yelled knowing it was too late. KD hit the ground an bit his lip to keep the screams of pain in. "what the hell's wrong with you Delaney?" Kimbrough snapped. "I lost my grip." "help him back in the chair before somebody sees this." The three of them helped KD up and sat him back in the chair. "sorry bout that mister Drake." Delaney said with a smile. "officer Delaney you got a wife or kids?" KD asked. "that's none of your concern." "well, if you do, watch out for 'em, it's a cruel world." "I think you better shut your mouth before you get yourself in trouble." Delaney replied through gritted teeth. "keep ya' advice ta' ya 'self." KD said with a smirk. Officers Kimbrough and Lennon rolled KD into the Milwaukee County Jail. "we finally got mister Drake here for you." Kimbrough said to the petite caramel complected nurse. "mister Drake can you roll over here please?" The nurse asked. "you need us to wait for him?" Lennon asked as KD made his way over to her. "naw, yall can go he won't be no trouble." "a'right have a nice day." "you to." She replied with a smile. When they made it out of the door, she looked at KD. "I can't stand those mutha fucka's." "we got somethin' in common then." KD replied. The nurse was used to being hit on and figured that's what KD was trying to do. "so, are your stitches holding?" "yeah, they straight, but can I ask for a favor?" "you can ask but that don't mean I'm a do it." She replied. "it ain't nothin' major, I just want some crutches." KD replied. "that I can do just give me a few minutes." As he was about to respond he heard his name being called by one of the deputies and rolled toward the booking area. "one of yall just called my name?" "through here, I gotta get you searched and up to the medical unit." "the deputy rolled him through a small door and motioned to

99

another deputy. "mister Drake could you stand for a second?" "I'm a need crutches, cuz I got stitches in my side, and I can't really put pressure on my legs." "Riley, can you see if Kelly ordered mister Drake some crutches?" Riley walked out of the booking area and to the nurse's station. "did you order crutches for mister Drake?" "not yet but I'll call now, he should have them in about ten minutes." When Riley made it back the other deputy had KD sitting against the wall. "so, what she say?" "she said they'll be up in about ten minutes." Ten minutes later the nurse brought the crutches in. "Riley, Banyon, what's goin' on?" she asked. "nothin' much, just waitin' on you to bring these damn crutches, so we can get mister Drake here on the medical unit." Riley replied. "well mister Drake deputy Banyon has your crutches, you take care of yourself." "what about my medication?" "your medication will be on the nurses cart except your Ibuprofen that'll be given to you, and you can keep that in your room." "a'right bet." "you ready mister Drake?" Banyon asked. "yeah, I'm ready." Banyon lead KD to the elevator and hit the up button. "mister Drake you're already famous with the inmates here, hopefully that doesn't turn out to be a bad thing." "I ain't worried 'bout it, this ain't my first go round." KD replied. "born convict huh?" Banyon replied. "naw, just been part of tha' system before that's all." "so have most of the people here mister Drake." When the elevator doors opened KD hopped on and gritted his teeth through the pain, not wanting to show weakness. "you ain't never met nobody like me, believe that." "I've seen all kinds." Banyon said. "see that's the problem, I'm one of a kind." KD replied as the elevator doors opened. "we're goin' to tha' left mister Drake." Banyon lead him to a beige metallic door and signaled the deputy behind the control desk. When the door clicked, he pushed it open. "you a'right mister Drake?" he asked after seeing KD wince in pain. "yeah, I'm straight." Banyon glanced at him as he hopped to the second door. When the first door closed the second one opened and they both walked in. "hey, Taylor I got mister Drake for ya' he's single cell." "a'right mister Drake, you're in room two." "a'right." He replied as he looked around. "hey Sal! Grab a couple blankets an take 'em to mister Drake's cell." "got it dep."

100

He replied as he stepped out of the broom closet and made his way downstairs. KD watched him as he washed his hands and walked over to a grey bin that looked like a garbage can, grab two blankets and two sheets. "is it a pillow in two dep?" "yeah, I think so, if not we'll get him one sent up." "is his brown bag in there?" "yeah, I made sure that he got the basics." Sal nodded and made his way to KD's cell. KD hopped behind him. Sal walked into the cell, turned on the light and began to make the bed, when he was finished KD hopped into the cell and leaned against the wall until the pain stopped, he couldn't wait to get the stitches removed so he could get rid of the crutches, but he knew that the crutches were better than the wheelchair and hospital bed he'd been in for a month. "good lookin' on tha' bed, I appreciate it." KD said as Sal walked out. "it's all good." "when the next time we come out?" KD asked. "I don't know they do shit when they feel like it around this mu'fucka." "ain't shit changed since the last time I was here." KD replied. "naw, just mo' beds fa' mo' niggas." "most definitely." KD said before nodding and hopping toward the bed.

Trina had finally called Peter Hopper and scheduled a meeting for one-thirty at the ponderosa on third and Martin Luther King. After getting off the phone she took a shower, dressed, and headed to the restaurant, when she arrived it was one-fifteen, she fixed herself a salad and ate hoping to pass the time. At one-forty-five Peter walked in and Trina waved him over to the booth. "miss Gibbs, I'm sorry I'm late, it's been a hectic day." Peter was about fifty years old, bald, very proper and expensively dressed. "don't worry about it, you here now so let's get to business." "a'right, let's do that." Peter reached into his alligator skinned briefcase, pulled out some papers and set them on the table. "what's all that?" "oh, all of this isn't for or about mister Drake, I just have to find his file." He replied shuffling through the papers. "augh, here we go." He said as he placed the rest of the papers back in his briefcase. "miss Gibbs I need you to read this and sign it." He said as he handed her the papers. "what's this?" "well, you're the only person other than mister Drake's mother who can get

101

money from his account, and this is just to show that you're responsible for my fee." "wait, wait, wait, what account? He never told me nothin' about no accounts, I gotta talk to him first." She replied. "I understand your predicament, so I'll call you in two days to see if you've made a decision, I'll also be visiting mister Drake around the same time." "a-a'right mister Hopper, thank you." "no thanks necessary and I apologize again for being late?" "no problem, I do have a question though." She said as they stood to leave. "ask away miss Gibbs." "how much is in this account?" "uh, well about ten-thousand dollars." "ten-thousand dollars!" She repeated loudly. Everyone in the restaurant turned toward them. "uh, I-I'm so sorry, excuse me." She said apologetically as they began walking out. "tell KD to call me I need too talk to him." "I'll make sure to tell him." "a'right mister Hopper, thank you, and have a wonderful day." "you to miss Gibbs." They shook hands as he placed the paperwork back into the briefcase and stepped outside.

TWO DAYS LATER

Grip was working KD's list when his phone rang. "hello." "you have a collect call from, KD, press one." Grip quickly pushed one to accept the call. "what up?" KD asked. "shit much." "did you tell Trina what I said?" he asked. "naw, not yet my nig." Grip replied. "click over an call her real quick." "a'right hold on." KD began blowing in the phone when Grip clicked over. He dialed Trina's number and clicked back over. "it should be ringin'" "hello." "baby, what up?" "oh my God, baby you a'right?" "yeah, I'm a'right, but I only got a few minutes, I need you to call correctional billing an take tha' block off the phone." "okay, I'll call soon as you hang up." "you talk to my lawyer yet?" "yeah, he'll be up there sometime around four." "good, I need you to come wit' em." "I was comin' up there anyway." She replied flirtatiously. "be careful and wear somethin' sexy." KD said. "oh! I need to talk to you about

102

somethin' tha' lawyer said." "we'll talk when you get here." He replied. "okay." She responded sadly. "love you." KD said. "love you to." Trina replied sadly before hanging up. Grip cleared his line and clicked back over. "so, what it do? Holla at ya' boy." "nothin' much, workin' shit out tha' best I can." Grip replied. "I feel that did you get ta' what we talked about?" "not yet, I can only do so much but I'm workin' on it." "I'm a have Trina drop you a few mo' dollars in about five days, so I can get you what I owe you." KD replied. "I ain't trippin' I know you got me, just work on gettin' out." "hey! Before I go, I need you ta' holla at somebody fa' me, it's a police friend of mine." "nigga is you crazy?" "I ain't crazy, I'm just reachin' out." KD replied. "what's tha' name?" he asked. "Delaney." "spell It." Grip replied. "d-e-l-a-n-e-y." KD replied spelling out the name. "it might take a while, but I'll let 'em know you checkin' on 'em." "good lookin'" "a'right, let me get off this phone, so I can get ta' that other thing you asked me bout." "a'right, my nig." "love." Grip replied. "fa' sho." KD hung up, grabbed his crutches, hopped back to his cell and thought about his next move. It was two-thirty-five and KD was sitting in his cell waiting for the door to buzz open, at two-forty-five the deputy called count and the doors buzzed open, everyone lined up in front of their cells. "KD! KD!" Someone called in a mild whisper. KD looked around and finally saw smoky an old school hustler turned dope fiend from the neighborhood. "what's up smoky?" "I gotta holla at y-." "Booker! No talkin'" Smoky stared at the deputy for a brief second before smiling. "no talkin' I got you." The deputy looked at them then continued with count. "count clear, lock in!" he yelled. When everyone turned to go back in their cells, he tossed a piece of paper to KD. "read that asap." KD slid the paper in his cell using his crutches. When he closed the door he hopped to his bed, sat down, and read the note. KD ripped the paper into pieces and threw them in the toilet, KD lay down to think, but must've dozed off because he woke up to the deputy knocking on the door. "Drake! You got a visit, get ready." KD got off the bed and slowly limped to the sink, he could feel the pain, but tuned it out. He quickly looked in the mirror, then waited for the door to open. A few seconds later the door buzzed open, and he limped out and looked at the clock. "what booth dep?" KD asked. "booth one." KD made his way to the booth, sat down, and waited a few minutes later the screen popped on and Tara's face appeared. KD

picked up the phone. "what's goin' on? Where Trina at?" Tara looked behind her nervously. "I-I don't

know but, I gotta call tellin' me ta' give you a message." She replied close to tears. "what's tha'

message?" he asked irritably. "pay backs a bitch." "what tha' fuck goin' on out there?" KD asked

angerly. "nothin', you didn't want ta' happen." Tara replied. "what tha' fuck that mean!" KD snapped.

"nothing." Tara said. "tell Grip ta' come holla at me, an yall go get my baby." "KD, I-I didn't mean that,

I-I just don't know what ta' do." Tara replied sadly. "don't trip, shit cool, I'll fix it." KD said shaking his

head. "We both know who behind this shit." Tara replied. "yeah, I'm a handle it don't worry" KD said

again. "I ain't worried I know you got it." Tara replied. "tell me if you need anything a'right?" Tears

began rolling down his face as he hung and limped out of the booth. Tara sat the phone down and wiped

tears from her eyes then walked away wondering what KD could really do from jail and why she should

keep risking her life, then she shook it off knowing KD would get things under control." As KD made his

way through the dayroom thinking about what he'd been told, smoky caught sight of him. "KD, what's

wrong man?" KD continued walking toward his cell focused on fixing things. "KD, slow up I gotta holla

at you." KD stopped so smoky could catch up. "what you wanna holla at me bout?" KD asked angerly.

Smoky handed him another piece of paper. "I found it on my floor when they buzzed the doors." KD

unfolded the note and began to read. When he was done reading, he balled the paper up and grabbed

smoky. "how these notes getting' in?" KD asked. "I don't know." Smoky replied. KD tightened his grip.

"find out who wrote this you got a gee comin' don't an I swear I'm a have you killed when you touch the

street." Smoky stared at KD before knocking his hand away. "you ain't gotta go that route wit' me." KD

sighed. "look, I'm goin' through some shit right now, can you just do what I asked?" "yeah, I'll look into

it." Smoky replied. "Drake! Booker! Off the stairs." The deputy yelled. KD and Smoky went their

separate ways, KD went in his cell and lay on his bed praying that Trina was all right, he also tried to

figure out how the notes were getting in. After a few minutes alone he headed back to the dayroom, he was still doing his best to hide the pain walking caused. "hey Kev, when you get done, holla at me." KD looked at the man that he had heard people call wink. "do I know you?" "naw, but I need ta' holla at you." KD walked over to the table and sat down. "talk." He said. "I heard bout ya' problem, an I got a friend who might be able to help." Wink replied. "I ain't got no problems my guy." KD replied. "call me Wink." "well, Wink I ain't got no problems." "a'right, I'm here wit' my ears open if you need me." KD got up and headed to the phones. When he got there, he sighed, picked up the receiver and dialed. A few seconds later his call was accepted. "I'm all over it." Grip replied as soon as he answered. "what happened?" KD asked. "all I know is, she called Tara and told her she was comin' ta' see you and she needed her to watch the house, when Tara got their the door was open." Grip replied. "find Bobby an talk to him again." KD replied. "I'm on it." Grip said. "a'right, what's up wit' tha' notes?" "notes? I only sent one, the one about tha' judge, and I been workin' on it, but he ain't goin', he won't do it." Grip replied. "well get close to him and give him a reason ta' do it." KD said through gritted teeth. "KD, that's a fuckin' Ju-." "I know what he is, an I don't give a fu-." "Drake, you're too loud." The deputy yelled. KD sighed but lowered his voice and got control of his anger. "look, we don't need them type of problems right now." Grip replied brushing KD's anger off. "my fuckin' girl missin' an I'm in jail, I already got problems, one more don't matter." "I ain't sure bout this move, but I'm a get on it." Grip replied. "good, I'm still workin' on that money, just give me a couple days." KD said. "fuck that money, I ain't trippin' on that shit." Grip replied. "a'right let me get off this phone, I gotta make another call." KD replied. "a'right, I'm a holla, oh! I got Drama number." Grip said knowing KD would want it. "let me get it." KD replied. "five-three-o-three, seven-four-five, ask fa' Drama." Grip said. You have one minute left the automated voice said. "Grip find my baby." KD said. "fa' sho." Grip replied before the call was ended by the operator. KD hung up and looked around for smoky, when he saw him, he walked over and tapped him on the shoulder. "let me holla at you real quick." Smoky got up and walked toward the gym. "what's the problem?" smoky asked as KD opened the door that lead to the gym. "what up wit' you tellin' wink

105

my business?" KD asked when they began walking. "I ain't told nobody shit." Smoky replied. "you the only one gettin' messages, so you had to tell 'em." KD replied through gritted teeth. "what I gotta lie fa'?" smoky asked. KD looked smoky in the eyes, turned and walked out of the gym. When he walked back into the dayroom he walked over to Wink. "let me holla at you." KD said. Wink made his last chess move and stood up. "what's up?" he asked. "let's talk in tha' gym." KD replied. When they made it to the door Wink let KD go in first. "what's up?" Wink asked again. "let's walk." KD replied. As they walked around Wink began to get nervous. "you said you wanna talk, so what's up?" Wink asked. "first off how you know my name?" KD asked. "I heard the dep say it." Wink responded. "the dep didn't use my first name." "it was on the n-." KD didn't give him a chance to finish his sentence, KD's punch caught him in the face causing him to fall against the wall. Wink quickly swung two punches, KD side stepped them and punched him in the face and head, at the same time the pain in his legs and side began to get the better of him Winks nose began to bleed, KD grabbed Wink around the neck and threw him towards the wall, then banged his head against it. When smoky and the other two people in the gym saw the blood they left quickly, smoky went to his cell and the other two told the deputy about the fight, as the deputy ran toward the gym he pressed his emergency button, alerting other deputies to the fight. As he entered the gym, he saw KD banging Winks head against the wall. "Drake stop it! Stop it right now!" KD continued to bang winks head against the wall, so the deputy grabbed him and threw him down, as he held KD down more deputies entered the unit. "everybody lock in! lock in now!" They yelled. While everyone was locking in more deputies entered the unit and headed toward the gym. "Myrion, call a medical emergency now!" one of the deputies yelled. Myrion called in the code fifty-one. "we have an inmate seriously injured." He said into the walkie-talkie. The reply was immediate and about two minutes later the medical team arrived on the unit. "what happened?" one of the nurses asked. "two prisoners came to my desk and told me there was a fight in the here, when I entered, I saw mister Drake banging Mister Samuel's head against the wall." He replied. "get an ambulance in route now!" one of the nurses yelled as Winks eyes closed and he lost consciousness. The other nurse called control to relay the message as the deputies watched the other nurses grab the first aid kit and break a vile of smelling salt under Winks nose. Wink twisted his head slowly, blinked, then closed his eyes again. "mister Samuel! Mister Samuel! We need you to stay woke for us." As the nurse was talking, they were told by one of the deputies that the ambulance was in the sally port. "check Drake and get him outta here.!" Two deputies picked KD up and lead him to a nurse who quickly checked his stitches. "he's okay." She said as the paramedics rushed in with a stretcher. When they lead KD out of the gym one of the nurses turned toward the deputy. "isn't that guy the one all over the news?" she asked. "yeah, that's him." The deputy responded. "you really think he, did it?" she asked. "of course, he was caught red handed." "I heard some of the other prisoners say he was set up." She said with a slight shrug. "well, I'm not the judge so I don't-." "excuse us, we need to get him outta here asap." The medic said. The nurse and deputy quickly stepped to the side and held the door, so they could exit.

CHAPTER 9...

THREE DAYS LATER

It was two 'o' clock Monday afternoon and Grip was sitting outside of the Milwaukee County Courthouse, watching people come and go, he wasn't worried about looking suspicious because the Benz he had stolen fit in perfectly with the surroundings. When his phone finally rang, he answered immediately. "yeah?" "he just left out the building through the tunnel." Drew said. "can you follow him 'til I get that way?" Grip asked. "yeah, but where you at?" drew replied. "I'm in tha' front." "you sho' this shit gon' work? Drew asked concerned. "ain't shit in life fa' sho Drew." Grip replied. "just hurry up and get this way." Drew replied. Grip pulled away from the curve, made an illegal U-turn and headed for a tunnel. "Drew, where you at?" Grip asked. "the red light by the hospital." Grip hung up, waited a brief second then dialed Drama's number. "what it do?" he answered. "we 'bout two blocks away, long as he don't make no unexpected turns, we good." Grip said. "I told you he live in the condos by the college, he gotta come this way." Drama replied. "we'll see lil nigga." "I been followin' 'em for two days, so-." Grips line clicked. "hold on this might be Drew." He said before clicking over. "hello." "you have a collect call from-." Grip quickly accepted the call. "what up my nig'?" KD asked. "nothin' handlin' business." "good, good, any news on my girl?" "naw, but we still workin' on it." Grip replied. "a'right, what 'bout my police friend?" KD asked. "I ain't got a chance ta' talk to 'em yet." Grip replied. "slow motion huh?" "yeah, slow motion." Grip replied. "after this I ain't gon' be able ta' call til' next week." KD said. "why?" "I'm in tha' box fa' beatin' this nigga named Wink half ta' death." KD replied. "man, you gotta chill out that shit ain't gon' look good at court." Grip said seriously. "I'm already fu-." "hold on real quick." Grip said before clicking over. Once he clicked over, he dialed Drama's number. "yeah?" "here we come, be ready." Grip said. "a'right." Drama replied. Grip clicked back over. "what's up wit' clickin' over on me?" KD asked. "I'm takin' care of that business like you asked, call me back next week." Grip said as he watched the traffic. "a'right." KD replied before hanging up. As grip hung up, he heard a crash and knew that there was no turning back. He and Drew stopped their cars, they knew that this mission had to go exactly as they had planned. Drew was the first to get out and head to the scene. "hey! Hey! Yall a'right?" Drew asked as he looked around. When Drama saw his chance, he cocked his gun and Drama did the same. "hey! Is you straight?" Drew asked again as Drama opened his car door, walked to the judge's passenger side door, and looked in, the judge was holding his head as blood gushed between his fingers. "the paramedics on the way." Drew said. The judge couldn't really understand what was being said and no matter how hard he pushed or kicked the door it wouldn't open. When Drama and Drew realized he was stuck they opened fire through the windows, the judge was shot ten times. As the judge sat in his car dying Drew and Drama ran though the gangway where their getaway car and new clothes waited. Grip got out of the car he was driving with a badge and gun in hand. "police! Everybody stay down!" no one bothered to look at his face, they stayed where they felt safe, the ground. What grip had done would give them a little time before the real police were called or so they thought, because when he made it through the gangway, he heard the sirens and they sounded close. "drive slow." Grip said as he closed the door. "we gotta get rid of these clothes." Drama said panicky. "what about yo' fingerprints?" Drew asked looking at Grips hands. "I wiped the inside as clean as I could." Grip replied. Drew and Drama held up their hands showing their gloves. Grip shook his head knowing he had slipped up and all he could do now was pray that he had wiped down the car good enough not to leave any prints or at least none that would be identifiable. He had been to prison once and swore he would never go back, during the rest of the ride he was silently praying that he had done a good enough job of wiping the car down to avoid being another victim of Milwaukee's throw away the key justice system.

Trina sat tied to a chair blind folded, all she could remember was hearing a woman screaming for help and thinking that it could be Tara, she opened the door and was tased, after that everything went black, now she was waking and trying to loosen the ropes that held her. "yo' ma' stop strugglin' ya' not getting' outta that shit." Pharaoh said confidently. "w-who-i-is you?" Trina asked. "I can't tell you all that ma, but I'll tell you this, ya nigga fucked up." Pharaoh replied as he eyed her body like a wolf eyeing a sheep for its next meal. Trina knew Bobby was behind her kidnapping. "so, Bobby got you doin' his dirty work?" Trina asked even though she already knew in her heart. "naw ma, money got me doin' it, but bobby asked me." Pharaoh replied still eyeing her body. "w-who is money?" Trina asked seriously. Pharaoh laughed. "I'm talkin' dead presidents ma, tha' green shit, Dolla Dolla bills ma." Trina figured since it was about money, she could talk her way out of what was going on. "how much he payin'? I'll get you double." She said. "I'm gettin' thirty fa' ya' head." Pharaoh replied knowing he was only getting twenty, but sixty was better than forty any day. "I can get that fa'-." "look at who we got here." Bobby said as he walked into

109

the room, he hadn't heard any of the conversation between Pharaoh and Trina. "you so much of a bitch you had ta' get somebody ta' handle ya' business." Trina said as she struggled to get loose. Bobby looked at pharaoh then punched her in the face. "bitch you should learn ta' keep ya' mouth shut; it might keep you alive." He said shaking his hand. Trina knew if pharaoh didn't let her go, she was dead anyway, so his promises and threats meant nothing. "I wanna know who killed Troy and MC, an I wanna know where Rock is." Trina remained quiet. "bitch you think I'm playin' wit' you?" bobby snapped before slapping her. Trina looked up at him then spit in his face and watched as he wiped it away. "you don't watch tha' news, do you? You stupid mu'fucka." Bobby punched her twice and watched as the blood dripped from her nose. "I can kill you whenever I want, so play nice." He replied as he ripped her shirt and squeezed one of her nipples hard enough to make her scream. "you dead if I live or not, so it don't matter what happens." She said angerly. "Pharaoh this bitch a lil' to tough, fix that." Bobby said. Pharaoh looked from Bobby to Trina, then punched her. "he screamed like a bitch before he died." She said quickly. Bobby laughed. "you ain't killed nobody except one of them punks in Carlo's house and Keema, and you was scared then." Bobby replied. "Pharaoh unclenched his fist and leaned against the wall to watch them talk. "the day he got snatched you got shot twice, Rock had on a black pair Prada jean with some white ones and a plain white shirt." "that don't mean shit except you workin' wit' whoever hit us, pharaoh beat this bitch till she talk." He replied and began walking away. "bobby! Bobby!" she screamed panicked. "don't get scared now, you put ya 'self here." "he had a tattoo on his chest that said loyalty, power, respect, and one on his back of a angel, that said watch over me." Bobby couldn't find words to match his anger, he knew Rock had gotten those tattoos when he was in Memphis and had only shown them to three people, Brian, him, and Keema. "Pharaoh." Bobby said softly. "what up dun?" Pharaoh replied. "kill her an dump her body in front of the county jail." He said barely above a whisper. "son you buggin' cuz I ain't dumpin' nobody in front of no cop shop yo'." "do it at two in the mornin' they either on break or changin' shift." Bobby replied ignoring Pharaoh's refusal. "yo b, I just said I ain't gon' be able ta' do it,

110

I'll dump her ass in front of her crib or somethin'." Pharaoh said as he shook his head. "you gon' dump her where I told you mu'fuka! Or you can get dealt wit' too." Bobby snapped. Pharaoh had never been worried about threats, but he knew Bobby was capable of anything right then. "don't ever threaten me again b, feel me." Pharaoh replied with a cold stare. Bobby didn't respond as he walked out the door. When the door closed Trina sighed in relief. "let's talk money." She said. "sorry ma, I like breathin'." Pharaoh replied. "but-I-I can get th-." "sorry ma, I gotta think 'bout me." Pharaoh replied before knocking her out. While she was unconscious pharaoh untied her and took her to the back of the abandon house, lay her on the mattress that was stained and ripped, then undressed her, when he had her undressed, he stood over her naked body, unzipped his pants and put on a condom. "might as well get somethin' else out the deal." He said as he got on top of her, once he entered her and began to thrust Trina regained consciousness. "g-get off me! Help! Help!" she screamed as she fought. Pharaoh got tired of the struggle, punched her until she lost consciousness again. After he finished, he took off the condom, put it in a bag, pulled his pants up, then began to kick, stomp, and punch her until blood dripped from her mouth, nose and ears, he knew that she was alive, so he put on his gloves, grabbed the sheet set he had bought and ripped the plastic open. When he got it open, he took the sheets out and wrapped her body in them, took the Glock forty bobby had given him, wrapped it in the semi-thick plastic and fired four shots into her stomach, chest, face and head at point blank range, as the echo of the gunshots faded pharaoh heard footsteps, and quickly turned with his finger still on the trigger waiting to see who was coming his way. "yo' don't creep up on me son, I almost unplugged ya' fuckin' x-box." He said when Bobby stepped through the door. "leave this on tha' bitch." Bobby said as he looked at the body and passed pharaoh the note with gloved hands. "listen dun, its gon' be war in tha' streets if them cats get down how you say they do, word life." Pharaoh replied. "it's already war so let it be what its gon' be." Bobby replied as he looked at his watch. "it don't seem like she was here no eleven an a half hours, its goin' on one-thirty, get movin' I want her there at two 'o' clock exactly." He said. "at least help me carry this bitch to tha' car." Pharaoh

111

replied. "you can't use tha' car, I told you it can be traced." Bobby replied. "I ain't stupid, I stole one."

Pharaoh said. "how long you had it?" bobby asked. "bout two, three hours." "it shouldn't be hot yet?"

Bobby replied as he and pharaoh carried the body out of the back door and to the car. "open the trunk."

Bobby let go of Trina's legs and walked to the passenger side of the brown delta '88' and pushed the

yellow button that opened the trunk, once the trunk was open, he helped pharaoh throw Trina's lifeless

body in, then walked to his truck. "take care of that." Bobby said nodding toward the trunk. "I'm a handle

me dun, just get my dough stacked an remember what I said." Pharaoh replied. "what you talkin' bout?"

he asked. "bout how you came at me yo'." Pharaoh replied. "I was a lil' upset I lost it my bad." Bobby

said with a sigh he couldn't wait until he could call Bruce and get rid of pharaoh. Pharaoh had been

driving for five minutes wondering why Bobby wanted the body dumped in front of the county jail, when

it hit him, he smiled. "that's a cold shot b, word life." As he turned the corner, he looked at his watch, it

was one-forty. "fuck it son I'm a do this shit now fuck waitin' till two 'o' clock." He turned at the next

corner, pulled to the curve and got out the car, he looked at the county jail building and the few officers,

then looked at his watch again. "close enough." He said as he popped the trunk. When he got out he

walked to the trunk, got back in the car and pulled off.

CHAPTER 10

Homicide Investigation Team better known as H.I.T. were the best homicide detectives in their districts

put together to solve cases others couldn't. The team consisted of detective Randall, Coldburn, and

Lincoln who had been out of action due to being shot earlier in the year. "hey Coldburn, I've been diggin'

into this Drake case an I'm comin' back wit' some weird shit." "like what Randall? I'm busy." "in the last

month and a half twelve people have been murdered and four had their bodies burned, all four involved

gasoline and out of those four it seems that they've all been tortured before death." "oo-kay, now tell me somethin' I don't know Randall." "you know the guy that got shot when his shop got torched?" "yeah, Bobby skyy, what about 'em?" "well, his wife and daughter were both killed, shot in the back of the head." Coldburn looked up. "did either of you know they found burned walkie-talkies in the shop?" she asked. "no, did you know he hasn't been questioned about the murders of his wife and daughter?" "hold up, that goes against protocol not to question family." "it's hard to question someone that no one can find." They were interrupted by a knock on the door. "come in! Coldburn yelled. Detective Williams walked in. "we got another body." He said sadly. "and the count keeps getting higher." Coldburn replied. "they found a body wrapped in a sheet on the curve." "on the curve where?" Randall asked. "in front of the county jail." "what!? Coldburn and Randall replied at the same time. "they found her during shift change." "do they know who it is?" "yeah, she had her id." "well, who was it?" "it was Trina Gibbs." Coldburn and Randall know right then that there was something major going down in the streets. "how was she killed?" Coldburn asked. "beaten and shot, we'll know more after an autopsy." "the whole state's gonna laugh at us, first the judge now this." Randall replied angerly. Williams and Coldburn looked at him, but Coldburn was the first to speak. "judge? What are you talkin' bout?" "haven't you been listening to the radio or watchin' the news." "what judge?" Williams asked impatiently. "Penderwall." "Penderwall, Penderwall, isn't he the judge that was going to handle the Drake case?" Williams asked finally placing the name with the face. "I don't know." Randall replied. "find Tara Harper now!" Williams snapped. "and when I find her, then what?" Randall asked. "take her to Paris or Disneyland, what the fuck do you think? Bring her ass in, she knows what's goin' on and she's gonna tell us." "oh, there was a note left with miss Gibbs body, I almost forgot." Williams said. "what'd it say?" Coldburn asked. "somethin' like, one of us has to lose or one of us has nothin' to lose, somethin' like that." "when will it reach us? Coldburn asked. "we'll get the case officially in about two hours from now." Both Williams and Randall noticed that Coldburn was kind of pale as they walked out. "what's wrong with her?" Randall asked. "you're behind on the latest gossip and back biting I see." "I try to avoid that shit, but this I wanna hear, so answer my question." "she's been fuckin' Penderwall for the last six months." Williams replied. "you're kidding right?" Randalls asked. "nope, Alex from the gang squad caught them coming out of the same hotel room." Williams replied. "that's crazy, aren't they married?" "yeah, but not to each other." "that's fucked up." "yeah, but everybody lives life their own way."

Inside the county jail everything and almost everyone was on lock down, the prisoners were told to stand in their cells for count and the only people out of their cells were swampers. Around mealtime the deputy buzzed doors as they passed out meals. When Sal made it to smokey's cell he was standing in the doorway. "why we on lock down?" he asked. "some crazy mu'fucka dumped a body in front of the buildin'." "Salazar, move on no door visiting." Downstairs in the hole as most prisoners called it KD was just receiving his meal. "mister Drake, what's goin' on this mornin'?" "shit much, waitin' on my lawyer." "he might not get in today." The deputy replied. "why not?" "some crazy son of a bitch left a dead broad in the street." KD dropped his tray. "I'll get you another tray an somethin' to clean that up with." "w-when that happen?" KD asked. "around two this mornin'." "do anybody know who she is?" "that I don't know." KD sighed. "can you get this tray?" The deputy waited until KD passed his tray through the slot, then called for another one. "I'll be back with the broom, dustpan, and mop." When the deputy walked away KD sat on his bed and wondered if his worse fears had come to pass. Ten minutes later the deputy was back. "sorry, I got busy the sheriff just told us judge Penderwall was killed yesterday." "who gon' handle his cases?" "nobody knows yet, and it'll probably be a few weeks before we do." KD finally got up, walked to the door and grabbed the broom, mop and dustpan. "your trays on the cart." "let me clean this shit up an I'll grab it." KD quickly cleaned his room and then asked for his tray.

Back at district five officer Allen was finishing a phone call with captain Reynolds. "yes sir, I understand, I'm puttin' my best men on it right away, bye sir." Allen hung up then used his cellphone to call Fredricks. "yeah, what's up?" Fredricks asked. "where the fuck are you?!" "I'm pullin' into the station now, why? What's up?" "get to my office now! And I mean right now." Allen said before hanging up. He paced his office for five minutes before Fredricks arrived. "What's up Al?" "close the door and sit down." Fredricks knew things were bad, so he sat down like he was told. "a'right tell me what's up?" Allen turned around and walked behind his desk and sat down. "I got twelve dead bodies within' two months, a judge who got gunned down in his car after he hit a stolen one, I got the captain chewing my ass askin' me what tha' fucks goin' on, and I don't know shit!" Fredricks threw his hands up. "whoa, whoa, whoa, what's this got ta' do wit' me?" "I know you got connections, I want every fuckin' snitch you got on tha' streets, in jail, an wherever the fuck else you got 'em workin' or brought in." "on what charges?" "I don't give a fuck make somethin' up!" "and while I'm doin' all that what you gon' be doin'? "tryin' ta' find out who had the nuts to drop a dead body in front of the county jail." "what tha' hell you talkin' bout Al?" "some mutha'fucka dumped a woman by the name of Trina Gibbs in front of tha' county jail." "whoever did it must be a cold hearted mu'fucka." Fredricks replied seriously. "I said the same thing." A few minutes later Fredricks walked out of the station and to his car, when he got in, he sat trying to figure out where Bobby could be. "the house by the lake." He said to himself as he pulled off. Thirty minutes later he pulled up to the gate and pushed the button. He waited a few minutes before anyone answered. "who dis?" "who tha' fuck is you son?!" "I'm here ta' see Bobby, tell 'em it's Fred." "hold on a minute." Pharaoh replied. Fredricks looked at his watch and sighed. It wasn't even two seconds before the gate was buzzed open, he drove up the quarter of a block driveway, parked, got out and knocked. Bobby answered the door and extended his hand, but Fredricks didn't shake it. "we need to talk." He said. "a-a'right, let's go on tha' patio." Bobby replied closing the door. "naw, let's go in tha' kitchen." As they walked to the kitchen Pharaoh walked pass smoking a blunt. "I see you got a

115

bodyguard." "naw, just a lil' help, kinda like an enforcer." Once they entered the kitchen Fredricks got

serious. "sit down." Bobby sat in the red wine-colored high back chair. "what's up Fred?" "I'm a ask you

this once and only once, why the judge and who did it?" "I saw it on the news, but I ain't have shit ta' do

wit' no judge." Fredricks slowly stood and began to pace, then he quickly slammed Bobby's head into the

table. "I know I said once, but I like you so I'm a ask you again." This time he pulled his gun from the

holster. "why the judge? An who did it?" Fredricks said through gritted teeth. "I told you I saw it on the

news, but I ain't have shit ta' do wit' no judge!" Bobby snapped as he rubbed his forehead. Fredricks hit

him in the face with the butt of the gun. "now's not the time ta' fuck wit' me Bobby." When pharaoh

heard the yelling, he ran into the kitchen with gun in hand but froze when he saw the gun pointed at

Bobby's head. "yo son, what you want me ta' do?" he asked. "put the gun down." Bobby replied. "you

sure dun? Cuz I can spread his shit all over the wall." "I said drop tha' fuckin' gun pharaoh!" Bobby

snapped. Pharaoh dropped the gun, Fredricks tapped Bobby on the head with the barrel of the gun. "seems

like I wore out my welcome, but I'll tell you this, whatever tha' fuck goin' on wit' whoever playin' shoot

'em up bang bang better stop, an if I find out you know about that judge, I'll be back you understand?"

Bobby nodded. "I can't hear you." "I understand." Bobby replied. "good." Fredricks replied as he walked

toward the kitchen door. "watch out nigga." Pharaoh moved to the side and let him out of the kitchen.

"stay in here til' you hear the front door close; I'd hate for Bobby to have to find a new enforcer." A few

seconds later the door was slammed, pharaoh picked up his gun an turned to run after Fredricks. "leave

him! It's cool." Bobby snapped. "who tha' fuck was that?" Pharaoh asked. "don't worry bout that, just get

me a towel and some ice." Pharaoh walked in the bathroom and grabbed a dry towel then walked out to

the refrigerator and began filling it with ice. "what was that shit he was talkin' bout a judge? I know you

ain't have me whack no judge b." "did that bitch look like a fuckin' judge?" Bobby asked. "naw."

Pharaoh replied. "that's cuz she wasn't, now I don't know who hit tha' judge, but I'm sho' as hell gon'

find out." Bobby replied as he held the towel to his forehead. After leaving Bobby's, Fredrick decided to head to the southside, he knew Taz would be out there hustling. When he turned on seventeenth and mineral, he saw Taz standing on the same corner he had busted him on eighteen months ago, he rolled down the window. "Taz, what's up?" Taz knew the voice but not the car, so he thumped his cigarette and prepared to run. "don't do it Taz, don't you fuckin' run!" he said as he slowed the car down. Taz saw his chance and took off at full speed through the store's gangway. "damn it!" Fredricks yelled as he hit the gas and sped down the block, he knew the route well, it was the same route he had chased others from bells click known as the one-eight mafia, as he hit nineteenth, he sped through the alley swerved to the right, and blocked it, Taz continued running through the alley and ran into the car. "let's talk." He said as he yanked Taz up from the ground. "what you want man? I ain't did shit." Taz replied. "we're goin' to Renae's to talk." Taz was glad Fredricks wasn't arresting him, so he decided to remain quiet. Fifteen minutes later they pulled up in the back of Renae's house, no one in the neighborhood knew Fredricks was a cop, once he stopped the car, he looked around then opened the back door and removed Taz's handcuffs. "let's go hurry up." Fredricks said as he went to Renae's door and knocked. "who is it?" "it's Fred." Renae rushed down the stairs and opened the door. "come in." she said stepping aside. Once they were inside Renae closed the and locked the door. "you know where to go stop actin' like a stranger." She said. All three of them walked up the stairs and into the living room, Renae went to the kitchen and came back with two cups of orange juice. "here you guys go." She said handing each of them a glass and sitting down, Renae caught Fredricks attention by sighing then crossed her legs to let him see that she wasn't wearing anything under the long pajama top. "so, what's the reason for the visit?" "I just need to talk wit' my friend Taz." Fredricks replied. "about what?" Taz asked. "can we have some privacy? I'll let you know when we're done." "no problem." She replied as she headed to her room. When her room door closed Fredricks turned to Taz. "who killed the girl and dropped her in front of the county?" "I don't know." Taz replied truthfully. "who shot tha' judge?" Fredricks asked. Taz sighed. "word on tha' street is, it was a hit." He replied. "what, like a mob hit?" Fredricks asked. "yeah, but I don't know if it's true."

117

"who said it was a hit?" Fredricks asked. "b-bell." Taz replied. "a'right, what about the fire and shootings at the auto shop?" "I heard it got burned down by some dudes he owed money to." "what dudes?" "I don't know ask Skeet an Bell." "what do you know about the house on Scott that got hit?" Fredricks asked. "somebody beat us to it, I seen it on the news." Taz said. "what about the gun shop?" "wasn't us." Taz replied. "look, go somewhere and lay low for a couple days, call me an I'll put some papers together, make it look like I busted you on some bullshit." Fredricks said. "can I get fifty bucks? My money's at the safe house." Taz said not wanting to admit he was an informant. Fredricks peeled off five tens. "get outta here." Taz headed out and Fredricks went behind him to lock the door. Renae came out of her bedroom and looked downstairs to see if Fredricks was coming back up. "he comin' back?" she asked. "not ta'night, so get to the bedroom." Renae quickly took off the long shirt she had been wearing and got in the bed, when Fredricks entered the room, he unbuckled his belt and pulled off his pants, Renae smiled as she stared at his erection. "I see you're thinkin' bout me Poppi." "of course, I am." He replied as he got in the bed. As soon as he was in the bed Renae reached for him, he lowered his head and began to suck on her nipples which caused them to pucker and harden, he rolled her left nipple back and forth between his teeth. "w-why you still got on ya' shirt?" Renae asked as she gripped his shoulders. Fredricks lifted the shirt over his head and threw it on the floor, Renae waited for him to ease into her, but he continued to play with her nipples, he grabbed the back of her head and began kissing her. "stop playin' an give me this dick." She said excitedly. Fredricks had never heard her talk that way, but he liked it, he quickly gripped her waist and began a steady grind. "Poppi! Poppi! Poppi!" She moaned loudly as she began breathing heavily. "say you want it!" Fredricks replied aggressively. "n-no-n-no." she replied shaking her head with passion. Fredricks began licking down the side of her neck, making his way to her shoulders, then down the middle of her chest, when he reached her navel he slowly licked around it and before going back up to her stomach he gave her a soft half bite, half kiss on her stomach and the sensation of pain and pleasure caused her to moan louder, when he heard her moan which was more like a sharp, quick intake of breath, he worked his way back to her nipples, took one of her nipples in his mouth and began to caress the other, Renae tried to speed things up the sensation was becoming more than she could bare. "st=stop teasin' me." She said softly. Fredricks didn't bother to reply as he gripped her ankles and spread her legs apart, he placed his knee on the bed, leaned over her, then used his teeth on the inner skin of her lower leg, Renae began to tremble, so he tightened his grip on her ankles and worked his way up her leg using his tongue, lips and teeth. Fredricks kissed, licked and softly bit her causing her to arch up to meet his mouth. Renae wished that he would just make her cum instead of teasing her, even though she complained in her mind, she was loving everything he did to her, Fredricks softly kissed her neck then put one finger inside of her to see if she was wet, when he felt the wetness between her legs he slowly slipped inside of her then slipped back out, when he felt her stiffen and squeeze him with her legs he thrust deeply, Renae wrapped her legs around his waist to show her satisfaction and Fredricks began to thrust faster and Renae began to move with him, Fredricks tightened his grip on her and continued to thrust until she bit into his shoulder. "oh! P-Poppi! Poppi! F-fuck me!" she screamed loudly. "yeah-you like it don't you?" Fredricks replied as he pounded into her. "o-o shit! I'm-I'm cummin'!" she screamed as she grabbed his ass hoping to push him deeper inside of her and when he thrust, she began to shake with another orgasm. Fredricks waited on her to relax then rolled off of her, Renae lay still breathing heavily for a few minutes, then headed to the bathroom, when she made it in the bathroom she went in the cabinet for towels, Fredricks walked up behind her as she continued to look for towels and grabbed her by the waist. "move Poppi, I gotta take a shower." Renae said as she pushed back against him, Fredricks ran his hands down the outside of her thighs, not paying attention to what she said. "stop playin' move." She said softly as he grabbed her breast. "who said I was playin'?" he replied. "move." Renae replied as she went to the medicine cabinet and grabbed a small bottle of bubble bath, as she closed the cabinet Fredricks kissed and licked her neck. "st-stop." She said breathlessly. Fredricks put his hand on the small of her back. "bend over." "what?" she asked playfully. "bend over." He repeated. Renae bent over and

119

gripped the sink and when he entered her, she pushed back against him, Fredricks held her waist and began to thrust deeper. "oh! My G-god!" She moaned as he stuck two fingers in her ass and kissed her neck. Fredricks continued to thrust with his fingers and dick, the mixture of pleasure and pain was driving her crazy. "n-not here, b-bed." she gasped. Fredricks slipped his fingers out then his dick and carried her to the bed. Once they made it to the bed Fredricks kissed her nipples which were already hard and sensitive, then he began softly kissing her from her chest to her stomach, but this time he continued past her stomach. 'd-don't go th-there I to-told y-." before she could finish Fredricks kissed her, then pushed her legs open. "Fred stop!" she yelled. Fredricks stopped for a brief second before putting his face between her legs and sticking his tongue into her as far as he could. "fr-sto-oh! Oh! Poppi! Poppi! Yes!" She moaned as he continued to lick and suck on her clit, when she felt herself reaching her peak, she grabbed his head and squeezed her legs together tightly, then went limp from the orgasm. "I thought you didn't like that." Fredricks said as he watched her tremble from the aftereffects of her orgasm. "I-I don't and I tol-." Before she could finish Fredricks grabbed her by the waist and gently flipped her over. "w-what are you doin'?" Renae asked as she looked back at him. "finishin' what I started in the bathroom." He replied, "I can't right now." Fredricks didn't say anything as he pulled her up by the waist, placed her hands on the headboard, pushed her legs apart and entered her from behind. When he slid in, she was still wet and warm. "oo! Shit! Give it to me!" she moaned as he began to thrust hard and deep. "you like that?" he asked as he wiped sweat from his face. "yes! Oh fuck! Yes!" she yelled matching him thrust for thrust as he pounded away. When Fredricks realized he couldn't hold back he came inside of her in long spurts and pulled out. Renae rolled onto her back, sticky from their sweat and looked at Fredricks, smiled and fluffed her pillow, a few minutes later she fell into a light sleep. Fredricks kissed the side of her face and walked to the bedroom door, he knew he could take her key, but decided against it. "Renae wake up, an come lock the door." Renae slowly got out of bed and walked him to the door. "you comin' back tonight?" "yeah, I'll be back." "bye Poppi." She replied softly as she watched him leave. Fredricks waved, got in the car and pulled off knowing he had to see Skeet and Bell.

CHAPTER 11

As Fredricks drove he picked up his cellphone and called the station. "officer Whitney, fifth district, how I can I help you?" "this is Fred, I need to speak with Al." "hold on, I'll transfer you." After a short wait Allen picked up. "what's goin' on Fred?" "you remember where the one-eight safe house is?" "yeah, what about it?" "I think you an a couple guys need to go check out what's goin' on over there." "why? What they got to do with anything?" "I don't know, it's just a hunch." "a'right, I'll check 'em out." "I gotta go." Fredricks said and hung up. He made a left on tenth and Mitchell, pulled up to Bells house and parked, he debated on whether he should sit in the car or get out and knock, Fredricks decided to knock so, he walked up the raggedy stairs and knocked. "who is it?" someone called out loudly. "it's Fred, is Bell here?" "hold on a minute." For a few seconds nothing happened then the door was opened. "come in." the small woman said. "what's up?" Bell asked. Fredricks glanced at Bells girlfriend. "can we talk in private?" "yeah, let's go in the back yard." Bell replied leading the way. "you to Skeet." Fredricks said. Bell turned and looked at Skeet. "I ain't do nothin'." Skeet said knowing what the look meant. "he didn't do nothin', this time." Bell looked at Fredricks and the look let him know that he didn't find anything funny. "a'right what's up?" Bell asked as they stepped into the backyard. "let me ask tha' questions, what do you guys know about the murders that've been going down?" Bell and Skeet looked at each other. "I think it has to do wit' Carlo's house gettin' hit, but I'm not sure." Bell replied. "I'll be checkin' on him an crazy when I leave." "what's crazy got ta' do with this?" Skeet asked. "how old are you now Skeet?" Fredricks replied ignoring his question. "I'll be fifteen in a month." Skeet replied. "a'right lil' man, what do you know about the judge that got hit?" Skeet looked at the ground then at Fredricks. "I-I heard it was a hit." He replied nervously. "from who?" "just around on the streets." He replied. "yeah, I figured that." Bell looked at Skeet. "what you doin' pokin' ya' nose in people's business?" he asked. "I-I didn't people just talk." "yeah, we gon' talk to, soon as Fred leaves." Bell replied. "one more question Skeet, who did the fire and shootings at the shop?" "somebody told you I was supposed to know about that shit or somethin'?" "maybe, now answer my question." "I don't know nothin' about it." Skeet replied. "you sure?" Fredricks asked. "yeah, I'm sure." "a'right, you guys stay outta trouble." Bell looked at Skeet and back to Fredricks. "we ain't never in trouble, right Skeet?" "damn right." "what I tell you bout cussin'? that's twice." Bell said before slapping Skeet in the back of the head. "I forgot man, chill." He said rubbing the back of his head. "who you tellin' to chill?" Bell asked as he grabbed him by his shirt collar. "nobody." He mumbled doing his best to hold in his anger. "go to you room tough guy." Bell said as he let go of Skeets collar. "but I ain't did nothin'." Bell turned and looked at him as he stomped up the stairs. "and don't slam that fuckin' door!" Bell yelled. "take it easy on tha' lil' guy, I like 'em." Fredricks said. "whatever, so what this about?" he asked as he gestured between the two of them. "bell, you know like I know that there's somethin' goin' on out here and it's big." Fredricks said. "it ain't us, if it was, you'd know." "I know, but I gotta look into everybody, an until this is over everybody's getting' pressure, so lay low and chill." Fredricks advised. "I'll do that." Bell replied. "good, good, if anything changes call me." Fredricks said as he searched for a card. "I know tha' number." Bell said never reaching for the card. "call Crazy an tell 'em I'm on tha' way." "a'right." "see ya' around." Fredricks said. "naw, I don't do tha' corner thing no more." Bell replied seriously. "keep it that way." As they were talking the phone rang and Fredricks smiled. "you might wanna answer that, it's important." He said. Bell walked over to the phone and answered it. "hello." Fredricks could hear the frantic but muffled caller explaining what happened. "a'right, I'll handle it give me an hour." As Bell talked Fredricks walked out, when he got in his car he placed a call, once the phone began to ring, he pulled off. "hello." "hey, my friend, how you been?" "I ain't no friend of yours Fredricks, what do you want?" "Mary, Mary, why so harsh?" "don't ever fuckin' call me that! You understand?" "look, I saved your ass now it's your turn to save mine." Fredricks replied. "meet me at the Cabana at nine-thirty." "I'll be there." Fredricks replied. "by yourself." He said making it a command not a question. The phone was hung up before he could say anything else. Fredricks smiled, it felt good to piss off Marzeno Coppanelli even though he was the head of Milwaukee's largest Mafia family, Fredricks made it to eighth and Arthur before he spotted Crazy walking out of the corner store. "hey crazy! Crazy!" he yelled causing crazy to quickly put his hand under his shirt. "Crazy, it's Fred!" Crazy removed his hand from under his shirt as he looked into the car. "what's up Freddy?" "get in we need to talk." Crazy looked around then got in. "where we goin'?" "let me ask the questions?" Fredricks replied. "yea a'right." Crazy replied. "tell me what's goin' on." Fredricks said as he pulled off. "what you mean tell you what's goin' on?" Crazy replied. "I need to know who burned down the auto shop." Fredricks said as he looked in the rearview to make sure they weren't followed. "I don't know I heard it was over some money." "whose money?" Fredricks asked. "how I'm supposed to know?" Crazy asked. "I don't know, but I need to know asap, there's been twelve murders in the last two months, and one was a judge, so what's goin' on?" "I don't know, I seen all that shit on the news, but whoever it is got some big nuts." Crazy replied. "yeah, real big nuts that are causin' major problems, and I don't like problems." Fredricks said with a slight sneer. "me either." Crazy replied once he realized what Fredricks was implying. "I bet you don't so who did the shop?" "I told you I don't know, I heard he owed somebody money and they came for it." "well, you be cool, cuz we're puttin' heat on everything movin' in Milwaukee." Fredricks replied. "good lookin' on tha' heads up." Crazy said knowing he had to tell his people. "no problem, one more question though." Fredricks replied. "what's that?" "why you walkin' round wit' the gun?" "the streets crazy right now, the Wild Boyz on deck again." Crazy said seriously. "the Wild Boyz? We locked them up it'll be damn near twenty-five years from now before one of them gets out." Fredricks replied confused. "these young dudes tryin' ta' put the Wild Boyz back on the map." "you think it's them doin' this shit?" Fredricks asked as a million things ran through

123

his mind. "I don't know, it's possible." Crazy replied. "well let 'em paint a target on themselves, we'll get 'em." Fredricks said confidently. "if you don't, we will." Crazy said clutching his gun. "no, you won't, you guys won't do shit, you understand?" "yeah, yeah I got it." Crazy replied moving his hand off the gun. Fredricks pulled to the corner of eleventh an Arthur. "get out." Fredricks said. Crazy opened the door and stepped halfway out. "talk to Carlo." He said before getting all the way out and closing the door. Fredricks pulled off and looked at his watch. "damn, only five 'o' clock." He said to himself as he headed to Carlo's house on the deep south side, when he arrived it was five twenty and there was a party going. He got out of the car, walked through the crowd into the house. "so much for security." He mumbled to himself when he saw Carlo and Alillah with dollar bills rolled and laying on a platter of cocaine. "Carlo usin' ya' own shit now huh? And Alillah you're too good lookin' for that shit." Carlo looked at Fredricks then looked quickly around the room. "what you want?" "call your goons off or shit gets ugly real quick." Carlo nodded and the guys turned back to the women they were with; he now knew that he had been watched the whole time. "we need to talk, now." Fredricks said. "bout what amigo?" "twenty-thirty an Scott." Fredricks replied. "let's go out back." Carlo said gesturing toward the kitchen, Fredricks looked around and put his hand on his gun which was now under his shirt. "lead the way." "I'll be back in a minute." Carlo said as he came from around the table, Alillah smiled and put one of the rolled bills in each nostril, put her face almost into the pile of cocaine and inhaled. "hurry back Poppi." She replied as she inhaled the powder. "let's get this shit over with." Fredricks and Carlo walked through the kitchen and out the back door. "so, what's up?" "who hit your house?" Fredricks asked. "I don't know I wish I did." "don't bullshit me you wouldn't tell me if you knew, would you?" "I'd have someone tell you where to find there fuckin' bodies." Carlo replied. "that much huh?" "they got me for seven ki's and forty-five thousand." "you serious?" "I think it was an inside job." "who hit the judge?" Fredricks asked. "I don't know, but word is the hit came from behind the walls." Fredricks laughed. "don't fondle my nuts a'right there's no way it came from behind the walls those calls are recorded." "you don't have to use the phone

124

letters only get read comin' in unless they go out to another prison." "who gave you the word that it came from behind the walls?" Carlo opened the door. "I don't do what you're askin'." He said as they walked back through the kitchen. "I'm not askin' you to snitch, I'm askin' for the jail or a name." Carlo walked back around the living room table and whispered in Alillah's ear, she nodded then spread and crossed her legs, showing off her crotchless panties. "it might be the county jail." She said. "no name?" She looked at Carlo. "talk to Wink." She replied. Fredricks quickly looked at Alillah's long tanned legs. "real name." "De'montay Samuels." "thank you." He said and turned to walk away. "hey Fred! Let her walk you to the door." Carlo said with a slight smile. "well lets go, I'm in a hurry." Alillah stood up and pulled down her dress so it would cover her thighs, when they reached the door, she looked back and saw Carlo turn his head, which was their signal, she pushed Fredricks against the door and spread her legs. "be careful she bites." She whispered sexually. Fredricks reached between her legs and grabbed the money out of the clip. "you like that don't you?" she asked with a smile. "very much so." Fredricks replied. "I'll ask Carlo if you can see her up close." Fredricks knew she was serious about asking Carlo, he had heard about their open relationship. "don't, I like not having to look over my shoulder for a hit squad." Alillah didn't respond as she opened the door, when he stepped on the porch, she waited for a second. "Fred." "yeah." He replied. "two things, first he always gives me what I want, second call us as soon as you know who hit us, we don't pay you for nothin.'" She replied before she closed the screen door. Fredricks watched as she disappeared into the crowded living room, when he got back to the car he sat and watched the scene for a few minutes, then pulled off, happy that he had finally gotten some useful information, he just hoped that the information would lead somewhere because so far, he had nothin' but dead bodies stacking up and that wasn't good at all, he had to figure out what he should do first, check on his first lead or wait and meet Coppanelli.

Two days into the lock down Peter Hopper finally made it in to see KD. "mister Drake, I'm afraid I have some bad news." He said. "what's goin' on?" Peter took a deep breath and released it before he continued. "I just talked to the coroner and-." "coroner? What the fuck you talkin' to a coroner bout?" KD snapped. "calm down, please, this isn't easy, first of all the state wants him to testify, an-." "is that the bad news?" he asked impatiently. "I'm getting to that." Peter replied as he took a deep breath and continued. "a friend of yours, Tara Harper is in the hospital." Peter held up his hand to stop KD from interrupting. "she wanted me to tell you the bad news." KD sighed. "so, tell me." "well, uh, there's no easy way to say this, but your girlfriend, miss Gibbs was murdered." "naw, it can't be, naw! Naw! Not her!" He said holding back tears. "I found out from the coroner that this is the most recent person brought into the mortuary." Peter replied as he placed a picture of Trina on a metal table on the screen. "those mutha'fuckas!" Peter physically flinched at the anger in KD's voice. "no one has been caught as of yet." He said. "I need you to let somebody here know so I can make a call." "I'll do that, oh! I know now is a bad time, but your preliminary hearing is two weeks away." "a'right, hey, what happened to Tara?" "she wouldn't say." "alright, I-I gotta go, I-I can't believe this." He said as the tears finally rolled down his face. "I understand and my condolences mister Drake." "can you call my mother and tell her what happened.?" "I'll do it as soon as I get outside." "tell her to pay for everything." "always mister Drake, I'll see you in two weeks, if nothing else comes up before then." KD walked to the door and knocked to be let out, a few seconds later a deputy opened the door. "bad news huh?" he asked seeing the look on KD's face. "what the fuck it look like?" "don't take it out on me mister Drake." The deputy replied. "just get me back to my fuckin' cell." When he made it to his cell he got in bed and cried himself to sleep.

As Peter was walking out of the county jail Fredricks was walking in, when he made it to the security checkpoint, he showed his badge and firearm. "you can't take your firearm into the visiting area." "give me a locker key." Fredricks replied showing his annoyance. "follow me please." A few seconds later they reached the hallway and a guard pointed to the lockers on the wall. "it's a new system we just got installed when you're done just come back here, you won't need me." Fredricks took a key from one of the lockers, opened it then placed his gun inside and closed it. "thanks." He said before heading to the elevator, when the doors opened, he walked to the desk. "I'm here to see De'montay Samuels." "your id please." Fredricks took his badge from his waist. "oh, officer I'm sorry, let me call up there so they can get him to the visiting room." The deputy said picking up the phone and dialing one of the four numbered extensions. "hey Quentin, I have an officer-." "Fredricks." "yeah, I have an officer Fredricks down here who wants to see a mister De'montay Samuels." After a few seconds the deputy seemed to cut whoever, Quentin was off. "a'right, I'll let him know, bye." When the deputy hung up, she shook her head. "he's across the street, it seems that he got the hell beat out of him by that guy who killed those people in that drug house." "thanks." He said as he headed back to the elevators. When he made it to the first floor, he headed to the locker area where he had left his gun. Once he made it outside, he ran across the street to the hospital. "I'm here to see De'montay Samuels." He said when he made it to the front desk. "are you a relative?" the nurse asked. "no, I'm an officer." He replied as he showed her his badge. "room two-ten, show the deputy your badge." "a'right thanks." "if you wanna thank me, I'm free for lunch we can get somethin' ta' eat." She replied with a smile. "what's your name?" he asked caught off guard by her straight forwardness. "Casey, Casey Ashton." "well Casey, if I don't get wrapped up in any more bullshit, I'll be glad to take you too lunch." "we'll see what happens, but just in case stop back so I can give you my number and if you're nice my address." Fredrick leaned on the counter. "I'll be very, very nice if you let me." He whispered. "just come back." She replied as she applied strawberry red lipstick to her plump lips. Fredricks nodded then headed to Winks room, when he reached the door, he showed the deputy his badge. "is he woke?" Fredricks asked. "yeah, he's woke but his jaw is wired up real good?" the deputy said. "can he talk?" "not really, I mean he can, but I don't know if you'll understand what he's saying." "you got some paper and a pencil or pen?" "nope, nothin' but my memo pad ask the nurse at the desk." Fredricks walked back to the desk and saw Casey standing there with her back turned, he had to admit that she had one hell of a body. "Casey." Fredricks spoke. "oh, you're back fast, you must be in a hurry." Casey replied. "not really, I need some paper, pen or pencil." She went to one of the cabinets and unlocked it, bending over to give him a good look at her ass. "here you go." She said as she handed him a memo pad and pen. "Casey, stop flirtin' an finish ya' rounds." Another nurse said. "gotta go." Casey said before walking away. Fredricks couldn't help shaking his head before walking back to Winks room. "can I go in?" "sure go 'head." The deputy replied as he opened the door. Fredricks walked in and closed the door behind him. "mister Samuels, I'm officer Fredricks, I need to ask a few questions if you don't mind." Wink nodded then gestured for him to take a seat in the chair next to him, Fredricks looked around the room, he hated hospital rooms, but he had a job to do. "mister Samuels what happened?" Fredricks asked. Wink gestured to the paper and pen. Fredricks passed them and waited, Wink seemed to write forever, when he finally stopped, he handed the paper and pen back. "somebody told you they had a message for you?" Wink nodded. "you were told to talk to the guy who killed the people in the drug house." Wink nodded again. "they gave you his name and promised you five hundred dollars." Fredricks said breaking down what Wink had written. Wink nodded again as Fredrick turned the paper over. "mister Samuels, what was the message? And who gave it to you?" Fredricks asked. Wink shook his head before ringing the emergency

128

button. "who gave it to you? What did it say?" he asked angerly. "mister Samuels, what's wrong?" Casey asked when she walked in. Wink pointed at Fredricks then the door. "you want him to leave?" she asked. Wink nodded. "I'm sorry, but you have to go." Fredricks nodded and let Casey lead him out of the room. "oh I forgot my names Fredricks." "I was going to ask when you came back to the desk." They walked to the front desk, and she quickly wrote down her information. "call or come see me." "I'll make sure I do." He said as he walked out. With that done he stopped at his car, hid his gun and headed back to the county jail. When he walked in the door, he had to go through the metal detector again, as he walked through the metal detector beeped. "can you turn your pockets inside out sir?" The guard asked. "it's my badge." Fredricks replied. "just put it in the basket an go through again." Fredricks took a deep breath and did as the guard asked. "thank you, sir." Once he reached the elevators he pressed the call button, when it arrived, he got on and pushed the button for the second floor, when he got off he walked back to the desk and a male deputy was there. He casually looked at his watch and saw that it was now five minutes after six, the shift had changed. "who you here to see?" The deputy asked as soon as Fredricks approached the desk. "Kevin Drake." He replied knowing that the deputy was going to be an asshole, the deputy nodded as if Fredricks had asked a question, then pointed to the visiting hours that were posted on the front of the desk. "you'll have to come back Tuesday." Fredricks angrily snatched his badge from his waist and showed it to the deputy. "I'm officer Fredricks from district five and it's important that I speak with master Drake." The deputy quickly glanced at the badge. "he's in the hole, you want a face to face or screen visit?" Fredricks thought for a brief second. "face to face would be nice." He replied. The deputy turned from the desk, grabbed some papers then turned back and picked up the phone quickly dialing a four number extension. "staggs, I gotta officer Fredricks down here who wants a face to face with Drake, can you come down here and escort him?" The deputy hung up. "I need your id so I can log ya' in an give you a pass." Fredricks reached into his back pocket, pulled out his wallet, then gave the deputy his id. "you can get it back when you leave." Fredricks nodded and walked to a row of chairs that were screwed down and sat, ten minutes later his name was called by a man who looked to be in his late fifties and had a stomach three sizes too big for his uniform. "you the police guy?" "yeah." "could you follow me please?" "right behind you." Fredricks replied. "I gotta tell ya' this guy Drake is having it bad right now, his girlfriend was the broad who dumped out front." Fredricks took the information to mind. "I know, that's why I'm here." Fredricks replied. For some reason the deputy didn't believe him. "can I see your badge? I don't wanna get my ass chewed." Fredricks unclipped his badge and showed it to the deputy. "thanks." "no problem, how long before we get their?" "oh, I gotta take ya' across the skywalk, so we can get you signed in up here and into a booth, the skywalks at the end of the hall to our left. Five minutes later he was led into a room by the deputy. "Drake will be brought out in about ten minutes." Fredricks nodded and waited for the deputy to leave, once he was gone Fredricks took out the few pieces of paper he had left from the hospital then searched for the pen, a few minutes later KD was led to chair on the other side of the glass, he was wearing a red segregation unit suit and a black Velcro waist belt to which he was cuffed. "who the fuck is you?" KD asked. "I'm officer Fredricks, I just want to ask some questions." "talk." KD replied. "first I wanna talk to you about your girlfriend." KD's eyes grew hard and at the same time brimmed with tears. "you know who did it?" he angerly. "not yet, I was hopin' you could help me with a few things." "I'm in here, how tha' fuck I'm a help you?" KD asked. "well, it seems to me that you gotta a name for yourself." "if you came here to bullshit I ain't got time for it." "mister Drake I know the deal so cut the bullshit, a'right." "what tha' fuck you talkin' bout?" KD replied. "mister Drake I know you weren't the only one who hit Carlo's house, cuz he's pickin' you guys off one by one." Fredricks replied thinking he had pieced everything together. "like I told you a

130

few minutes ago, if you came to bullshit I ain't got time." KD replied. Fredricks slammed his fist down on the aluminum ledge that doubled as a table. "I know you got hired by Coppanelli to shut Carlo down, but the shits going too far, all I need are some names and you get a slap on the wrist." KD knew that Fredricks didn't know what he was talking about, he didn't know Coppanelli, and he was done listening. "talk to my lawyer cuz I don't know what tha' fuck you talkin' bout." Fredricks shook his head and smiled. "mister Drake, did you know that the guy you beat the shit out of is one of Carlo's hit squad." Fredricks replied. "what you say?" KD asked. "you're either hard of hearing or you just learned somethin'." Fredricks replied. "so, Carlo killed my girl?" "if I knew I wouldn't tell you, I mean somebody might get seriously hurt and I can't have any more of that." KD got up and kicked the door to get the deputies attention. "what if I told you that no matter what happens the streets ain't never gon' be safe til' I-." "mister Drake you ready to go?" the deputy asked while opening the door. "yeah, I'm ready." He replied. "until what mister Drake?" "Jesus come." He replied as the deputy led him out. "Drake, how you feeling?" the deputy asked as he led him to his cell. "not too good, why?" the deputy shook his head. "well, uh, I heard about your girlfriend and I'm sorry, I lost my wife two years ago and I feel the pain every day." The guard asked. "pain only makes us stronger." KD replied. "true, but it never stops hurting." KD could only nod as they stood in front of his cell. The deputy sighed as KD stepped into his cell. "you need some books or something?" The guard asked. "naw, but I do need to make a phone call." "your lawyer already arranged it for you, if I don't come back another officer will bring the phone." He replied as he walked off. Exactly five minutes later KD heard the phone being rolled down the hall. "if you got an arranged call yell out your cell number." The deputy said loudly. "two-seventeen dep!" The deputy rolled the phone to his door, opened the food slot and handed him the phone. "what's the number?" the guard asked. "come on now dep, I don't want nobody trying to call my number." KD replied. "do you want the call or not?" "four-one-four three-four-four-twenty-two eleven." KD called out. "you got ten minutes." KD nodded and waited to be asked his name. "you know who." He said when the time came. A couple of seconds later his call was answered. "what's goin' down?" "nothin' much, listen I only got ten minutes, remember my police friend?" KD asked. "yeah, I remember, what's up?" Grip said. "forget 'bout that, an find out 'bout this cat named Carlo, he owns that house on twenty-third an Scott." KD replied. "I got you my nig'." Grip replied. "one mo' thing." KD said. "what's that?" Grip asked. "go visit Tara and try ta' find Brian or his lil' brother." "I got you, what's up wit' court though?" "my prelim in two weeks." KD replied. "you know who ya' judge is?" Grip asked. "naw, not yet." KD replied. "you need some money on ya' books?" Grip asked. "naw, but I'm a call mom's next week or I might just write her an have her straighten you." KD replied. "I'm straight fa' now." Grip replied. "a'right, just let know." KD replied. Grip didn't know if he should say anything but decided that he had to. "I heard 'bout what happened man, my condolences." Grip said softly. "good lookin', I know it's serious in the streets, keep tabs on my momma." "that's already took care of, I got drew and drama on it." "speakin' of them lil' niggas, how they takin' it?" "they doin' as expected, they wanna go out." Grip said. "tell 'em I said to hold-." You have one minute left the operators voice interrupted. "love my nigga." KD said. "love." Grip replied. When the phone hung up the deputy unplugged it and KD handed him the receiver. "mister Drake, sounds like you're Makin' plans for somethin'" "naw, just checkin' on family and friends." KD replied. "well, you got your call, you need anything else?" the guard asked. "naw, but I do got a question though." "what's that?" the guard asked. "what's your problem wit' me?" KD replied. "well mister Drake to be honest I don't like any of you, if Pulley wouldn't have told me he promised you a phone call I wouldn't have given you shit you murderin' sonofa bitch." KD smiled. "you got issues dep, an fa' the record I ain't no fuckin' murderer." KD replied. "sing your song to the judge, it's people like you who make me wish Wisconsin had the death

132

penalty." KD shook his head as he stepped away from the door and sat on his bunk. "fuck you dep! Mutha'fuck you!" The deputy smiled as he walked down the hall rolling the phone in front of him. KD sat in his cell hoping that God would hear at least one of his prayers. "they'll be restin' in piss before this over, I promise you that." He said to himself, hoping Trina could hear him from heaven.

CHAPTER 12

Back at fifth district Allen was talking to Davis and Moby. "have either of you spoke to miss Harper?" "yeah, we talked to her at the hospital, but the doctor said she can't be moved." Davis replied. "why the fuck not?" "she found out her friend was that broad who got dumped in front of the county, an she passed out, hit her head pretty hard, she won't eat or nothin', she only talked to us for a few seconds." Moby replied. "anybody watchin' her?" Moby and Davis looked at each other but didn't answer. "who tha' fuck's watchin' her?" "Williams from H.I.T. has her under twenty-four-hour watch." Davis replied. "get the fuck outta my office!" Davis and Moby got up and walked out the door. When they were gone Allen locked the door, went back to his desk, took the plate out of the drawer then took a dollar bill, rolled it up and took a sniff. As he switched the bill to the other nostril someone knocked on the door. "who the hell is it!" He yelled angered by the interruption. "it's Corbail sir, we got some of those one-eight mafia fuckers." "I'll be right out." Allen got up, put the plate in the drawer and locked it, then grabbed the small mirror from his file cabinet to make sure there were no traces of cocaine under his nose. When he was satisfied with his inspection, he unlocked the door and walked out to see who had been rounded up. "hopefully we got some top mutha'fuckas." Corbail said. Allen walked into the hallway leading to the holding cells and stopped. "question 'em, check 'em for warrants,

133

whoever clean can go." "what! It took us four hours to round them up." "do I look like I give a fuck? Do what I said, and nobody knock on my door unless its life or death." He said as he opened his door and walked in. At nine-thirty Fredricks pulled up to the cabana club, a known mob restaurant, and handed his keys to the valet. Once he made it through the door one of the hostesses came over to him. "welcome to cabana club, are you expecting other guest, or would you like a table for one?" "I'm a guest of mister Coppanelli's." The hostess's eyes lit up when he said Coppanelli's name. "right this way sir." She spoke. He followed the hostess and looked at her ass as they walked, when they reached the back of the restaurant she pointed to the booth. "I hope you enjoy your meal." Fredricks nodded and took his seat. "mister Coppanelli will be with you in a minute." She whispered as she lay a menu on the table. Ten minutes later Marzeno Coppanelli walked into the restaurant and was led to the booth, when he reached the table Fredricks stood and extended his hand, Marzeno sat without extending his hand. "I see you still have a grudge." Fredricks replied. "you cost me a quarter of a million dollars." Marzeno said angrely. "well, I guess we can get this over with." Fredricks replied. "what do you want?" "whoever killed the judge." Fredricks replied seriously. "I don't know nothing about no judge gettin' hit." Marzeno said as he looked around the restaurant. Fredricks slammed his hand down on the table. "don't fuckin' play games with me, cuz I have enough to bury you in federal prison!" customers began looking their way and Marzeno didn't like it, he looked around and smiled at the guest, the smile reassured them that everything was fine. "don't you ever fuckin' threaten me you understand!" Marzeno said as he turned back to the table. "it's not a threat, it's a promise, now who handled the fuckin' hit on the judge!" Fredricks snapped. Marzeno stood up and motioned for the hostess, when she arrived at the table, he wrote on the back of a napkin gave it to her, then walked out of the back door, when Fredricks tried to follow Coppanelli's bodyguards blocked the way, Fredricks heard a car pull off and sat back down, the hostess handed him the napkin. "meet me at the loft in thirty minutes." He mouthed as he read the message to himself, he knew exactly where the loft was, it was the place he had once saved Marzeno's life, he placed a twenty-dollar bill on the table and walked out. Once outside he waited for the valet to bring his car which took five minutes. When the valet gave him the keys he quickly pulled off and headed to the loft. It took twenty minutes to get to the loft, when he pulled up, he parked his car and walked to the front door, when he walked up the stairs, he was let in by Coppanelli's son Domenico. "Fred, what's up? I heard you embarrassed the ol' man." Fredricks smiled and extended his hand, Domenico took that moment to punch him in the stomach, Fredricks fell to the ground gasping for air, as he tried to catch his breath Marzeno walked out of the back room. "pick 'em up!" Domenico and the bodyguard who had been standing behind the door lifted him from the floor. "hold 'em up." As they held him Marzeno pulled his gun from his waist band and hit him across the head. "how dare you embarrass me and think you can get away with it!" He screamed as spit flew out of his mouth in rage. Fredricks was still trying to see straight when the second blow came. "work 'em over and send him home." Marzeno said wiping his gun on Fredricks shirt. Domenico and the bodyguard let him fall to the floor, Marzeno walked out of the room leaving his son and bodyguard to do the rest of the work for him, after five or ten minutes of punching and kicking Domenico and the bodyguard put Fredricks in the his car and left him to make it home by himself, Fredricks drove home then limped and half limped half crawled to his door, when he finally unlocked the door he stumbled into his living room and saw a young man sitting there. "W-who are you?" Fredricks asked wondering if Marzeno had sent someone to finish him off. "do dirt, but everybody just call me dirt." Fredricks shook his head to keep from passing out. "w-what do you want?" "what I want is fa' my people to be left alone." Do Dirt replied as he looked Fredricks over. "you need ta' sit down." He said nonchalantly. Fredricks spit blood and fell into the recliner that do-dirt was just

135

in. "look, I run the Wild Boyz now an word is somebody told you it was us rackin' up bodies, but you got my word, we ain't got nothin' ta' do wit' what's goin' down." Fredricks tried not to laugh but couldn't help it, even though he knew how much pain it would cause and as he laughed, he winced, began to cough and spit blood. "T-take m-me to a hosp-hospital, I think my ribs are broke." Fredricks said. Do Dirt used his shirt to pick up the phone and dial nine-one-one. "it's a police officer beat up real bad, he need help." He said as soon as the operator picked up. The operator asked for a name, "just get here, the address is twenty-four-ten West Clarke Street." He said before hanging up. Once he hung up Do Dirt wrote a number down and put it in Fredricks pocket. "call me so we can finish talkin'" he said as he walked out of the house and down the street to the rooming house his mother owned. The police and ambulance swarmed the house as do dirt watched, it took about three seconds for them to bring Fredricks out and put him in the ambulance. Rough times were on the way and there would be blood on somebody's hands, do dirt just hoped that the blood didn't belong to anyone he knew, little did he know that the Wild Boyz were in for a war from the one-eight mafia, and little did Marzeno, and Domenico know that before the police and ambulance had arrived that Fredricks had spoken their names into the phone and the person on the other end gladly promised to handle the situation within a week from the time the phone hung up.

TWO DAYS LATER

Marzeno and Domenico sat inside a bulletproof limo that they knew wasn't bugged. "pop, I don't know nothin' bout no judge, it didn't come from me, we had no reason." Domenico explained. "I wanna know who it was, an I want his balls delivered on a silver platter ya' understand? I want the bastard that did this." Marzeno yelled angrily. "I'll put the word out, we'll find 'em pop."

Marzeno smiled. "it's good cuz they hit the sonafa bitch good, real good, but they stepped on our toe's, I want what they got." "I'll get it done; somebody knows who did it." Domenico replied full of confidence. "offer money." Marzeno replied as he tapped on the divider. Nicolino 'curtains' Ferri was the driver and had dreams of being made one day, every time he opened Marzeno's door he hoped to hear the words, meet me at Nunzio's to talk, and this time was no different. "have a good day boss." Nicolino said as he opened the door with a smile. "you too Nicky." Marzeno replied. As Nicolino closed the door and let his boss pass, Domenico's phone rang. "yeah?" he answered. "no bad deed goes unpunished, take a last look at daddy." "who is this!" "pop! It's a h-." the explosion of the limo cut short his last words and his life, Domenico was dead, the force of the explosion caused Marzeno to be tossed into the window of the loft, and Nicolino was running around with fire and death consuming his body, the people inside the loft ran outside and dragged Marzeno inside, then did their best to save Nicolino, but to no avail, Domenico and Nicolino died, victims of a ruthless hit, someone called nine-one-one and within minutes the fire department and ambulance were on the scene, Marzeno was taken to the hospital with minor injuries, some of his bodyguards who were in the loft followed the ambulance to the hospital and once they arrived they waited orders from the boss or his daughter Kyla who was on her way to the hospital with private bodyguards for her father and vengeance for her brother, Kyla arrived at the hospital at eleven-thirty with four bodyguards and her father's best friend and advisor Alphons Linquiti. "we're here to see Marzeno Coppanelli." She said politely but sternly. The male nurse behind the desk flipped through a few papers. "room sixty-three a, second door on the right." "thank you." She replied as She walked away followed by the bodyguards and Alphons, when they made it to the room a doctor walked out. "excuse me, I'm mister Coppanelli's daughter how is he?" the doctor smiled. "he's a tough old man, he's been raising hell asking for a phone." The doctor replied. "can we go in?" Alphons asked. "go ahead, he should be ready for release in a few days, we'll know more after a few more test." He replied and walked away. They walked into the room and saw him sitting up in the bed turning channels, Alphons was the first to speak. "who did this?" he asked. Marzeno turned off the tv. "I don't know, but I want people dead! Like my son, dead!" He yelled. "poppa, calm down, we'll find out who did this I promise." Kyla said stepping forward and placing her well-manicured hand on his shoulder. "I want Fredricks dead you understand? And find Carlo." He said. "anything else poppa?" "make sure everybody knows I'm a'right and that it's business as usual." He replied directing his attention to Alphons, they nodded then kissed him on the cheeks. "I'm leaving bodyguards outside your door." Kyla said. "listen to her talk, she's gonna be tough like her ol' man." "yeah, she might be a lil' tougher, you should hear the mouth on her." Alphons replied. "poppa, I know you're gonna hear about it, so I'll tell you first, don't get mad, but I told Benitto I was gonna ram his cazzo down his throat if he didn't stop following me around like a sick puppy." Alphons laughed. "see what I mean? Wait til' you hear the rest." Marzeno looked at her. "what did you do?" he asked seriously. "nothin' poppa, I just called him a figlio di putana." She said casually. "I'll take care of it." He replied. "thank you, poppa." She replied ever daddy's little girl. "bye sweets." Marzeno replied. "bye poppa." Kyla replied as she and Alphons walked out of the room.

At the county jail KD was getting prepared for his preliminary hearing, he knew that the odds were stacked against him, but he was fighting for his life, at twelve 'o' clock the deputies appeared at his cell. "Drake! You got court." One of them yelled. "face forward and put your arms out the trap" once KD did as he said the deputy cuffed him and called for his door to be buzzed. "open two-seventeen, two-seventeen." When the door buzzed open the deputies wrapped the black Velcro belt around his waist and locked it with a pad lock, then quickly patted him down and walked him to the elevators. "so today the big day Drake?" one of the deputies asked. "naw, just my preliminary, nothin' major." A few minutes later he was walked out of the elevator and led to the waiting area, placed in a room and uncuffed, ten minutes later a deputy came to the waiting area. "Drake! Your lawyers here." KD walked to the door and the deputy led him to a room closely resembling an interrogation room. "Peter what's up?" "we need to talk business and quick, so let's do this and get it over with." KD sat in the chair. "what's goin' on?" he asked. "I need you to wave your prelim." "wave it? Why?" "they're going to bind you over for trial regardless, it saves us both a lot of time." "a'right do it, but don't fuck me over." "you know I'm not going to fuck you over." When they were finished talking KD was led back to the waiting area, which was a six by six room holding ten other people, one toilet and a sink, when he went back into the waiting area there were three guys talking about how the Wild Boyz had a Twenty-thousand dollar cash hit on anybody who tried to implicate them in anything that was going down in the street, and how the mob was looking for the people who did robbery on twenty-third. KD sat and listened, knowing there would be a lot more bloodshed and lost lives, while he was thinking one of the people who had been talking began to stare at him. "hey youngin' ain't you tha' boy that been all on tv?" "yeah, that's me, why?" the man shook his head. "you gotta lotta trouble on yo' back." The man replied sincerely saddened. "ol 'school, I'm a beat them charges like Rocky." He said confidently. "I hope so, but then what? I know you heard what I said, 'bout the mob." "I ain't w-." "Drake! Let's go." KD walked to the door and was cuffed by the deputy and led into the court room, once he was settled into his seat the clerk read off the complaint number, and the charges, then the preliminary began. "mister Drake, we are here for your preliminary hearing, and I've been advised that you do not wish to have this hearing, is that correct sir?" the commissioner asked. "yes." KD replied. "I'm holdin' up a preliminary hearing questionnaire and wavier form, is that your signature near the bottom of this form?" "yes." KD

139

said. "prior to signing this form, you read it yourself and it was read to you, is that true?" the judge asked. "yes." "did you understand its content before you signed it?" the judge asked. "yes." "this tells me you are twenty-nine years of age and you've completed ninth grade." "yes." "did anyone make any threats against you to get you to give up this hearing?" the judge asked. "no." "did anyone make any promises to get you to give up this hearing?" "no." "did you-and you did discuss your decision to waive this hearing with your attorney?" "yes." KD replied. "and was he available to answer any questions you might have?" the judge asked. "yes." KD replied. "counsel, is this your signature at the bottom of the form indicating that you read the form to him and were present when he read it himself." "yes," Peter replied. "did you discuss with him his rights to a preliminary hearing and the decision to waive that hearing?" "I did." Peter replied. "do you believe this waiver is a voluntary waiver?" "I do" "I do find his waiver to be a voluntary waiver knowingly, intelligently, understandingly, made, I will accept the same and bind the defendant over to the circuit of Milwaukee county for trial, the next court date, may three at eight-thirty for scheduling conference in judge Christenson's court, branch thirty-seven. KD nodded to Peter as the deputies came to lead him out of the courtroom and back to the waiting area. After everyone returned, deputies called names and connected the prisoners to chains, and leg shackles, by three 'o' clock KD was back in segregation waiting to use the phone the next day, when food was passed out he refused, he was too busy thinking about what the old man had said to him earlier that day, he still had some connections with the older Wild Boyz, he knew he would have to use them before a war started, KD knew the mob had him outnumbered, so he had to think of a way to even the score, he thought about reaching out to Brian's lil' brother, then remembered that Brian was marked for death for his betrayal, which KD was still piecing together.

Alillah hung up the phone, ran out of the booth and to the car where Carlo was waiting. "let's go." "I love it when you're all business." Carlo said as he pulled off from the pay phone and headed towards the one-eight safe house, Alillah took her phone out of her purse and began to dial, when she finished, she sat quietly and waited for an answer. "hello." The soft male voice said. "what you doin'?" she asked adding the heavy Latino accent to her voice. Bell and Alillah had met at the probation office on the southside and had got along until she found out that he was a member of the one-eight mafia. "shit, chillin' at the crib, why? What's up?" Alillah tapped Carlo and smiled. "I wanna see you." She said. "what time?" Bell asked. "right now, if that's cool." Alillah replied. Bell smiled to himself as he thought about how it would feel to have her legs wrapped around him. "not right now but what about nine?" Alillah repeated the question playfully so that Carlo could tell her what to do. "yeah, nines cool." She replied after Carlo nodded. "a'right, I'll pick you up." Bell said trying to hold back his excitement. "okay, well I got some errands to run, so call me later and I'll tell you where to meet me." "how bout you call me?" Bell replied. "a'right bye." Alillah said and hung up. "turn back, we'll get to him later." Carlo turned around and headed towards theirs house. "I want you to be careful til' this shits over." He said seriously. "I'm always careful baby." She replied. They both relaxed as they rode towards home to plan Bells execution, as they got closer to their house Alillah began to have a bad feeling. "don't stop somethings not right." Carlo looked in the rearview mirror and then out of the windows. "what's wrong baby?" Alillah asked. "you see those two cars in front of the house?" Carlo replied. "Yeah, I see 'em what about 'em?" he replied. "I think they're Marzenos people but let's not find out okay." Carlo nodded and drove pass the house with his hand on a mac eleven. "we'll get a hotel for the night." He said as he rubbed her thighs. "okay, but make sure they don't follow us." She replied as she smiled, spread her legs a little wider than they had been. Carlo watched the rearview as he continued to drive, so Alillah slid down the seat so

141

Carlo could slide his finger inside of her, and when he did, she was instantly wet, Carlo smiled but didn't say anything. Alillah didn't care that he didn't say anything, she just wanted to cum, the thought of dying and killing always made her horny.

Tara was checking out of the Mount Sinai Hospital when she heard the news of Domenico Coppanelli's murder, she had a funny feeling that it had something to do with KD and his mission for revenge. Tara was still under police guard which she didn't like, but could do nothing about, as she changed the channel a nurse walked in. "well, miss Harper, you're looking a lot better, how do you feel?" she asked. "better than when I first got here." KD replied. "well, you're on your way home now, that should make you feel better." The nurse replied. "yeah, that makes this feel a lot better." "all you gotta do is sign these papers and you're on your way." Tara signed the papers then waited for the nurse to leave, once she was gone Tara began to get dressed, as she was dressing detective Williams walked into the room. "miss h-." "get out! What the fuck you doin' in here?" she yelled embarrassed that he had caught her putting on her panties. "I' I'm sorry." Williams said as he quickly stepped out and closed the door, Tara quickly pulled her panties up, then put on her pants and shirt, when she finished, she began to look for her shoes, when she couldn't find them, she opened the door. "where the fuck my shoes at!" Tara asked the nurses and doctors that were behind the desk looked up in shock and surprise. "they're at your house, you were brought in barefooted." Williams said. "well can I get some damn footies or somethin'!?" She snapped as she looked at the people who were staring. Williams looked down and smiled. "you have pretty feet; you don't need footies." Tara went back in the room and slammed the door as hard as she could, Williams looked at the nurses and doctors. "she's emotional right now, her friend was killed." The nurses and doctors understood so they returned to their normal duties, a couple of minutes later a nurse walked in with a pair of

142

footies, her release papers and prescriptions. "alright miss Harper you're set to go." When the nurse walked out of the room Williams stood. "is she ready?" the nurse nodded and continued walking. "you ready to go to the station?" "do you know how to knock?" Tara asked. "I don't have to knock." Williams replied. "look, I ain't got time fa' this shit, what you want me ta' come ta' the station fa?" Tara asked. "questioning?" "about what?" "you'll find out when you get there." Tara sighed as she and detective Williams walked out of the room and headed toward the front entrance, once outside Williams directed her to his car. "no squad car?" she said nervously. "I figured you wouldn't want anyone thinkin' you work for the police, so I drove my own car." "good cuz I don't need them troubles." She replied. Williams opened the door for her, then went to the driver's side and got in, once she was in the car she leaned back. "thank you." She said. "for what?" Williams asked. "for openin' the door, most people don't do that anymore." Tara responded. "I'm not most people." He replied as he started the car. "I guess not, where'd you cop the Benz?" she asked when he pulled off. "the mob." He replied. Tara quickly grabbed the door handle then looked at him. "I'm jokin', I got it as a gift from my parents." Williams replied seeing her fear. "I wish I had people who'd buy me a Benz." Tara said with a slight smile. Williams noticed that the conversation had gotten personal. It took twenty minutes to get too the station, but Williams enjoyed the whole ride, which wasn't hard since he felt that Tara was the most beautiful woman he had met in years. "well miss Harper, this shouldn't take to long." Williams said after opening her door. "call me Tara, and I hope not." She replied with a slight smile. Once they walked inside the station Tara got nervous again. "you want somethin' ta' drink?" Williams asked. "yeah, a soda would be nice." Tara replied. "I'll be right back." Williams said as he walked off. "ok." Tara replied as she watched him walk off. Tara knew she liked him, but couldn't figure out why, she even thought he was kind of sexy. While Tara was left to her thoughts Williams had signed back in and retrieved his messages, as he walked to the soda machine flicking through his messages he saw a message from Allen, he decided to take Tara her soda before going to see what Allen wanted, when he made it to the machine, he began to slide the coins in. "fuckin' dollar ten for a sixteen ounce." He said to himself as he pressed the button. "always complainin' about somethin'." Someone said behind him. Williams looked over his shoulder and saw Allen standing there. "Al, I was on my way to see you." He said. "really, about what?" Williams passed him the pink slip. "oh yeah, what's up with the Harper situation?" "she's in the front waitin' to be questioned." "good, take her to one-nineteen." Allen replied. "a'right." Williams walked back to the front and handed her the soda. "thank you." She replied with a smile. "no problem, you ready to get this over with?" Williams asked. "yeah, the sooner the better." Tara replied sooner. "a'right follow me." Once they reached room one-nineteen Williams opened the door and let her in. "so when we gettin' started?" she asked. "we're waiting on a few people." Williams replied. A couple of minutes later Allen and Davis walked into the room, they all exchanged greetings then Allen and Davis sat down, and Allen placed a tape recorder on the table. "I'll be recording this if it's okay with you miss Harper." Allen said. "it's cool wit' me, what's all this about?" she asked. Davis cleared his throat. "this is about the murders of your friends Robert "Robbie" Green, also known as Mano, and Star James." "I was already questioned about this." Tara said. "we just want to go over it again, you've might've remembered something that might help." Allen said. "I don't have anything to remember." Tara replied. "do you know Star James?" Allen asked. "I've met her, but I don't know much about her." Allen looked at Davis and smiled causing her to wonder if she had slipped up somehow. "how long have you known her?" "we went to the same middle school, but we wasn't best friends or nothin' like that." "well, I've done a lil' research, it seems that your friend Robert and Star were a couple." This was news to her; she was surprised that neither of them had bothered to tell her. "I don't know nothing about that." Tara replied. Allen could tell that she was telling the

144

truth. "I believe you miss Harper, but I want you to know that whatever mister Green, Drake, miss James and mister Drake's girlfriend were involved in has gotten a lot of people killed and I'm going to solve this fucking case, so be very careful." Tara knew a threat when she heard one and she knew what she had to do, but she had to contact Grip and Trina's family, she knew she would hear from KD sooner or later. "is that all mister Cantz?" she asked. Allen stopped the recorder. "yes, you can go, but please stay in the state." He replied. "can I please get a ride home now?" she asked irritably. "Williams take her home." Tara stood and walked toward the door. "where are your shoes?" Davis asked when he noticed that she only had on a pair of footies. "at home, why?" Davis shook his head. "nothin' never mind." He replied. "those footies keepin' your feet warm?" Williams asked. "yeah, I'm cool, just get me home." Tara replied. Williams opened the door. "you ready?" Tara nodded and walked out the door followed by Williams. "that didn't hurt to much now did it?" Williams asked. "you sound like the mu'fucka who took my virginity." Tara replied. "is that a good thing or bad thing?" Tara sighed. "never mind, let's just say I'm glad it's over." Williams led her out of the station and back to his Benz, when they were in the car Williams put a CD in. "hope you like rap." Tara laughed. "come on now, of course." Williams hit play on his remote and cam'ron came on Tara couldn't believe a homicide detective knew anything about cam'ron and dipset, but here she was listening to cam'ron rapping about shooting dice and wearing minks. Tara bobbed her head to the music and Williams watched as he drove, when they arrived at her house she got out of the car. "thanks." "no problem, you just get those sexy feet into some shoes." "I will, hey don't you got a card in case I remember somethin'?" Williams fumbled around looking for a card, but finally settled on writing his cellphone, house and office number on a piece of paper. "I always answer my cellphone." He said as he handed her the paper. "if I remember anything I'll call that number first." Williams couldn't believe he was flirting with a suspect, but he was, and he would continue

145

to unless she stopped it, Tara went up the stairs, let herself in then went back to the door and waved.

CHAPTER 13

Alillah and Carlo checked into the super eight motel at seven 'o' clock, they both checked in under their own names and asked for separate rooms even though they would only be using one, Alillah went to room one 'o' one and waited on Carlo, five minutes later he knocked on the door holding a duffel bag which held three hundred and twenty thousand dollars, two mac elevens, two thirty-eights, a nine millimeter and a weeks' worth of changing clothes, they always left the duffel bag in the trunk in case of situations like the one they were in. "you a'right?" Carlo asked as he closed the door. "yeah, I'm fine." Alillah replied. Carlo sat the bag down and opened it, then gave Alillah the nine-millimeter and two clips. "keep the safety off at all times." Carlo replied. "baby stop worrying I'll be okay." Alillah said. "these ain't street punks we're playin' with, this is the mob, so take this serious." Alillah lay on the bed. "I am takin' it serious." Carlo picked up the phone and began to dial, when the phone began to ring Carlo sat on the bed. "si." "Diablo, what's up?" "nothin' much where are you?" "don't worry about that I need a favor." "okay boss." "I need you to do a security check, make sure my house an the block are safe then call Alillah's phone." Carlo replied. "a'right, I'll take some people with me." Diablo said. "just get it done." Carlo hung up and turned to Alillah, she closed the windows and blinds so that she could walk around naked. "baby you're beautiful." Carlo said as he watched her. "so, you say." She replied. Carlo took her by the hand and led her back to the bed and they made love

146

until morning, Carlo woke up and felt around to make sure Alillah was still next to him, then grabbed her phone and called Diablo, the phone rang, but no one answered, he hung up and called Hector. "hello." The man answered. "where tha' fuck is Diablo!" Carlo snapped. "I don't know, why what's wrong?" Hector asked. "I pay you good right?" "yeah boss." Hector replied. "I give you whatever you want right?" Carlo asked. "yeah boss." Hector replied. "then why the fuck can't I get one damn security check done!" Carlo snapped causing Alillah to wake up. "I'll get it done boss." Hector replied. "good, good that's what I like to hear, and when you see Diablo shoot him." Carlo said. "o-okay boss." Hector replied. Carlo hung up as he saw Alillah sit up with her breast showing above the blanket. "what's wrong baby?" she asked worriedly. "nothin' you hungry?" Carlo replied. "Carlo, you're lying." "it's nothin' to be worried about, I sent Diablo to do a security check, but hasn't called to let me know anything." "you're right, its nothing to worry about, so let's get something to eat." Carlo picked up his clothes and walked in the bathroom. "I gotta take a shower, I stink." he said. Alillah sniffed. "sex is a good smell." She replied. "yeah but sweat and must ain't." Carlo said as he closed the door. Five minutes later he came out of the bathroom and Alillah went in, ten minutes later she came out naked, she liked to dress in front of Carlo, once she was dressed, they went to the car, but they both looked around and under the car before they got in and drove up the road to an all you can eat at restaurant. When they made it inside Alillah sat down and Carlo went to fix their plates, as he walked away Alillah's phone rang. "hola." "Hola senorita, let me speak ta' Carlo." Hector said. "hold on a minute." She replied as she watched Carlo walk toward the table with two plates, when he made it to the table, she held out the phone. "it's Hector." She said. Carlo set the plates down and grabbed the phone. "hola amigo." "senor I have bad news." Hector spoke softly. "what is it?" Carlo asked with anger building. "two houses were hit this morning, and Diablo is dead." "what did I lose?" Carlo asked. Hector was quiet for a while. "What did I lose!" Carlo asked again.

"thirty-six thousand cash and twenty kilos." Hector replied quickly. "mutha' fucka!" Carlo snapped as he slammed his fist down on the table, Alillah knew it was bad, she put money on the table and guided Carlo outside. "who did it?" he asked. "I'm using every resource we have, but no one knows." Hector replied. "find out! Find out! And kill them!" Carlo snapped. "si, si, I'm on it." Hector replied. "don't talk, do it! I want answers tonight." Carlo said through gritted teeth. "fuck! Fuck! Fuck! Mutha'fuckas shit!" Carlo snapped handing Alillah back her phone. "what is it?" Alillah asked. Carlo got in the car. "somebody hit two of our houses this morning, Diablo's dead and the mutha 'fucka's got away with thirty-six thousand cash and twenty kilos, somebody has to die, this is too much." He said running his hand through his hair. Alillah got in the car, started it up, then pulled off and headed back to the motel, when they got there, they grabbed their bags and left headed toward the southside. Carlo drummed his fingers against the dashboard. "Alillah, call your friend Bell and see what he knows." Alillah picked up the cellphone and dialed Bells number, the phone rang but no one answered. "nobody answered." She said. "call Fred." Carlo asked. Alillah dialed the number and waited for an answer. "hello." He answered sounding like he was in pain. "hola mister Fredricks." "Alillah, I don't have time for games, what up?" Alillah handed Carlo the phone without responding. "somebody hit me twice this morning I need names." Carlo responded. "look, you know my situation, I got worked over by Marzeno and friends, I'm laid up for a while." Carlo sighed. "don't worry about them they've been took care of, I did you a favor." Fredricks remained silent, he hadn't thought about what would happen when he called Carlo and told him that Marzeno had hired the people who hit his house, now it was them slapping him in the face, he knew that Marzeno would figure out he had something to do with it, he had to find out what was going on and fast or he might not live through the night, Carlo was waiting on him to say something, but he was growing impatient. "Fred, you there?" he said. "yeah, I'm here." Fredricks replied. "good, like I was saying, I did

148

you a favor, so I want one in return, you know how it works." Fredricks couldn't think of a way out, he had used his phone to call Carlo, so he couldn't turn Carlo in because he would be hurting himself. "right now, is not the time for fuckin' games!" Carlo snapped. "I told you, I'm laid up, I just came back got back from the hospital." "I don't give a fuck if you just came from mars, you owe me!" "what the fuck do you want Carlo?" Fredricks yelled causing pain to shoot through his body. "I want names by tonight." He replied then hung up the phone. After a few seconds he began to do drumbeats on the dashboard again. Alillah grabbed the phone and put it on her lap but remained quiet not wanting him to take his frustration out on her, she had experienced that once a few years back and that had been enough to learn a lesson.

KD was being released from the segregation unit, and back to general population. At seven-thirty the deputies came to his door. "Drakes, you ready to go?" one of them asked. "yeah, I'm ready." One of the deputies attached a Velcro waist strap to the door as the other deputy opened his food slot. "put your hands out of the trap." KD complied and put his hands out of the trap so the deputy could handcuff him. Once he was cuffed the other deputy called to have the cell opened. "open cell two-seventeen, two-one-seven." It took a few seconds for the door to buzz open, and when it did, they stood to the side. KD knew the routine, so he turned and faced the wall as one of the deputies put on the Velcro waist strap and connected it to the handcuffs. "close two-one-seven." As the door began to close the deputies led him down the hall. He watched as the deputy walked with the blankets which held his property, once they reached the double doors the deputy sat the blankets on the floor and took him to another cell, connected him to the door and waited for him to walk in. "what size mister Drake?" one of the deputies asked. "two x shirt and pants." KD replied. One of the deputies walked off, it took five minutes for the deputy to come back with clothes. "strip." The officer said. KD began to strip down and
149

change clothes, once he was dressed the deputies called to have the cell buzzed open. "open the strip cell." The door was opened and KD was allowed out without the Velcro waist band or handcuffs, he picked up his blankets and followed the deputies to the elevator, when they arrived on the unit everyone was still in their rooms waiting to come out, the officer behind the desk took KD's paperwork from the deputy. "Drake you're in sixteen." The deputy said. "that a single cell?" Drake asked. The deputy nodded and buzzed the door open. KD walked into the cell. "close it behind you!" the deputy yelled. KD threw his blankets on the bed and closed the door. After making his bed KD laid down, as he got comfortable the doors buzzed open, KD got up, walked out of the room and stood in front of his door like the other forty-nine prisoners on the unit, after the deputy stated his rules, he looked at all of them, then sat down. "dayroom opened!" he yelled. KD quickly made his way to the phone and dialed Grips number, after a few seconds the automated operator asked him to state his name. "it's me." He stated. The line was silent and then there was a click letting him know that someone had answered, a few seconds later the automated operator came on letting him know his call was connected. "what up?" Grip asked. "shit man goin' through a thang." KD replied. "I already know man." Grip said with a sigh. "you straight out there?" KD asked steering the conversation to business. "yeah, but shit getting' hectic." Grip replied seriously. "what's goin' on?" "two of Carlos places got hit, Marzeno's son and bodyguard got blew the fuck up and word is it's bout ta' be a whole lotta shit." Grip replied not concerned with being recorded. KD hadn't expected this news, but he wasn't surprised. "what's up wit' bobby?" he asked. "somebody offed his wife and daughter, so he been layin' low." Grip replied. KD laughed. "be expectin' some money in tha' mail." He said. "good lookin'." "Grip replied wondering how KD was going to send him money. "you heard from Drama and Drew?" KD asked. "yeah, we been waitin' ta' hear from you." Grip said. "I just got out the hole, so it's good." "bet, I'll let 'em know." Grip replied. "let 'em know my momma takin' care of everything, so don't trip." "I got you, anything else?" "naw not right now, but once I holla at Tara, I'll let you know." KD replied. "just call me and let me know tha' business." Grip said. "fa sho'." KD hung up and went back to his cell to think about what he had just been told, ten minutes later he went back to the phone, this time he called Tara, after stating his name he waited to see if the call would be accepted, after a few seconds of silence he was connected. "hello." "what's up? You straight out their?" "I'm cool, but shit getting' crazy, I'm stayin' strapped especially after wh-." "I already know, so what's the deal?"." KD said cutting her off. "it's hot, the detects questioned me bout Mano and Star, did you know they were fuckin'?" Tara asked. "naw, who told you that?" KD asked. "the dicks." Tara replied. "look, just be cool, go to the funeral then lay low." KD said. "I'll be there, but this shit getting' deep." Tara replied. "don't worry bout it, Grip handlin' it, but I need you." KD said. "I know, but after this I'm out I'm through." Tara replied. KD couldn't believe what he was hearing. "Tara don't let this shit shake you up." KD replied. "we talked money KD, not this shit." Tara replied. "some of this shit come wit' getting' money, it'll cool down." KD replied. "look I love you like a brother, but after this I'm out, I'm through." Tara said sadly. "just think about it, but fa' now just keep ya' ears ta' the street and be careful." KD replied. "I'll do that." Tara said. "they didn't deserve what happened to 'em." "I know, but what goes around comes around." KD didn't know if she meant that towards him or the situation. "let me get off this phone, so I can call my mom's." KD replied. "a'right." Tara said sadly. "you sure you a'right?" KD asked. "a'right as I can be wit' tha' shit that's goin' on." Tara replied. "you need anything?" KD asked. "yeah, a vacation." Tara replied. KD laughed. "I'll send some money yo' way." He replied. "take care of business first." Tara said. "I will." KD replied. Before the operator could interrupt KD hung up and went to watch tv, with some of the other prisoners. When KD hung up Tara made sure that all of the windows and doors were locked, once she was satisfied she sat down and watched tv, she wasn't really focused on what was going on in

151

the show she was watching, she was to busy thinkin' about all of the things that had been going on and how she wanted to settle down and live a normal life, she went in her pocket and took out the paper that detective Williams had written his numbers on then picked up the phone. As she dialed his cellphone number, she thought about what she would say if he answered. "Williams." He answered barely containing himself. "this is Tara Harper, you told me to call you." "yeah, what's up?" Williams asked. After a few seconds of silence, she sighed. "are you goin' to tha' funerals on Monday?" she asked. "I was thinkin' about it but somebody else might cover it." Tara felt like she was getting nowhere. "would you like to have dinner with me? I'm payin.'" Williams said hopefully. "I'd like to have dinner with you, but I'm paying." Tara asked. "you wanna pick tha' day?" she asked sarcastically. "tonight, I'll pick you up." Tara had been caught by surprise by the way he had taken control. "a'right, ta'night." She said still fighting the shock of what she was doing. "start getting ready I'll be there at eight." Tara looked at the clock sitting on top of the tv. "it's only six 'o' clock." She replied. "yeah, and by eight you'll just be finished picking out what you wanna wear." Williams replied. Tara laughed. "I see you got jokes." She said. "yeah, a couple." Williams replied. "okay mister comedian." She said. "my first names Elliot." He said. "well, you already know my name." Tara replied. "yeah, I do, and wear somethin' with open toe's, I like your feet." Williams said hoping he wasn't pushing it. "I might but let me see what I'm a wear first." She replied flirtatiously. "cool, I'll call when I'm on my way." Williams replied. "okay." Tara said before hanging up. After hanging up Tara thought about where the date would lead, what it would mean and why she made it.

After his conversation with KD, Grip decided to hit the streets to see if he could find Doobie, Brian, Bobby, or Travis, and so far he had come up with nothing, it was like they had dropped off the face of the earth, he sparked a blunt and rolled down thirtieth and Concordia hoping to

152

see Brian or Travis, as he made it to the middle of the block he saw a group of young guys in black hoodies, he knew that they were members of the Wild Boyz, so he blew the horn, some of them turned to look at the car, he saw Travis in the crowd and stopped the car in the middle of the street. Travis remembered Grips car, but he knew if he ran, he would be considered a punk by the rest of the click. Grip got out of the car and walked towards the crowd. "what tha' fuck you want?" one of them asked as he stepped onto the sidewalk. "I came ta' holla at my man's right here." He replied pointing to Travis. The boys looked at Travis and saw the fear. "I don't think he wanna holla at you, so won't you leave before you get fucked up." Grip looked at the boys. "mind ya' business lil' dude an let me do me." He replied as he walked over to Travis and grabbed him by the arm. "let's go talk." He said. "naw, I'm straight, we can talk right here." Travis replied. When the oldest one out of there group saw that Travis was nervous, he stepped in between them. "I think it's time fa' you to move around pimp." Grip quickly punched him in the face and pulled a nine beretta from his waist. "I told yall to mind ya' business, Travis get ta' movin'." Travis took slow steps toward him, but he placed his body on the fence. "you know what it is, yall fall back." Grip said as he kept his eyes on the boys. Everybody did as he said not wanting to be the one to get shot. "Travis walk wit' me, and if you run, it better be faster than a bullet." Travis walked to the street and towards Grips car. "you know you fucked up right?" Grip said as he opened the door and let Travis in, once he got in Grip started the car and pulled off. "you'll be dead by tonight, when dirt find out." Travis said. "that'll make two of us." Grip replied. Once Grip felt he was far enough from the scene he pulled over and opened his door. "get out." Grip said. Travis stared at him without moving. "nigga you ain't deaf get out!" he repeated. As Travis got out of the car Grip looked around then popped the trunk. "get in." Grip said calmly. "I ain't gettin' in no trunk, fuck what you talkin' bout." Travis replied. Grip shook his head then punched Travis in the face and stomach, when he bent over from the punch Grip hit him in the head with the gun and put him in the trunk and closed it. He looked around again then got in the car and pulled off. Thirty minutes later he pulled up to the safe house he used for emergencies, parked the car, got out and opened the trunk. "get out." He said knowing Travis was scared to death. Travis climbed out of the trunk and fell, Grip waited for him to get up and when he didn't move, he kicked him. "get the fuck up!" Grip said. "I can't feel my fuckin' legs." Travis replied. Grip closed the trunk and yanked him up. "you better stand yo' ass up and walk!" Travis half stumbled, half walked to the house, when they reached the door Grip stopped. "put ya' hands on top of ya' head an don't move." He said. Travis did as he was told, and Grip unlocked the door and pushed it open. "go." He said pushing Travis into the house and closing the door, once he locked the door, he turned on the light in the living room. "sit right there." He said pushing Travis into the house and closing the door, once he locked the door, he turned on the light in the living room. "sit right there." He said pointing to a wooden chair. Travis hesitated but sat down. "how old are you?" Grip asked. "Seventeen why?" Travis asked. "cuz you in some grown man shit, you gon' have ta' make some grown man choices." Grip replied. "what the fuck you talkin' bout? What I do?" Travis asked confused. "it ain't what you did it's what yo' bitch ass brother did, I wanna know where he at?" Grip replied. "I don't know." Travis said. "so, you gon' play tough?" Grip replied as he pulled the nine from his waist and slapped him with it, blood came from his mouth and forehead as he fell to the floor holding his face. Grip lifted him up from the floor then hit him again, Travis fell to the floor unconscious, while he was unconscious Grip grabbed a rope out of the closet and unplugged the extension cord from the wall then he pulled the chair Travis had been sitting in closer to the stove. "wake up nigga!" Grip said as he slapped Travis back to consciousness. Travis woke up slowly and grabbed his face. "get in the chair." Grip said pulling him up by his shirt. Travis stumbled and grabbed the chair, then sat down, Grip stared at him for a brief second, then turned on the stove. "look, I ain't finsta

154

play games wit' you, so we gon' cut the bullshit, tell me where Brian at or I'm a fuck you up." Travis was still shaken from the pistol whipping and angry for being scared. "Dirt gon' kill you fa' this." Grip punched him in the stomach then grabbed his hand and held it over the flame. Travis screamed and Grip let go. "talk nigga! Where ya' brother at?" Grip asked. "I-I don't know where he at?" Travis said as he began to panic. "you got his number, call 'em fa' me." Grip said. "I-I can't do that." Travis replied. Grip pulled the nine from his waist and pointed it at his forehead. "well what tha' fuck I need ya' fa?" he said slowly adding pressure to the trigger. "Okay! Okay! I'll call 'em." Travis screamed close to tears. Grip grabbed the phone off the table. "what's tha' number?" he asked. Grip dialed the number Travis gave him and waited on the phone to ring, when it rung, he put the phone on speaker. "ask him where he at?" he said putting the gun to the back of his head. "hello." Brian answered. "what up bro? where you at?" Travis replied. "chillin' at Nancy crib, why? What's up?" Brian asked. "I'm on my way there." Travis replied. "be careful." Brian replied. "fa' sho." Travis replied. Grip hung up. "who tha' fuck is Nancy? An where she stay?" he asked. "naw it don't work like that?" Travis replied keeping the tremble of fear out of his voice. "what tha' fuck you talkin' bout?" Grip asked. "I ain't tellin' you shit, you gon' take me wit' you an I'll show you how to get there." Travis replied. "what, you think I'm a let you set me up?" Grip replied shaking his head. "ain't no set up, I wanna live." Travis replied. "what you livin' got ta' do wit' tellin' me where Brian at?" Grip replied. "if I give you tha' directions, then you don't need me, but if I gotta show you, you need me alive." Grip knew he could get the information he wanted but still decided to play the game. "if you breath to hard, you dead, you hear me?" Travis nodded. Grip hit him with the gun knocking him unconscious again, after he finished untying him, he slapped him to wake him back up. "let's go nigga, an don't do nothin' stupid." Travis sat for minute letting his head clear, then got up and walked toward the door, when they made it to the car, he let Travis get in first. "reach under the seat, it's a towel and a

155

bottle of water under there, clean ya' face an shit." Travis reached under the seat and grabbed the towel and water, then began to wash his face, occasionally, he would flinch because of the pain, when he was finished, he threw the bottle and towel out the window. "which way we goin'?" he asked testing Travis. "I don't even know where the fuck we at." "good." He replied and pulled off. Once they were away from the safe house Travis felt safe. "where tha' fuck we at?" he asked as he looked out of the window. "don't worry bout that." Grip had a bad feeling but pushed it out of his mind. He began thinking of how he was going to handle this and make it to the funeral tomorrow. It took thirty minutes to reach an area that was Travis recognized. "which way we goin'?" Grip asked. "make a right on the next block." Grip made the turn on national and continued to drive. "when you make it to twenty-seventh make a right an park in front of the apartments." When they arrived, Grip grabbed the nine off his lap. "get out an walk slow." He knew that Brian would probably still have the tech nine, so he was being careful. They walked up the stairs and entered the hallway. "what number?" grip asked looking at the intercom. "seven." He rang the buzzer and waited on an answer, he kept the gun hidden in case someone came in. when no one answered he rang the buzzer again. "who is it?" Grip motioned for Travis to answer. "it's me Nancy, open the door!" there was a loud buzz and the inside door clicked, Grip pulled it open and let Travis go in first. "when we get up there knock an don't try no bullshit." He said as they made it to the elevator. "so, you gon' kill me now?" Travis asked. "naw, I ain't gon' kill you, when I know Brian here fa' sho you can go." Grip replied. Travis knew Grip was lying but he wasn't worried to much because he had a trick up his sleeve, when the elevator doors opened Travis smiled to himself. When they reached the apartment Grip stood off to the side and motioned for him to knock, when he knocked there was a brief silence. "hold on Travis." A few seconds later the door was unlocked and opened, Grip moved from his hiding place and pushed the door all the way open using Travis as a ram. "move back bitch, where that

156

nigga at?" Nancy looked Travis. "ya' own brother! You- you did this ta' ya' own brother!" she snapped. "shut up! On tha' flo' both of yall." Grip replied. When they were on the floor he closed and locked the door. "Brian bring yo' bitch ass out here." "he gone, he left thirty minutes ago." Nancy said holding back tears. "you better not be lyin' hoe." Grip snapped. "I swear he gone." She replied. Grip opened the closet door then closed it back. "mutha'fucka!" he snapped. "where he go?" he said tapping the barrel on his leg. "I don't know." Grip liked that the woman wasn't scared, but he was wasting time. "bitch! I ain't got time fa' this shit, where he at?" Grip asked. "I told you I don't know, he left." Grip looked around the room trying to figure out what to do next."

CHAPTER 14

Brian knew something was wrong when Travis repeated what he said, so he had kissed Nancy and left with the car keys, he was now on his way to dirt's so that he could tell him what was going on, once he got there he got out of the car and knocked on the door. "who the fuck is it?" a deep voice asked. "it's Brian." The door was opened by one of dirt's bodyguards, he quickly pulled Brian in the house and searched him. Brian knew not to come to the door strapped, he had left the tech in the car, after the search the guard nodded, and the other bodyguard knocked on the door he was standing in front of. Dirt walked out with a mac-11 on a shoestring and greeted him. "I already know what's up, some nigga snatched ya' lil' brother." Dirt said as if it was an everyday thing. "how you know?" Brian asked. "cuz, he snatched him while he was wit' my people." Dirt replied. "why they ain't do shit?" Brian asked. "they young but believe me they got dealt wit'." Dirt said coolly. "if I tell you what all this about will you find me a lay low spot?" he asked. "let's go to the garage." Dirt said. Everyone followed dirt and Brian to the garage. "what's the deal?" Dirt asked once they were in the garage. "it's KD, ever since bobby crossed him shit been crazy." Dirt laughed. "KD! Get tha' fuck outta here, KD ain't rollin' like that." He said. "naw, but he gotta plug wit' this nigga named Grip he got all types of straps and shit." Dirt had heard Grips name around town a little bit, but he didn't know much about him. "who hit tha' judge and Domenico?" Dirt asked. "I don't know, but KD been on the news lately an that judge was 'posse ta' handle his case, it's two and two." Brian replied. "yeah, you might be right, but you know KD used ta' be one of us, right?" Dirt said coolly. "how much?" Brian asked knowing why dirt had mentioned KD's pass affiliation. "protection is priceless, but if I'm a step to KD I need more details." "he was trying to get back in the game on his own." Brian offered up, knowing that he had to be careful. "is that right? KD was tryin' ta' make big moves huh?" Dirt asked rubbing his chin. Brian nodded. "did you help set 'em up?" dirt asked. Brian hesitated. "yeah, cuz bobby promised me two-hundred-fifty-thousand." He said. Dirt whistled. "that much huh? He must be movin' up in tha' world." "yea, I mean he been bussin' moves fa' a minute." Brian replied. "so yall the ones that hit Carlo?" dirt asked. "yeah, that was us." Brian said dropping his head. Dirt nodded and hit him with the Uzi. "yall tha' ones who hit Shaymo to then huh?" dirt asked as if he hadn't hit Brian. Brian shook his head. "that was KD and them I ain't have shit to do wit' that." He said fearfully. "call bobby!" dirt said as he threw Brian the cellphone. "w-what you want me to say?" "nothin' just get 'em on the phone." Dirt replied. Brian dialed the number and waited for an answer. "yeah." Bobby answered. "this b, what's up?" "you can come ge-." Dirt snatched the phone. "bobby what's up?" he said. "w-who this?" bobby asked nervously. "that's not important right now, what's important is the bad news I been gettin' from ya' boy." Dirt replied. "what bad news?" bobby asked. "first I wanna know somethin'." Dirt replied. "what's that?" bobby asked. "did yall hit Shaymo?" dirt responded. "hell naw, why would we do that?" bobby asked. "I don't know, but Brian told me somethin' different." "Brian don't know shit! If he said it was us, he Makin' it up." Dirt looked at Brian. "you ain't makin' this shit up is you b?" Dirt asked with a smile. "n-naw I ain't makin' shit up i-I can tell you what they got." He said nervously. "stay by tha' phone, I'm a call you back." When he hung up, he put the phone in his pocket. "what they get?" dirt asked knowing that only a few people knew. "fo-forty-eight p-pounds and thirty-six thousand." Brian replied. "yall know Shaymo was one of my mine, right?" dirt asked. "I-I ain't never hear that." Brian replied. "yeah, yall gone have ta' cut me in." Brian nodded as if it had been a request and not a demand. Dirt took the cellphone out of his pocket and pressed redial then waited on bobby to answer. "hello." "what's goin' on?" dirt asked. "I should be askin' you." Bobby replied. "I want you to break bread." Dirt replied. "what you mean break bread?" "yall hit Shaymo an Carlo, I want a cut, especially since Shaymo was one of mine." Dirt explained. "I don't know what you talkin' bout." Bobby replied still sticking to his story. "bobby don't fuck wit' me! I know what it is an I want in." dirt snapped but quickly regained his cool. "what I get out tha' deal?" bobby asked. "I make it safe for you an yours ta' walk tha' street an I find the nigga who hit ya' wife and daughter." Dirt replied. "h-how you know bout that? I paid good money ta' have that kept quiet." Bobby asked shocked and saddened. "I got ears everywhere bobby." Dirt said with a slight laugh. "I got protection." Bobby replied getting back to business. "one person bobby? You should know better." Dirt said smoothly. "how much?" bobby asked. "I want twenty-thousand off the move on Carlo, an I wanna know who was involved wit' hittin' Shaymo." Dirt replied. "I'll set it up, you'll have ya' money on Thursday." Bobby said biting down on his lip so hard he drew blood. "good, glad we could do business." Dirt replied. "tell Brian I said nobody likes a snitch." Bobby said after a deep sigh. "I'll relay the message." Dirt replied before hanging up. "I'm a get ya' brother fa' you cuz he one of mine, but I gotta problem." Dirt said. "what's that?' Brian asked. "you, you the problem." Dirt replied as his bodyguards grabbed Brian from behind. Brian tried to fight but it was no use, as he continued to struggling dirt grabbed a silenced Glock out of a drawer that was supposed to hold tools. Brian had been

159

beaten down and was no longer fighting, when the guards stepped away from him dirt pulled the trigger repeatedly until he had emptied the whole clip into Brian's body. "drop his body in front of his house, and somebody clean this shit up." Everyone began to move quickly as dirt walked back in the house, his bodyguard followed him as he walked toward the bathroom. "hold up." The bodyguard said as he walked into the bathroom and looked around, once he was finished, he walked back out. "it's good." He said. Dirt walked into the bathroom and began to undress, when he was finished, he tossed the clothes in the hallway. "burn 'em." He said as he stepped into the tub. The bodyguard took the clothes and walked away. Fifteen minutes later he got out of the tub, got dressed and called bobby. "hello." "when can I meet you?" dirt asked. "what you need to meet me fa'?" bobby asked. "ta' make funeral arrangements fa' Brian." Bobby was silent for a few seconds. "what tha' fuck are you talkin' bout?" bobby asked. "I don't like mu'fuckas playin' wit' me an that's what you doin'" dirt replied. "what's this funeral arrangement shit?" bobby finally said. "I don't like snitches; they make it bad fa' tha' game." Dirt replied. "a'right let's cut tha bullshit, how much you want?" bobby asked. "you playin' again I told you I want twenty-thousand from the Carlo move, and I wanna know who was involved in hittin' Shaymo." dirt responded. "what you mean who was involved?" bobby asked. "names bobby, I want names." Dirt replied trying to mask his irritation. "KD." Bobby replied. "who else?" dirt asked quickly. "they all been dealt wit' except a bitch named Tara." Bobby replied. "I don't kill bitches, so you deal wit' that." Dirt said. "nothing to handle." Bobby replied. "good, I'll be to see you." Bobby hung up and looked at pharaoh. "I want him dead before Monday, how much?" bobby asked. "twenty grand and a point in the right direction, I'll do the rest." Pharaoh replied. Bobby nodded and walked out of the room leaving pharaoh to think about how much money he'd made in the last three weeks, bobby went to his room, closed the door and lay on the bed.

Things were starting to look better, he was hoping to be able to show his face and money on the street within the next two weeks, all he had to do now was wait and let everything fall into place.

KD sat in his cell waiting to hear from his lawyer, he couldn't help but to focus on his next court date, he was ready to get everything over with so he could put together his next plan. It was one 'o' clock when the door was buzzed open. "drake! Visit." The deputy yelled. KD went to the sink washed his face, brushed his teeth, then went to his door and waited to be buzzed out. When the door was opened, he walked out to the tier. "what booth?" he asked. "booth one." When he made it to the booth his lawyer was sitting there. "peter what's up?" KD asked. "well depending on how you look at it I got good news." Peter replied. "give it to me." KD said. "you start trial next month." Peter said with a smile. "good, good, I'm ready." KD replied. "make a list of people you want as witnesses, so I can start the subpoenas." "Witnesses to what? I was unconscious in a house wit' some dead mu'fuckas, I ain't got no witnesses." KD replied. "I was seeing if you were paying attention." "this my life, of course I'm paying attention." KD replied. "good, now sit there and listen you can ask questions when I'm done." For the next half an hour peter discussed the facts of the case with him. "I'm not pleadin' guilty." KD said when peter was finally done talking. "I'll have a private investigator get in touch with you." Peter replied. "yeah, we'll talk." KD replied as he sat the phone down. When the visit was over he went back to his cell and lay on the bed, hoping that his next move would work out for everybody, but he knew things could get worse, peter had told him so, but he had also told him that murder was the easiest case to beat and he was willing to take his chances on that, especially since pleading guilty was a one way trip to life in prison, which Wisconsin was handing out to black people like candy on Halloween.

161

People filed out of the New Creation Church on thirteenth and Center headed to the cemetery, the funereal had been so packed that people had to stand outside, the preacher who had known Trina's family for thirty years had shed tears as he spoke of her going to heaven. After everyone had said a few words, people were allowed to make rounds to see the coffin which held their friend and loved one, her sisters were the first to go by the coffin, they both cried as they kissed their sister one last time, then her brothers went, when drew made it to the casket he bent down an put his face next to his sisters. "we gon' handle it big sis, we gon' handle it." He said before the tears ran down his face. Drama kissed her on the forehead. "take that to heaven wit' you." Once they had sat down their mother walked to the casket and touched her daughters face for what would be the last time. "lord why! Why my baby!" she screamed. Drew and Drama went to the front of the church and lead their mother back to her seat, after that everyone went past the casket. "you beautiful girl, I love you." Tara said. When everyone had had their turn to speak and go past the casket it was time to go to the cemetery. Drew, Drama, two of Trina's uncles, and two of her best friends carried the casket to the hearse and shut the back door, when Tara walked out of the church, she saw KD's mother, she walked over gave her a hug and kiss on the cheek. Thank you so much for everything the funeral was beautiful." She said. Before KD's mother could reply, Trina's mother came out, she looked at them as if deciding whether to love or hate them before walking over. "tell KD I love him." She said before heading to the limo that was waiting to take her to the final resting place of her oldest daughter. Tara saw detective Williams and another officer standing across the street, she gave a slight nod, and got in her car. When she locked the doors she reached under for her gun, pulled it from under her seat and sat it in her lap, started the car and pulled off, she followed the rest of the cars as they drove to the cemetery, when they were a block away, she put the gun back under the seat and reminded herself to take pictures so she could show KD how beautiful the funeral was. It took thirty minutes to get the casket into the ground, once it was lowered everyone threw flowers on the casket and walked away. Tara was the last person to throw flowers on the casket. As she walked away, she began to feel like she was being followed, so she sprinted to her car, when she made it, she grabbed her gun quickly. As she started the car there was a knock on her window, she swung quickly with her finger on the trigger and saw detective Williams and another officer, she quickly dropped the gun on her lap and rolled the window down. "turn the car off." The officer said with his hand on his gun. Tara did as he said. "unlock the door." Williams said. "what the hell you doing wit' a gun?" Williams asked. "keepin' yall from standin' around doing whatever the fuck yall do at my funeral." "do you have a license to carry it?" Williams asked as he stared at her. "y-yeah, I got one." She replied as she picked up on the tone of his voice. "can I search the car?" Tara nodded her consent and climbed out. Williams searched knowing she didn't have a license for the gun, but he also knew he wouldn't arrest her, he grabbed a paper from the glovebox. "a'right." He said as he slid out of the car and made as if he was reading it, the officer that he was with knew something wasn't right. "let me run it." He said. "no need it's stamped." Williams replied. "it could be fake." He replied. "I've been doing this for decades; I know a real fuckin' license from a fake one." Williams replied angerly. "a'right, a'right, I'm just a little wired." Williams understood why he was wired and took it easy on him. "well miss Harper, be careful with that and keep it under your seat." "am I free to go?" she asked. "yeah, get tha' fuck outta here." Williams replied. Tara grabbed the paper then slowly got back in the car, sat back, took a deep breath and started the car, it was time for her to go home and chill for the day, she couldn't believe she had almost killed two people. "this shit drivin' me crazy." She said to herself. It took her an hour to get home, when she walked in the she had three messages on her machine, she checked the messages, one of them was from detective Williams, she knew he would be calling, she went to the next message, it was from Grip he only

163

left a number, the last message was from detective Williams asking why she hadn't called back yet. Tara laughed then decided to return calls, she listened to the number that Grip left then picked up the phone and dialed. The phone rang twice before it was answered. "h-hello." A feminine voice said. "a friend of mines called me from this number." "hold on." Nancy said shakily. Grip got on the phone, but kept the gun pointed at Nancy and Travis. "yeah." He said. "what's up?" she replied. "I'm wit' Travis, but Brian ain't here." He said. "be careful." She replied. "always." He said glancing around. "don't stay on the phone to long." "I know, how was the funeral?" "it was beautiful, now get the fuck off the phone." "a'right, I'm a handle this and be bout my business." Tara hung up. "shit ain't lookin' to good yall." Nancy looked at Travis, then to Grip. "what the fuck you talkin' bout?" "both of yall follow me." Travis and Nancy got up as Grip walked backwards towards the bedroom, once they were in the bedroom he looked around. "both of yall get on the bed." He said as he grabbed a pillow and walked to the side of the bed that Travis was sitting on. Travis knew he had to make a move or die so as Grip walked closer to the bed he kicked out with both feet causing Grip to fall backwards, as he fell he squeezed the trigger twice, the shots made Travis hesitate and that gave Grip enough time to get too his knees, but Nancy took the chance to jump on his back, as she grabbed him around the neck he flipped her over his shoulder causing her to hit to hit the dresser with a hard thud, Travis had made it to the closet and grabbed the gun that he kept stashed there, he had knew that the forty-five would come in handy. "stop mu'fucka!" Travis yelled. "what you gon' do wit' that nigga?" Grip asked. "move and find out." Grip decided not to test him. "throw ya' heat over here." Grip slowly hit the clip release and watched the clip fall then threw the gun towards Travis, when it landed on the floor Travis smiled and pulled the trigger and nothing happened, he squeezed again and heard the click. Grip charged him like a bull seeing red and started to punch him, when he went limp Grip grabbed his gun and put the clip in, he quickly released the

164

bullet from the chamber, and fired three shots, two into Travis' face an one into Nancy's head, he then unplugged the phone, grabbed the pillow and headed out the door, he looked around and saw people opening their doors and coming into the hallway, he decided to do the only thing he could do and began to fire shots into the hallway as he ran down the stairs hoping the pillow covered his face, when he fired the shots people began to run back into their apartments or fell to the ground, most of the people didn't get a chance to see his face. Grip ran to his car and hopped in, he threw the pillow and phone in the backseat, started the car and pulled off. Grip got on his cellphone and dialed Tara's number. "hello." Tara answered. "what's your address?" he asked. "twenty-twenty three west center." Grip hung up and headed to Tara's house, when he pulled up, he parked quickly, ran up the stairs and knocked on the door with his gun in hand, Tara looked out saw Grip, then opened the door, when she saw the gun, she pulled him inside. "what tha' fuck wrong wit' you?" she asked. "I fucked up, I fucked up bad." Grip replied panicked. "slow down, what happened?" she asked. Grip sat his gun on the table and paced the floor as he told her what happened, when he finished Tara was quiet for a few seconds. "what tha' fuck was you thinkin'?" she asked. Grip could only shake his head. "first we gotta get rid of the car, burn it, the gun to." Tara said. Grip threw her the keys. "drive my car, I'll follow in yours." He said. "let's go hurry up." She said as she caught the keys. It took them a half an hour to drive downtown, once they were there Tara pulled into an alley across the street from the mall, Grip went into the trunk and grabbed the gas container he kept for emergencies, Tara watched as he wiped the car down, took off the plates, and began to pour gasoline over it, she looked around knowing that the fire would gain attention quickly. "hurry up! We been here to long already." Grip reached in his pocket and grabbed his lighter and flicked it. They watched as the car caught fire then hopped in her car. "pull off! Pull off!" Grip said panicked. Tara put the car in reverse and backed out the alley and no one paid attention as they drove slowly away from

165

the alley and the burning car. Grip continued to look in the sideview mirror until they made it out of the downtown area, when they reached her house a detective car was sitting in the front, so she kept driving. "what the fuck tha' dick's doin' in front of yo' shit?" Grip asked. "I don't know but let's find out." Tara replied. "you strapped?" Grip replied. "hell yeah, ever since that shit with Trina I been holdin' this bitch down." Tara said showing him the gun. "let's be careful wit' how we play this." Grip replied. "it is what it is, fuck it." She replied. "fuck it then lets get it over with." Grip said. Tara turned the car around and went back towards her house, when they pulled up, she put the gun on her lap and waited to see what would happen, when the people in the detective car didn't get out Grip sighed. "fuck this shit." He said as he got out of the car and walked toward her house, when he got to the stairs the door to the detective car sprung open. Tara slowly eased out of the car as the men walked towards her house, Grip was putting his hand on his gun. "move that hand up real slow." One of the officers said. "a'right, just don't let ya' finger get itchy." The officer said. As the two men watched him move his hands slowly into sight Tara waited to get a good shot, when she got close, she saw the man with the gun remove something from his hip, then she recognized the other man as Williams, so she tucked her gun and came from behind the car she had been hiding behind. "what tha' fuck goin' on?" Williams turned around at the sound of her voice. "good, you're a'right." He said. "yeah, I'm a'right, why you fuckin' wit' my homeboy?" Tara asked. "your homeboy was lookin' a lil' suspicious." "leave 'em alone, what you doin' here?" she replied. "look, I know you tough an all but there's a hit out on you." Williams replied. "hit! What the fuck you talkin' bout?" she asked looking around. "your friend miss Gibbs was involved with Kevin Drake, right?" Williams asked. "yeah, why?" Tara asked. "well miss Harper, mister Drake and some people we haven't identified got involved in some serious shit, and now it's hittin' the fan." Williams replied. "okay, what I'm suppose to know bout this?" Tara asked. "hey, you on the stairs, you heard of the Wild Boyz?" Williams asked.

166

"yeah, I heard of 'em." Grip replied. "well, they boss ain't to happy about mister Drake puttin' his hands in they pocket." The officer with Williams sighed. "tell 'em about Marzeno's hit, you might as well put it all on the table." He said. "what the fuck he got ta' do wit' all this shit?" Tara asked. Williams sighed and glanced at the officer. "it seems that Drake had his hands in his pockets to." Williams replied. "so now what?" Tara asked. "first we're gonna get you some clothes, then we're takin' you to a hotel." Williams replied. "I'm not goin' less my friend can come." Tara replied seriously. "take his weapon, an make sure he ain't got no warrants. "put your hands up and don't move." "no problem." Grip replied. The officer did the search quickly, took the gun and handed it to Williams, he took the gun and tucked it into his waistband. "if he doesn't have any warrants we forget about the gun, but if a warrant pops up so does the gun." He said. The officer took Grip to the car too check for warrants. "why you didn't call me?" Williams asked. "I got busy." Tara replied. "who's he?" Williams asked. "he's a friend of mines and KD." Tara replied. Williams shook his head. "what!" Tara asked. "what's goin' on?" Williams replied. "what you mean, what's goin' on?" Tara replied. "we'll talk about it in a minute, what do you need out of the house right now? We can get the rest later." "I can get my own shit." Tara replied. "no, you can't, so give me the keys." Tara did her best to hide her smile as she threw him the keys. "I would kiss you, but you'd probably get fired." Williams knew that she was serious. "go to the car and wait." He said smiling. Tara went to her car and got in, as Williams unlocked her front door the explosion rocked the car, it took a few seconds before they realized what happened Tara knew there was no way that Williams had survived that blast, she was losing everybody who got close to her, first Mano, then Trina, now Williams, it was to cut the losses, but their was nothin' she could do, in her mind it was like being raped all over again, but this time it was KD's fault, he had brought her into this, but she knew how to fix it even though it went against everything she stood for, she knew there was no other way. After the officer finished calling the

167

explosion in, she waited for him to come to the car. "you got a phone I can use?" she asked. "yeah." He said as handed her the phone, she dialed as the tears rolled down her face. "is this detective coldburn?" she asked when the phone was answered. "yes, it is." Tara sighed. "this is Tara Harper; we need to talk but only on my terms." Tara said sadly. "a'right come to my office." Coldburn replied. Grip sat in the back of the squad car unaware of the call that was taking place.

CHAPTER 15

TWO MONTHS LATER

It was ten 'o' clock Wednesday morning when KD and his lawyer walked into the courtroom, Peter had just finished telling KD about the explosion at Tara's house and the call that had been placed to Coldburn, he didn't bother to reply to the news, his mind was on the courtroom and his trial. When he walked into the courtroom he saw Drew, Drama, Angela, Grip and his mother, when he was seated the judge nodded as if confirming something to himself. "let's begin." He said. "state of Wisconsin v. Kevin Imani Drake 02cf003785 appearances." The clerk said into the microphone. "Matthew Arieff for the state." The DA replied. "Peter Hopper, in person with his client Kevin Drake." "noted, start with the proceedings." The judge replied. "your honor there really isn't a lot to say on this, this is nothing, but a maximum case, mister Drake is a ticking time bomb when he's out, this is a young man with a juvenile history going back to the ninety's with burglary while armed where a friend of mister Drakes was killed during the crime, possession of a dangerous by child for which he was sent to the juvenile detention center, and then to prison which he just left five months ago, and all of that pales in comparison to the five counts of murder and the one count of home invasion, along with impersonating an officer, he was also a known member of the Wild Boyz in nineteen ninety one, and escaped going down with his friends during their indictment, he has never gained full employment, has no education, he's a clear and present danger when he's out." The D.A. replied. "mister Hopper." "your honor my client and I have spoken and he's told me that yes he did go in with the intent to rob the people who were in the home, he also states that someone, he doesn't know who, but someone set him up to take the fall for the murders, as you know my client was found unconscious on the floor, suffering from three close range gunshots wounds from a shotgun that was found on the scene of the crime, if it wasn't for the bulletproof vest he was wearing he would more than likely be deceased. "mister Hopper do you have anyone you wish to call to the stand?" the judge asked. "their were no witnesses to the crime as far as I know of except for two ladies who said they saw the police going in and out of the house." The judge nodded. "mister Arieff, do you want to call any witnesses?" "yes, your honor I would like to call officer Chavez to the stand." Officer walked to the stand and was sworn in, when he sat down the district attorney sighed. "officer Chavez, will you describe for the court what you saw when you entered twenty-five 'o' one south Scott?" he asked. "I and my now deceased partner came into the house with guns drawn, due to being called in by dispatch after a nine-one-one call saying that officers were under fire, when we went in I saw what I believed to be two officers seriously injured, I went over to one of them checked for a pulse and there was none, I told this to my partner and he checked the other guy and said he was breathing." The officer said. "do you remember anything else?" the D.A. asked. "yes, there were bodies on the stairs, in the living room, and blood all over." "is it true, that two of the victims were a sixteen-year-old girl and her mother. "we also found a woman murdered execution style." The district attorney went to the table and grabbed a packet of pictures that were taken at the crime scene. "I would like to enter these pictures into the record as exhibit A." he said as he passed them to the jury. Upon seeing them members of the jury shook their heads and passed the pictures around the jury box and then back to the district attorney, when KD saw the reaction that the jurors gave to the pictures he looked at peter. "what you gon 'do bout that shit? I ain't kill them people." KD replied. "I'll handle it don't worry a'right." KD poured a cup of water and sat back in his chair. It took ten minutes for the D.A. to finish his questioning and when he was done Peter walked to the witness stand. "officer Chavez you stated that my client was seriously injured when you arrived at the scene, is that correct?" "yes, that's correct." "when you saw all of the bodies what was your first reaction?" peter asked. "I-I was shocked it was like a slaughterhouse in there." The officer said. "I've seen the pictures, as have the jury and I want to ask you a few questions, when you checked the people, you thought were officers, what went through your mind?" peter asked. "I just wanted to make sure they were alive." Peter nodded. "you found a shotgun on the scene of the crime, is that right?" peter asked. "yeah, that's right." The officer said. "when you found the shotgun, how did you find it?" peter asked. "we were securing the house with other officers, when my partner found the shotgun in the living room where that guy was." Chavez said pointing at KD. "for the record officer Chavez is pointing to my client Kevin Drake, officer Chavez, was my client conscious or unconscious?" peter asked. "he was unconscious." The officer said. "did you see any signs of injury?" peter asked. "yes, he was bleeding from his mouth, and side." Peter picked up the shotgun. "I would like to enter this shotgun into the record as exhibit b." he said. "noted for the record." The judge replied. "is this the shotgun you found?" Chavez reached for the shotgun and peter handed it to him. Chavez looked at it for a few seconds. "yes, it is." He replied. "did you get any prints from it?' "yes, but they weren't useful." Chavez said. "did my client have on gloves?" peter asked with a slight smile. Chavez was silent for a few seconds. "no." he finally replied. "was anyone killed with the shotgun?" peter asked. "yes." Chavez replied. "how many?" "two, it would've been three with your client." Chavez replied. "thank you." Peter replied. Chavez was told that he could leave the stand, once he stepped down peter sat down. "mister Drake, I can get two cases dropped with no problem, but we're going to have too fight like hell on these other ones." Peter replied. "that's what I pay you for." KD replied. "at two 'o' clock they were still going through testimonies from different officers, at three-thirty they called for recess. "I know shit's looking bad right now, but it'll get better." Peter told him. "don't bullshit me, they finsta lay me down on this shit, just get my appeal ready." KD said. "its not over til' it's over, and it's up to the jury." Peter replied. "so, what's the next move?" KD asked. "we try to get the police to say it's possible you were set up, and we try to discredit Tara." "cool lets run wit' that." KD replied. "a'right, I'll get tha ball rollin'." Peter said. They were called back into the courtroom at eight the next morning to resume the trial, peter began by calling one of the women to the stand. "can you state your name for the record?" he asked politely. "yes, my name is lenette Jenkins," "a'right, miss Jenkins, what did you see on the day in question?" "I saw about five or six police cars block off the street, and they all had guns I knew that they were goin' ta' get the drug dealers who lived there, so I watched from my window, they ran into the house and then I heard some loud booms and pops, so I called nine-one-one." "did you see anybody leave the scene?" "yeah, I saw two or three police officers run to their car and speed off." "didn't you find it strange that police were leaving the scene?" "yes, I found it strange as hell." She responded sincerely. "did you tell the police or the nine-one-one operator this?" peter asked. "no, I didn't." she replied. "thank you." Peter said. The D.A. didn't have any questions, so she was allowed to step down. When she stepped down the D.A. turned toward the table KD was sitting at. "I call Tara Harper to the stand your honor." KD knew about the police call that Tara had made to detective Coldburn, but he couldn't believe that she was really testifying on him, he still hadn't found out why. She was lead into the courtroom by four armed deputies and detective coldburn, she had talked to coldburn for two and a half hours working out what she wanted and another half an hour talking to the D.A. to receive a deal, when she walked in, she heard KD's mother mumble bitch under her breath, Grip shook his head sadly, Drew and Drama did the same thing. "miss Harper, how are you?" he asked. "I-I'm fine." She replied doing her best not to look at KD. "good, good miss Harper do you know the man sitting at the table to your left?" "y-yeah I know him." She replied. "can you tell the court how you know mister Drake?" "w-we friends." She replied. "okay, oh! I almost forgot; can you state your name for the record?" "T-Tara Harper." She stated. "thank you, miss Harper." "you're welcome." She replied. "a'right miss Harper, how long have you and mister Drake been friends." "about five or six years." She responded still not looking KD's way. "is mister Drake a good friend?" "I would say so." She replied. "miss Harper what do you know about the day in question?" "Kevin had been workin' with a dude named bobby to set up the robbery and he asked-." "I object! Your honor, there is no mention of this person bobby in the record, whoever it is can't say if this is true or not." "strike miss Harper's mention of unknown person from the record as hearsay." The judge replied. "let's try this again miss Harper, other than the part you just mentioned do you know anything else?" "yes, I do." "okay can you tell the court what else you know." "yes, I was asked by mister Drake to be part of the robbery." KD dropped his head. "lift your head! Peter whispered harshly. "and did you participate?" the D.A. asked. "y-yes." She replied. "can you tell the court how you participated?" "I sat by the phone and waited on somebody to call me in case something went wrong." She replied. "and if something went wrong and this call came, what were you supposed to do?" even though Tara had told the D.A. the whole story she hesitated at this part and took a deep breath. "I was supposed to come with my gun and help out however I could." She replied. "and did you ever get that call?" "y-yes." She replied quietly. "I'm sorry miss Harper can you repeat your answer?" "yes, I got the call." She replied a little louder. "and what did you do?" "I went to the house and made my way in and saw all these people laid on the floor, and some other people running around." "Running around doing what?" "well, they had duffel bags and they was just goin' in and out of the rooms." Tara replied. "do you know what they were doing when they were going from room to room." "I don't understand the question." "I'll rephrase it, did you see anyone place anything in any of the bags?" the D.A. asked. "no." Tara replied. "okay, now I remember you saying something about a gun, where did you get a gun from?" the D.A. asked. "Kevin, I mean mister Drake got it for me." "do you know where mister Drake got the gun from?" "yes, he got it from a friend of his." Tara replied finally accepting what she was doing. Grip looked at Drama and Drew, then at the courtroom doors. "do you know his friends name?" Peter objected. "your honor, this mystery person can't defend himself." He said. "mister Arieff, please refrain from the mystery person defense." The judge said sternly. "your honor miss Harper is willing to give us the name of the person she is speaking about." The D.A. said. Peter couldn't believe he fell for that trick, by stating that the mystery person couldn't defend himself he gave the D.A. the burden of proof, meaning that if the D.A. didn't have a name, he would have to leave the line of questioning, but if he did have the identity, he would have to share it by Wisconsin state law. "continue mister Arieff." The judge said as he looked through paperwork.

"miss Harper, I'll repeat the question, do you know his friends name?" The D.A. replied. "yes I am." Tara said. "okay, miss Harper, can you please state the name for the courts record." The D.A. asked. "A-Andre Prin." She replied. Grip calmly made his way out of the courtroom hoping to make it out of the courthouse, but that hope was shattered when he made it to the hallway and detective Coldburn along with two deputies stood waiting for him. Back in the courtroom the D.A. continued his questioning and after five minutes he placed everything he could in the jury's lap, now it was Peters turn to question Tara. "miss Harper, you're receiving a deal of some sort for testifying, aren't you?" Peter asked. "yes, yes I am, I was told that for my testimony the D.A. would recommend five years in prison to the court." Tara replied. "oh, so it's not a deal it's a recommendation?" peter asked. "yes, that's right." Tara replied. "ok I just wanted to clear that up miss Harper, have you hid anything from the courts?" he asked. "no, I have not." She replied. "are you a murderer miss Harper?" Tara was caught off guard by the question, just like he wanted her to be. "miss Harper, please answer the question." He said after a few seconds. "no, I'm not a murderer." She finally answered. "where are you from?" Peter asked. "I was born in Indiana." Tara replied. "how long have you lived in Milwaukee?" he asked. "about seven or eight years." She replied. "why did you leave Indiana?" peter asked. Tara dropped her head. "I-I was raped." Peter didn't know that, but he knew she was telling the truth, and he had lost points with the jury. "miss harper have you ever fired a gun?' "yes." Peter had set the trap. "when?" he asked. "well, i-it was twice, once when I got, well after I got raped and once when I went to the house Kevin told me to go to." "did you hit anyone either time?" peter asked. "I don't know about the time after I was raped, but I only shot in the air at that house with Kevin." He knew that he was making things worse, so he stopped his questioning.

.   THREE WEEKS LATER

KD sat in the holding area waiting on the jury to come back with their decision, it had been a long process and he was ready to get it over with. "mister Drake, how you feeling?" Peter asked as he entered the cage which separated him from the prisoners. "anxious." KD replied truthfully. Well, they should be back in twenty or thirty minutes." "we been waiting for two hours, what the fuck takin' so long?" KD asked. "relax, the longer they take the better." Peter replied confidently. "yeah, a'right." KD agreed restlessly. An hour later KD was still waiting. It was three-thirty when the deputy came to the waiting area. "Drake, they ready for you." The deputy said. KD stood, wiped the sleep from his eyes and took a deep breath. "a'right, I'm ready." He said. The deputy unlocked the cage and waited for him to exit, when he exited a deputy escorted him to the courtroom, once KD was seated the judge nodded to the deputy and he went to speak to the jurors. "has the jury reached a decision?" the judge asked when the deputy returned. "yes, they have your honor." The judge nodded. "are both parties available?" he asked. "yes your honor." Peter and the D.A. replied at the same time. "a'right, we begin, please seat the jury," the deputy walked to the small door and knocked, the twelve jurors walked out and took their seats. "mister Hopper, does your client wish to speak?" the judge asked. "no he doesn't your honor." Peter replied. "noted, I have been informed that the jury has reached a verdict, is that true?" the foreman stood. "yes your honor." "what say you?" the judge asked seriously. "as to count one murder in the first degree we find the defendant guilty, as to count two murder in the first degree, we find the defendant guilty, as to count three murder in the second degree as a party to a crime, we find the defendant not guilty, as to count four murder in the first degree we find the defendant guilty, as to count five possession of a fire arm by felon we find the defendant guilty, as to count six impersonating an officer, we find the defendant guilty." KD didn't show any emotion as the foreman finished reading off their decision, reporters began making their way out of the courtroom in hopes of getting comments from the jurors and witnesses. KD knew from the beginning what the outcome would be, so it was not a surprise to him at all. As the judge called for order in the court KD looked at Peter and saw the disappointment on his face. "get my appeal ready." Peter nodded and handed him a yellow piece of paper. "fill this out." Peter replied. As KD filled out the paper the judge sat silently. "sentencing will take place on June thirteenth at twelve-thirty." Peter and the D.A. checked their date books and agreed. The deputies came and led KD out of the courtroom and back to the holding cell, once inside he was uncuffed and locked in the room with three other people, they hadn't been their before and they hadn't come with him on the van. "what they do you for you?" "shit, fucked me over." "what judge you have? Another man asked. "Axelmann." KD replied. "damn I heard dude rough as a mu'fucka." As they were talking the outter door opened and Peter walked in. "mister Drake, I just came to give you a copy of your notice of intent to pursue post-conviction relief, and to see how you're holding up. "I'm straight, I just wanna know how much time you think I'm a get." KD asked. "truthfully I don't know, but I would say under these circumstances and with it being a high-profile case you're looking at a minimum of seventy years." "seventy years minimum! Hell naw." KD snapped. "I'm not going to sugar coat things for you, you don't pay me to do that, this is the reality of the shit that they say happened, we lost the first, so we come back for a second." Peter replied. "just check on my momma and tell her don't worry." "will do mister Drake." He replied then tapped on the door. The deputy opened the door and let him out. It was twenty-minutes later when the deputies came and brought all of them out of the room to be shackled and led through the hallways and back to the jail or the buses taking them up north. As everyone talked about what happened at court, KD remained quiet and deep in thought, he had never imagined things going down the way they had, but he couldn't change what happened, he could only deal with what was going on at this point. As he made it to the jail, he looked at all of the people who were acting as if being locked up was part of a normal day and shook his head. He wasn't going to cry about his time, whatever it might be, but he wasn't going to accept it either, he was a fighter and wouldn't stop fighting. After being placed back in the holding cell KD lay on the hard concrete block and thought about everything that had went down, he wasn't sure if it was worth it, but it had already happened, it all started with a lick that turned into three murders, he had committed two of the murders and got away with them, but the third one wasn't his fault, bobby's son was slipping and he wasn't going to leave the money or weed to save Martin when he was going to die anyway, they say what goes around comes around, and it had come around twice as quickly, so quickly he hadn't been prepared for it, he had only been out of

176

prison five months, five long months filled with death and drama, and top it all off in the end he knew that everything he had worked for was gone, his money was going to his lawyer, well the money he hadn't spent on revenge, funerals, and payoffs, he had lost all of the people who had real love for him. Mano had been killed, Trina, Star, both dead and for what? KD sat up and thought about his life, he was so sure he would get rich off of his plan that he hadn't thought of anything else, as the thoughts of strip clubs, smoking weed, and having fun ran through his mind Tara's face popped up. KD had never thought that she would do him the way she was, not only him but Grip to, as he thought about everything the holding cell door opened. "Drake! Lawyer visit." KD stepped toward the door wondering why Peter would be there to see him again. The deputy handcuffed him and led him to a room and cuffed him to a metal ring embedded into the concrete. "he'll be here in a second." The deputy said. A few minutes later Peter walked into the room and sat down. "mister Drake, I have bad news and good news, which do you want first?" "give me the bad news first." KD replied. "miss Harper is going to be a witness for the feds against you and mister Prin." "feds! What the feds got to do with this?" KD asked. "when mister Prin was arrested, the D.A. talked a judge into giving them search warrants for his house and they found guns, lots of guns, and he's willing to testify against you and Tara for a deal." "fuck! What kinda deal he gettin'?" KD asked. "I don't know yet, but you'll know when I do." Peter replied. "a'right what's the good news?" KD asked. "well, you might not think i-." peter hesitated. "just tell me." KD said. "the D.A. isn't giving miss Harper a deal, well not the deal they were going to give her s-." "what's the good news in that?" KD asked. "I was trying to tell you it might not be good news to you, but I do have a question." "what!" KD asked showing his irritation. "are you willing to testify against them?" Peter asked seriously. "no." KD said. "mister Drake, listen and I mean really listen, you can end up in state and federal prison for the rest of your life, just the bulletproof vest is a minimum of fifteen years, not to mention the

177

possession of firearm by felon, I'll try to get you a deal and we'll still do an appeal." "I'm not turnin', fuck that." KD said. Peter sighed. "listen! Mister Drake, get it through your brain, you are fucked, fucked, there is no way that you're not goin' to do time, but how much is up to you, you have two people willing to testify against you in federal court, one of which has already testified in state court to save her ass, right now your friend mister Prin is in the interrogation singing like Pavarotti, and believe me he's intent on saving his ass not yours, so you can keep your loyalty and use it for the people who give a fuck about you or you can look out for yourself." Peter said truthfully. KD knew that Peter was only trying to do what he thought was best, but he couldn't see himself snitching on anybody, no matter how much time he was facing. "it's not happenin'." "you better think about it mister Drake." Peter replied. "ain't nothin' to think about, I said no." KD said angerly. "mister Drake you're a better man than me because if I was in your situation I'd jump on a deal." "that's why you, you and I'm me." KD replied. "and I'm glad I'm not." "is their anything else you wanna tell me?' KD asked. "not at this point, but after I find out what's going on with mister Prin, and Miss Harper, I'll contact you." Peter replied. "a'right, we'll get at me." KD replied as he stood up. "alright mister Drake, think about what I said and let me know." Peter said. "I ain't gotta think about it I said no and that's what it is." When the visit was over, he was returned to his cell, he knew that he would be going up north soon so he began to think about the future, he knew he had to come up with something and when he did the streets would pay for the.........BETRAYAL OF A STICK-UP KID.

TO BE CONTINUED.

178

Made in the USA
Columbia, SC
09 November 2022

70524954R00098